P9-AON-628

THE INHERITANCE

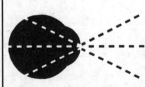

This Large Print Book carries the
Seal of Approval of N.A.V.H.

THE INNKEEPERS SERIES

THE INHERITANCE

ROCHELLE ALERS

THORNDIKE PRESS
A part of Gale, Cengage Learning

GALE
CENGAGE Learning·

Farmington Hills, Mich • San Francisco • New York • Waterville, Maine
Meriden, Conn • Mason, Ohio • Chicago

LIBRARY OF CONGRESS CATALOGING-IN-PUBLICATION DATA

Names: Alers, Rochelle, author.
Title: The inheritance / by Rochelle Alers.
Description: Large print edition. | Waterville, Maine : Thorndike Press, 2017. |
  Series: The innkeepers series | Series: Thorndike Press large print
  African-American
Identifiers: LCCN 2016059120| ISBN 9781410499219 (hardcover) | ISBN 1410499219
  (hardcover)
Subjects: LCSH: African American women—Fiction. | Large type books.
  Classification: LCC PS3551.L3477 I54 2017 | DDC 813/.54—dc23 LC record
  available at https://lccn.loc.gov/2016059120

Published in 2017 by arrangement with Dafina Books, an imprint of
Kensington Publishing Corp.

Printed in the United States of America
1 2 3 4 5 6 7 21 20 19 18 17

To Nancy Coffey — agent and friend. Thank you for the lengthy chats about the sister-girl road trip that blossomed into *The Innkeepers.*

I also dedicate this series to my editor and friend, Tara Gavin, for believing in my vision to create stories about women who are given a second chance at love no matter their age. Thank you for taking this journey with me.

"Because you got a double dose of trouble and more than your share of contempt, your inheritance in the land will be doubled and your joy go on forever."

— Isaiah 61:7

CHAPTER 1

Smiling, the doorman touched the shiny brim of his cap with a white-gloved hand. "Have a good day, Ms. Lowell."

Hannah DuPont-Lowell returned his smile with a warm one of her own. "Thank you, Max."

Her smile still in place, she inhaled a lungful of warm air. It was mid-May, a glorious morning, and her favorite time of the year. The daytime temperature was predicted to reach seventy-eight degrees; the weather in New York City had gone from a damp and chilly spring to summer overnight, forcing her to modify her wardrobe.

Today she'd selected a navy-blue linen gabardine pantsuit with an emerald-green silk blouse and navy kitten heels. Hannah favored wearing lower heels because they were not only comfortable but practical. Since moving to New York, Hannah found herself walking everywhere: the three blocks from her apartment building to the office, and whenever she didn't eat lunch in the bank's cafeteria it was the half mile to her favorite French-inspired café; on weekends it was either strolling to Battery Park or to the South Street Seaport.

Hannah didn't meet the eyes of the stoic guard standing outside the historic four-story structure in the Stone Street Historic District that housed the private international investment bank where she'd worked for the past five years. No matter how many times she greeted him with a smile he never returned it. She wondered if he even knew how to smile. She knew his job was to monitor everyone coming into and leaving the building, but a nod of acknowledgment would have been nice. And it wasn't the first time she reminded herself she wasn't in the South, where most people greeted strangers with a nod and "mornin'," or "good evenin'."

Whenever she returned to New Orleans for vacation or family holidays, she unconsciously settled into her childhood home training. She'd been taught never to sass older folks, nor use profanity in their presence, and to speak when spoken to. In another two years she would celebrate her sixtieth birthday, and old habits were still hard to ignore.

Hannah swiped her ID before punching the button for the elevator to the second floor where the bank's legal offices occupied the entire space. The doors opened, and she came face-to-face with the attorney who ran Wakefield Hamilton Investment's legal department like a drill sergeant. Lateness — his pet peeve — extended from not coming in on time to not completing a project by a pre-determined date.

"You're wanted in the small conference room. Now!" he snapped when she hesitated.

Hannah resisted the urge to snap to attention and salute him as she stepped back into the elevator. The doors closed, shutting out his cold ice-blue eyes and the thin lips that were a mere slash in his corpulent face. The car descended to the first floor, and a minute later she entered the conference room. She recognized the occupants seated at a round oaken table: CEO, CFO, and a member of the bank's security staff. The three men rose to their feet.

CEO Braden Grant gave her a steady stare. "Please sit down, Ms. Lowell."

She sat, the others following suit. Hannah didn't know why, but she felt like she'd been summoned to the principal's office because of an infraction. A shiver raced over her body and it had nothing to do with the frigid air flowing from overhead vents. She rarely, if ever, met with the bank's senior officers.

Braden continued to stare at her. "Ms. Lowell, I'm sorry, but we're terminating your employment, effective immediately."

The CFO pushed an envelope across the table. "We've direct deposited three years' severance and the last quarter's profit sharing into your bank account, and we'll also cover the cost of your health insurance coverage for one full year. Earlier this week the board of directors held an emergency shareholders' meeting, and the stockholders voted to merge with another institution. The result is the entire New York operation will move to Trenton, New Jersey, this coming weekend."

She inhaled deeply in an attempt slow down the runaway beating of her heart. Talk about being blindsided. Five years ago she'd resigned her position with a prominent law firm in midtown Manhattan to work for the bank, and it had been her plan to stay long enough to retire at sixty-seven.

"Am I the only one being terminated?" she asked, after an uncomfortable silence.

"No. Unfortunately, we've had to lay off

half our employees," the chief financial officer replied in an emotionless monotone, "including upper management *and* support staff."

Hannah saw his mouth moving but she wasn't listening to what he was saying because she'd suddenly tuned him out. She knew that someday she would go back to her roots, because she'd always yearned for a slower pace in which to live out the rest of her life. It was apparent that day had come much sooner than she'd planned.

Braden cleared his throat. "Is there anything else you'd like to ask or say, Ms. Lowell, before security escorts you to your office so you can retrieve your personal belongings?"

Her lips twisted into a cynical smile as she tucked a platinum strand of hair behind her left ear. He really didn't want to hear what she really longed to say. She stood, the others rising with her. "No. Thank you for everything. You've been most generous," Hannah drawled facetiously, when she wanted to curse them soundly for disrupting her life without prior notice.

She viewed the merger with skepticism, because there had been no discussion or rumors of a merger among any of the employees. She complimented herself for not losing her composure. If her mother had been alive there was no doubt she would've been very proud that her daughter had retained her ladylike poise, and poise was everything to Clarissa DuPont. Picking up the envelope, Hannah dropped it into her handbag and left the conference room.

The first thing she saw as she entered what would no longer be her office was the banker's box on the desk. It took less than ten minutes to remove laminated degrees from the wall, family photos, personal books and magazines off a credenza and store them in the box. She surrendered her ID badge, and the guard carried the box until they arrived at the entrance to the building.

It was apparent the CFO hadn't lied about the number of terminations, as evidenced by more than a dozen employees huddled together on the sidewalk. Their shock was visible. Those who were crying were comforted by their coworkers. She approached a woman who'd worked in human resources.

"Did you know about this?" she asked Jasmine Washington.

Jasmine shook her head, raven-black wavy hair swaying with the gesture. "Hell no!" she spat out. "And as the assistant director of personnel you'd think someone would've given me a heads-up."

Hannah glanced away when she saw tears filling Jasmine's eyes. She knew Jasmine had recently gone through a contentious divorce, even going so far as to drop her married name, and now being unemployed was akin to dousing a bonfire with an accelerant.

Recently certified public accountant Nydia Santiago shifted her box. "I don't know about the rest of you, but I could use a real stiff drink right about now."

Tonya Martin, the bank's former assistant chef, glared at Nydia. "It's nine flipping thirty in the morning, and none of the local watering holes are open at this time."

"I know where we can get a drink," Hannah volunteered. "Y'all come to my place," she added quickly when they gave her incredulous looks. "I live three blocks from here and y'all are welcome to hang out and, as you young folks say, get your drink on."

Tonya shifted an oversize hobo bag from one shoulder to the other. "Count me in."

Nydia looked at the others. "I'm game if the rest of you are."

Hannah met Jasmine's eyes. "Are you coming?"

"I guess so."

"You don't have to sound so enthusiastic, Jasmine," Nydia chided.

Hannah led the short distance to her

apartment building. As the eldest of the quartet, she suspected she was in a better position financially than the other women, who were nowhere close to retirement age. And she didn't know what possessed her to invite them to her apartment, because she rarely socialized with her coworkers outside the office. She occasionally joined them at a restaurant for someone's birthday or retirement dinner, but none of them had ever come to her home.

The doorman gave Hannah a puzzled look, aware she'd left less than an hour ago. He opened the door to the air-cooled vestibule, nodding to each of the women. She wasn't about to tell him she was jobless, because New York City doormen were notorious gossips — at least with one another.

Tonya glanced around the opulent lobby with a massive chandelier and mahogany tables cradling large painted vases overflowing with a profusion of fresh flowers. "How long have you lived here?" she asked Hannah.

Hannah smiled at the chef, who had a flawless henna-brown complexion and dimpled cheeks. Lightly graying curly twists were pinned into a neat bun on the nape of her neck. "Almost eight years."

16

"And how long has it been since you left the South?" Tonya had asked another question. "Your down South was showing when you say 'y'all.'"

"I really never left," she admitted. "I go back to New Orleans at least twice a year."

"Do you prefer Louisiana to New York?" Nydia questioned.

Hannah waited until they were in the elevator, punching the button for the twenty-sixth floor, and then said, "It's a toss-up. Both cities are wonderful places to live," she answered truthfully.

She'd spent years living on the West Coast when her naval officer husband was stationed in San Diego, but after his second — and fatal — heart attack, her life changed dramatically, allowing her to live her life by her leave. Hannah gave each woman a cursory glance. She felt a commonality with them despite their differences in age, race, and ethnicity. And despite being educated professionals, they were now four unemployed career women.

The doors opened and they exited the car, their footsteps muffled in the deep pile of the carpet that ran the length of a hallway decorated with framed prints of various New York City landmarks. Hannah stopped at her apartment door, swiped her cardkey, waited for the green light, and then pushed opened the door to what had become her sanctuary. The dwelling was high enough above the streets that she didn't hear any of the city's noise and she could unwind at the end of a long, and an occasionally hectic, workday.

"Please come in and set down your boxes next to the table." A bleached pine table in the entryway held a collection of paper-weights in various materials ranging from sterling to fragile cut-glass crystal. Hannah watched Nydia as she made her way across the open floor plan with a dining room, liv-ing room, and floor-to-ceiling windows.

"This is what I'm talking about," Nydia whispered, peering down at the cars and pedestrians on the streets below. "My boyfriend and I are looking for a place to live together, but nothing we've seen comes close to this." She turned, giving Hannah a long, penetrating stare. "How much do these apartments sell for?"

"Every apartment in this building is a rental."

Nydia grimaced. "And I can imagine the rents would be more than paying a mort-gage."

She didn't have a comeback for Nydia, because Hannah never had to concern herself with mortgage payments. She'd inherited a house in New Orleans' Garden District that had been in her family for two centuries. She kicked off her shoes, leaving them under the table.

"Y'all make yourself comfortable. There's a bar under the credenza in the dining room, and I also have chilled champagne in the fridge if anyone wants a mimosa or Bellini."

Jasmine dropped her handbag on one of the straight-backed chairs flanking the table. "A Bellini sounds wonderful."

A smile parted Hannah's lips. "And I don't know about the rest of you, but I've never been able to drink on an empty stomach, so if you can wait for me to change into something a little more comfortable, I'll whip up something for us to eat."

Tonya nodded. "I'm with you. If you don't mind, I'm willing to cook."

Pressing her palms together, Hannah whispered a silent prayer of thanks. Even though she was a more than adequate cook, it had been a while since she'd prepared a meal for someone other than herself. "Check in the fridge and use whatever you want." She'd planned to empty the refrigerator of perishables in the coming week anyway before she left to attend her high school's fortieth reunion.

CHAPTER 2

Hannah walked into her bedroom and closed the door, shutting out of the sound of voices coming from the living/dining area. She made her way over to a double dresser, peering into the mirror at the image staring back at her. It was if she were seeing the real Hannah Claire DuPont-Lowell for the first time in years; she recalled studying her reflection on her wedding day, which now seemed a lifetime ago.

Then she'd been fresh-faced twenty-one-year-old college graduate who was about to marry a young naval officer. She hadn't been in love with Robert Lowell, yet had accepted his proposal because she'd given him her virginity. He also had other favorable assets: He belonged to one of Louisiana's wealthiest families and he'd graduated from the U.S. Naval Academy. Two days before the ceremony she panicked, telling her mother she didn't want to marry Robert, but Clarissa, with her own inimitable powers of persuasion, reminded her that if she called off the wedding, the DuPonts would become the laughingstock of New Orleans' society. However, that was decades ago, and she had to deal with the here and now.

There were a few lines around her green eyes and the skin on her neck wasn't as firm as it had been years before, yet she refused to resort to plastic surgery or fillers to hold back time. She ate healthy foods, exercised regularly, and had a standing appointment at a local beauty salon for a trim, facial, and full body massage. Wavy platinum blond silver-streaked hair framed an oval face with a flawless peaches-and-cream complexion, which allowed her to forego makeup without appearing washed out.

She picked up a hairbrush and brushed the chin-length bob off her forehead, holding it off her face with a narrow elastic headband. After taking off the pantsuit and blouse, she left them on an armchair and slipped into an oversize white t-shirt and a pair of cropped cotton slacks. After washing her hands in the en suite bathroom, Hannah rejoined the other women in the kitchen. Like her, they'd all shed their shoes and sat barefoot on stools at the cooking island.

"Something smells good," she said, garnering their attention.

Tonya glanced up from the stovetop, smiling. "Jasmine and Nydia want pepper and ham omelets. Do you want the same or something else?"

"I'll have what everyone's having."

Tonya pointed to two flutes on the countertop. "I didn't know which one you'd like, so I made both."

Hannah reached for the flute with the peach nectar. "I'll drink both."

"Damn!" Tonya drawled, laughing.

"Go get them, lawyer lady," Jasmine teased. "One is enough for me."

"Y'all are playing yourselves," Nydia said. "I intend to be pissy-eyed drunk before I leave here today, because I know I'm going to have it out with my boyfriend. Now that I don't have a job, we won't be able to move in together."

Hannah sat on the remaining stool. "Doesn't he have a job?"

Nydia sipped her mimosa, staring at Hannah over the rim. "He doesn't have what I'd call a traditional job. Right now he works part-time as a waiter during the day and sings with a Latin band at night and on the weekends. He's recorded a demo record, but so far he hasn't been able to sign with a label."

Tonya turned a perfectly done omelet sprinkled with grated cheddar cheese along with warm cherry tomatoes onto a plate for Jasmine. She gave Nydia a direct stare. "At fifty, I'm old enough to be your mama, and I'm going to tell you the same thing I tell my daughter. Don't hook up with a man who can't match what you bring to the table. You can offer him moral support, but once you start opening your wallet to help him, you'll never close it. Am I right, Hannah?"

Hannah felt three pairs of eyes staring at her. What did Tonya expect her to say? She'd never been faced with that dilemma. "I suppose you're right, even though I never had to take care of a man. My late husband was a career naval officer and my son knew early on that he wanted to be a pilot. After graduating from the Air Force Academy, he became a test pilot and now flies commercial jets."

"Lucky you," Jasmine said. "But that's not going to solve Nydia's problem."

Tonya took a long swallow of her Bellini, and then quickly wiped out the omelet pan with a damp cloth. "Nydia wouldn't have a problem if she just took care of herself and not a grown-ass man. Where's he living now?"

Nydia ran a hand over dark-brown curls. Her large hazel eyes in an alizarin-brown complexion were filled with indecision. "He's living with his sister. I suppose I'm anticipating something that probably won't happen at all."

"I believe you're deluding yourself," Hannah stated in a quiet tone. "The fact you mention having it out with your boyfriend means you've had arguments about this in the past."

"Listen to the voice of wisdom," Tonya stated confidently. "Hannah and I have lived long enough not to steer you wrong."

"Thankfully, I don't have that problem because, thanks to Hannah, I was able to get my fair share from my ex for what had been *our* business," Jasmine announced proudly. She speared a forkful of omelet, and then popped it into her mouth.

A slight frown furrowed Nydia's forehead. "You didn't tell me you were Hannah's client."

Hannah gave Jasmine a disapproving glance. Jasmine had sought her out for legal advice, and she'd been forthcoming when advising her what she could do to get a share of the import/export business the former interior decorator had established prior to marrying. Hannah had also cautioned Jasmine not to tell anyone about their meetings, but now it was of no consequence because she doubted whether she would see her co-workers again after today.

"I wasn't, but she did steer me in the right direction because I suspected my attorney was being paid off by my ex," Jasmine explained. A smile tilted the corners of her generous mouth. "She became my guardian angel when I was at a low point in my life."

Nydia applauded. "Talk about sisterhood."

Jasmine shook her head, frowning slightly. "Sisterhood aside, now I have to think about what I want to do next."

"What business did you have with your ex?" Tonya asked Jasmine.

Jasmine reached for her flute and took a sip of the champagne infused with orange juice. "We bought and sold Asian artifacts. I was an interior decorator in a former life. I met Raymond Rios during a trip to the Philippines when I went there to buy several pieces for a client. We dated long distance for a year before we married."

Hannah drained her cocktail, her eyes measuring each woman seated at the breakfast bar. They all had options because of their ages. Nydia was in her early thirties, Jasmine in her forties, and Tonya had recently celebrated the big five-oh, while she would celebrate her fifty-ninth birthday before the end of the year. Even with a law degree, she still would have a problem securing a position with a salary matching what she'd earned at Wakefield Hamilton. And she didn't want to go online searching for companies or firms looking for someone with her experience.

"How long were you married?" Nydia asked Jasmine.

"Twelve years. And before anyone asks, we never had children — at least not together. What I didn't know was that my dog of an ex had an affair with another woman. After he became a baby daddy, and unbeknownst to me, he had a vasectomy, so that ruined my chance of having a child with him." Jasmine downed her drink. "I think that's enough true confessions for one day."

Tonya shook her head. "Don't worry, Jasmine, he'll get his."

A sardonic smile flittered over Jasmine's features. "He got his when I got the condo, the car, and when I sold the business, he walked away with only ten percent instead of half. He eventually moved in with his side chick. She lives in public housing in Brooklyn with three badass kids all from different daddies."

Nydia applauded loudly, and then raised her flute in a salute. "I've always said karma is a bitch."

Hannah laughed, touching her empty flute to the others. Jasmine hadn't given her an update on her ex-husband's fall from living the high life. "Here's to happy endings."

"Happy endings," the others chorused.

Hannah sobered as she mulled over the next phase of her life. "I don't know about the rest of you, but I plan to take the summer off and then decide what I'm going to do."

"I'm going to do the same," Tonya said, ladling a perfectly turned-out omelet on a plate for Hannah. "My daughter's home from college and I want us to spend some time together before she goes back to Atlanta for her senior year."

"What are you going to do after she goes back?" Hannah asked Tonya.

"I'm going to go job hunting. I don't believe I'm going to have a problem getting another position, but the difference is I'm going to have to start at the bottom again. That's going to take some getting used to after being assistant executive chef for the past four years."

Pale eyebrows lifted slightly when Hannah angled her head. "Why don't you come down to New Orleans and visit with me for a while?"

Again, she didn't know why she felt the urge to stay connected to her now former co-workers; maybe it was because she didn't have a sister and hadn't formed any close friendships with the women with whom she'd attended college or when living on base, and it made her acutely aware of how sterile her social life had become. If it hadn't been for her cousins, there would be no women in her life. Even as a military wife she'd kept her distance from the wives of the other naval officers because they were cliquish and prone to idle and occasionally malicious gossip.

Tonya whisked eggs until they were fluffy before she turned them into the omelet pan with sautéed ham and peppers. "If I decide to come, then I want to bring my daughter with me."

Hannah's smile was dazzling. "Please bring her. There's more than enough room for anyone who wants to come."

"How much room are you talking about, Hannah?" Nydia asked.

"The house has eighteen bedrooms and

two guesthouses." A swollen silence followed her reply. Her smile fading, she gave each woman a long, penetrating stare. "What's the matter?"

"You live in an eighteen-room mansion?" Jasmine questioned, breaking the silence.

She nodded. "Yes. I inherited it from my father, who inherited it from his father, and every generation as far back as two hundred years."

Tonya narrowed her eyes. "It's a plantation house." The question was a statement. Hannah nodded. The chef went completely still, the ladle suspended in midair. "There's no way I'm going to stay in a house where my ancestors once worked as slaves."

Hannah recoiled as if she'd been impaled with a sharp object. "What are you talking about?"

"Your house, Hannah," Tonya spat out. "If it's at least two hundred years old, then your people were slaveholders —"

"Stop it!" Hannah shouted at the same time a rush of blood suffused her fair complexion. "You know nothing about me or my family, yet you —"

"I'm with Tonya," Jasmine interrupted, cutting off whatever Hannah attempted to say. "Although people see me as Filipino I'm also African American. My father's people come from North Carolina."

Shaking her head, Nydia held up a hand. "As a Puerto Rican I'm staying out of this shit."

Anger and resentment made it nearly impossible for Hannah to think coherently. Tonya and Jasmine were judging her unfairly. She counted slowly until she eventually regained her composure. "I'm not going to lie and say one of my ancestors didn't own slaves, but it's not what you think."

Resting her hands on her hips, Tonya glared at her. "Now you say you know what I think?"

"No!" Hannah shouted. "And dammit, let me finish."

She must have gotten through to the chef. Tonya nodded. "I'm sorry. Explain."

"As the son of a wealthy French shipbuilder, my fifth great-grandfather, Etienne DuPont, sailed from Marseille to Haiti in 1779 where he set up a sugarcane plantation. He purchased a number of West African slaves to work in the fields, others as household servants, and some as boiler men at the sugar mills. Etienne refused to marry any of the daughters of the European colonists because he'd fallen in love with an *affranchise* — a free mulatto woman. Margit lived with him as his mistress and gave

31

him a son and three daughters. Things changed when Haiti claimed its independence from European rule and Etienne's younger brother, Jean-Paul, convinced him to leave the island and settle in Louisiana where he'd started up a shipbuilding company. Etienne appointed Jean-Paul as his agent, directing him to purchase land for a sugarcane plantation in the Louisiana territory."

Hannah felt a measure of satisfaction as the three women were seemingly spellbound when she told them Etienne's mistress wouldn't leave Haiti with his children unless he freed his slaves and took them to Louisiana as free people of color.

A hint of a smile curved Tonya's lips. "Did he?"

Hannah broke into a wide, open smile. "Of course he did. After all, his mistress was a free woman and not his property. Margit, realizing the power she wielded over Etienne, persuaded him to draw up a legal document making their son his legal heir and agreeing to have their children educated in France."

Tonya winked at Hannah. "What's the expression? Once you go black, you don't go back."

A becoming blush stained Hannah's

cheeks. "I wouldn't know anything about that." She'd researched her family's history after uncovering several trunks filled with diaries, letters, family Bibles, and legal documents dating back to the early eighteenth century. Many were yellowed, fragile, and a few were covered with mold. When she called the archivist at the local historical society to donate the items, the woman was so excited she couldn't stop stuttering.

Smiling, Jasmine leaned forward, meeting Hannah's eyes. "What happened to Etienne and Margit after they moved to Louisiana?"

"That's a very long story, but if you're willing to come to New Orleans, then I'll give you an in-depth history about the Du-Ponts."

Crestfallen, Jasmine's smile quickly faded. "That's blackmail, and you of all people should know that's illegal."

Tonya managed to look contrite. "I'm sorry I accused your folks of owning slaves, although initially they did. And I accept your invitation to come and visit you in Nawlins. But, I have to tell you now that I don't like flying, which means I'll rent a car and Samara and I will drive down."

Hannah smiled in smug delight at the same time she inclined her head. "Apology accepted." There was something about the

33

three women she liked, and she didn't want whatever fragile camaraderie they'd just fostered to end once they walked out the door. Although she planned to spend the summer in New Orleans, she wouldn't have the company of her cousins; they'd made plans to go abroad with a group of retired schoolteachers.

Nydia made a sucking sound with her tongue and teeth. "Why are you dragging your feet, Jasmine? Why don't you join Tonya and her daughter? Because you've got nothing here stopping you from going."

Jasmine glared at the accountant. "Neither do you," she countered.

"Hello," Nydia drawled. "I do have a boyfriend."

"A boyfriend who's looking for a woman to take care of him," Jasmine said accusingly. "Don't be like me, chica. After we were separated, my ex told me he never would've hooked up with me if I hadn't had a viable business. That was my first mistake, because the big three-oh was staring me in the face and I wanted to be married. My second mistake was letting him take control of a business in which I'd invested my blood, sweat, and tears to make a success." She held up a hand when Nydia opened her mouth to interrupt her. "And you would be very successful if you were a tax accountant. Rent an office in your neighborhood and do taxes from January to June and you'll probably make enough money where you won't have to work for the rest of the year."

"She's right, Jasmine," Hannah said. "I doubt at fifty-eight that I'm going to spend the rest of my life working for someone else."

Nydia pulled her lip between her teeth, and then asked, "What would you do? Open your own practice?"

"No," Hannah replied, shaking her head. "I've been thinking about turning the house in New Orleans into an inn." She didn't tell them she'd spent countless hours researching what went into operating an inn. Once she felt confident about going into business for herself, she'd applied for the permits and licenses to convert the historic home from a personal residence to a business.

"Don't you mean a bed-and-breakfast?" Tonya questioned.

"No. I mean an inn where folks will want to stay the night or longer. I haven't planned to offer meals because I would have to use the floor I need for my personal space."

Leaning against the back of the stool, Nydia nodded. "It looks as if you've really got yourself together."

Hannah smiled. "Honey, let me tell you that if I didn't have it together at my age, then I doubt if I'd ever get it together. Husband or no husband, women have to take care of themselves or they'll wind up royally fucked, because they'll have to depend on someone to dole out whatever crumbs they decide to give you. Did I say something wrong?" she asked when the trio stared at her with shocked expressions.

Tonya was the first to react. "I just didn't expect our little Southern belle to drop the F-bomb."

She didn't tell the others that she'd spewed a litany of curses once she'd uncovered her husband's ongoing affairs with a number of different women after his first heart attack, which resulted in her moving out of their bedroom. "Sometimes it's necessary to make a point."

"You've made your point," Jasmine said under her breath. "I've never been to New Orleans, so count me in. I have a Yukon Denali so, Tonya, you and your daughter can ride down with me."

Nydia blew out an audible breath. "Count me in too. I've always wanted to visit the Big Easy, and I'm willing to help with the driving."

"We can all help with driving," Tonya

added, "including my daughter. We'll have a sister-girl road trip, stopping at night to check into a hotel before getting back on the road in the morning."

"I'll map out the route," Jasmine volunteered, "and I'll confirm the reservations at whatever hotels you prefer. We should exchange numbers, and then coordinate a time that's convenient for everyone."

Hannah laced her fingers together in a prayerful gesture. "Whatever you decide, I'll make certain y'all have a good time." She gave them the number to her cell and home in New Orleans.

It was nearly noon when she contacted the concierge to call a car service to take the three women home. Hannah didn't know whether she would see them again after their visit, but at least she would be left with lasting good memories of her time at the bank instead of remembering being unceremoniously dismissed without prior notice.

CHAPTER 3

Hannah stared out the window as the jet began its descent, and then glanced at her watch. The nonstop flight left New York on time and was scheduled to arrive on time. She made the reservation to leave at six in the morning because she wanted to spend a few hours with her cousins before they left for their European vacation. A wry smile flitted over her features as she realized she was going home and had no timetable as to when she'd return.

Familiar landmarks came into view as the plane touched down at the Louis Armstrong New Orleans International Airport. After retrieving her carry-on from the overhead bin, she followed the signs leading to ground transportation. A taxi pulled up to the curb, the driver getting out and taking her bag and storing it in the trunk, while she got in and settled back against the leather seat.

"Where to, madam?"

Hannah hadn't realized she'd closed her eyes and dozed off for several seconds until hearing the cabbie's voice. "The DuPont House in the Garden District."

She knew her current sleep patterns were out of sync. Now that she was unemployed, she stayed up well past midnight watching movies she'd missed and many others she'd seen but were personal favorites. It had been a little more than a week since the layoffs, and she still contemplated her future. And though she'd talked about turning the DuPont House into an inn, the thought of overseeing it alone was more than daunting. The few times she'd broached the subject with her cousins, they were reluctant to begin another career as innkeepers.

Reaching for her cell phone, Hannah tapped the button for her son's residence. It rang twice. "Lowell residence." The feminine voice on the other end of the line was cheerful.

"Hello, Karen."

"Mother! How are you?"

"I'm well, thank you. I'm calling to let you know I plan to spend the summer in New Orleans and would like to schedule a time when I can see my grandbabies."

"Are you taking sick leave?"

"No. I'm just not working this summer."

She wasn't quite ready to tell her son and daughter-in-law that she'd been terminated. Both were overprotective, while not realizing she was more than capable of caring for herself. Her son checked in with her every Sunday night, and when he was out of the country Karen either called or emailed her. "When is a good time for me to see my little darlings?" she asked again. She enjoyed interacting with her eight-and ten-year-old grandsons; the past two years she'd taken them to popular theme parks.

A groan came through the earpiece. "I'm so sorry, Mother. I made plans to send the kids to Hawaii to stay with my parents for the summer. But I promise to bring them to New Orleans a week before they're scheduled to return to school. I'll tell Wyatt to put in for vacation and we'll all come together."

Hannah bit her tongue to keep from chastising her daughter-in-law about not checking with her before planning the children's summer vacation, when Karen knew she always scheduled time during the summer months to reconnect with her grandchildren. When her son and his family had lived in Texas she saw them more often; however, once Wyatt accepted a position with a carrier with international flights, they'd relocated to a Los Angeles suburb.

"Okay." The single word lacked emotion. "Don't forget to send me pictures of them in Hawaii."

"I won't. I'm going to ring off because I have a dental appointment. I'll have the kids call you tomorrow. Right now they're at a birthday sleepover."

"Kiss my grandbabies for me and give Wyatt my love."

"I will. Good-bye, Mother."

Hannah ended the call, staring out the open side window. The drive from Kenner to New Orleans was accomplished quickly, and she experienced an emotion she couldn't quite identify when the taxi maneuvered up the winding path to the historic house where she'd spent her childhood and adolescent years. In the past she'd come for a visit; but now she had no idea how long she would stay. She'd paid her rent several months in advance, emptied the refrigerator of perishables, and arranged with the post office to forward her mail to her New Orleans address.

The taxi came to a stop, and the fragrance of roses and jasmine came through the open windows, reminding Hannah that she'd truly come home. The sight of the antebellum mansion set back behind wrought-iron gates and surrounded by lush gardens and ancient oak trees draped in Spanish moss never failed to take her breath. The rose-colored limestone Greek Revival–style house, with pale pink marble columns, a wraparound porch, and tall black-shuttered windows was one of the finest homes erected in the historic Garden District.

The front door opened, and Paige and LeAnn DuPont walked out onto the front porch. The last time they were together had been Christmas, and seeing them again made her aware of how much she'd missed them. With the exception of a few distant cousins whom she'd never met, they were Hannah's only link to the past. Sixty-six-year-old Paige and LeAnn, sixty-eight, were fiercely independent free-thinkers who'd come of age during the time of civil rights and anti–Vietnam War demonstrations.

As a girl, Hannah overheard her father's younger brother complain that he panicked each time the phone rang whenever his teenage daughters left New Orleans over the summer to join the many civil rights workers coming down from the North to register blacks to vote. Although the sisters had elected to remain single, they had never lacked male attention or companionship.

She paid the fare, retrieved her carry-on

bag from the driver, and walked up to the porch, which held many happy memories for Hannah. It was where she'd sat with her parents, grandparents, and brother whenever the intense summer heat abated enough for them to sit outside. All were gone except Paige and LeAnn, who'd taken up residence at DuPont House at Hannah's request once she decided to move to New York. LeAnn had sold her house and Paige rented out her condo to a young teacher at the school where they'd taught together.

LeAnn went on tiptoe, pressing her cheek to Hannah's. "Welcome home, little cousin."

Easing back, Hannah angled her head. At five-nine, she was nearly a half head taller than the sisters, who'd inherited their mother's petite body, dark hair, and dark eyes. "When am I going to stop being your little cousin?" she teased.

LeAnn placed an arm around Hannah's waist. "It's not about height, Miss Daddy Longlegs, but age," she countered.

Hannah wrapped her arms around her cousins' shoulders, leading them into the house. The first thing she noticed in the expansive entryway was the number of bags. Seeing the luggage made her more than aware that she wouldn't see them for months. Their vacation itinerary included touring Europe, Russia, and China.

She strolled into the parlor, sat on a bench covered with a faded needlepoint cushion, and slipped off her running shoes. "My being laid off came at the right time, because we won't have to close up the house." Whenever Paige and LeAnn went on vacation, they either arranged for someone to housesit or they closed up the house completely.

Paige combed her fingers through her short salt-and-pepper hair, frowning. "I still can't get over folks firing you without proper notice."

"I wasn't the only one. Half the bank's employees were terminated because of the merger."

"How did you react when they told you?" LeAnn asked.

"I didn't," Hannah replied truthfully. "I was too shocked to say anything, and then I realized they'd done me a favor. My life didn't stop because of what I think of as a setback. Getting fired is only one piece in the puzzle of my life, and now I need to complete my future."

"If you'd known you wouldn't be working, you could've come with us," Paige said, folding her body down to a Louis XV–style chair, while her sister sat on a matching loveseat.

Hannah wanted to tell Paige there was no way she wanted to be away from the States for months on end. Whenever she and Robert had embarked on an extended vacation, she always experienced an intense longing to return home.

"I don't mind hanging out here, because it's been years since I've spent more than a month in this house." At that time she'd buried her father, and then extended her stay to settle the estate.

Paige scrunched up her pert nose. "Are you still thinking about turning this place into an inn?"

"Yes. I've filed for the permits and licenses, and as soon as they're approved, I'll put everything into motion. Of course, I'll have to move my bedroom downstairs, because I plan to use the second-story bedrooms for guests." There were nine upstairs bedrooms and nine on the main floor.

LeAnn smiled. "It appears as if you've really thought this out. And I've always said out of evil cometh good."

"Amen," Hannah said under her breath.

There came another pause, this one longer than the previous one. LeAnn crossed and uncrossed her legs. "What about staffing the house?"

Hannah tried unsuccessfully to hide a smirk. "Don't worry. You guys won't have to lift a finger. I plan to hire a housekeeping staff." A local maintenance company gave the house a thorough cleaning twice a month, and the gardens were maintained by a family of landscapers who'd worked for the DuPonts for many years.

She pushed to her feet. "I'm going to take a shower, and then y'all can give me an update on your love lives."

LeAnn rolled her eyes upward. "There's not much for me to tell. I gave John his walking papers when he started talking about us living together. And when I asked him where we'd live, he had the unmitigated gall to open his mouth and say DuPont House."

Paige giggled like a little girl. "I felt sorry for the poor man after LeAnn gave him a tongue-lashing he'll probably remember for the rest of his life." She sobered quickly. "What about you, Nah? Is there anyone special you want to dish about?"

Hannah smiled. It was only in New Orleans that family members referred to her by the childhood nickname her brother had attached to her. "Not a one." Her cousins knew she'd gone out with two men after moving to New York, but neither relationship progressed to the point where she'd want to sleep with either of them. Twenty-nine years of marriage to a philandering husband had left her distrustful of the opposite sex.

She left the parlor, picking up the bag off the porch, and walked into the great room with its curving staircase leading to the second story. She remembered her mother going into vapors whenever Clarissa found Hannah sliding down the banister to land unceremoniously on the black-and-white marble floor. Her prim and proper mother failed to realize her daughter had inherited the dormant wild DuPont streak, which surfaced every few generations. Clarissa's greatest fear was her daughter would turn out like her brother-in-law's daughters who refused to become proper DuPont women. Fortunately for her mother, Hannah had become the dutiful daughter, marrying well and making her a grandmother.

Her steps slowed as she stared at the rug running the length of the hallway. Not only had it faded, but portions were noticeably threadbare. Although she hadn't had to sell off priceless antiques and heirloom pieces to maintain the upkeep of the historic mansion, Hannah realized many of the paintings and rugs were in need of restoration. She stood in the doorway to her bedroom staring at the furnishings that portrayed an air of gentle Southern tradition. Creamy-white fabric draping the canopied mahogany bed, a pale sisal rug, and a pedestal table with two pull-up chairs with beige brocade seat cushions complemented the cream-colored wallpaper dotted with sprigs of lavender. A sitting area with a floral loveseat, bookcases filled with first-edition classics, and a window seat beckoned one to come and sit a while. She marveled how different this space was from her New York City bedroom where the no-fuss, functional furniture mirrored her big city state of mind.

Unconsciously she'd morphed into the laid-back Southerner when talking to Paige and LeAnn. When in New York she was forced to slip into the armor needed to communicate and navigate the city of more than eight million people. She talked fast, moved even faster, and there was little or no time to reflect on what had happened during the day because the instant her head touched the pillow she fell asleep, only to wake up and begin the grind again.

Grind. Hannah froze when the single word came to mind, lingering like a temporary tattoo. It was the first time she'd likened her career to a grind. She had always wanted to be a lawyer, like her father, but at her mother's insistence she'd gone into education because Clarissa felt it was a more genteel profession for a woman. It wasn't until her son had gone to school on the base she'd begun studying to take the LSAT, scoring high enough to be accepted into Stanford Law, but finally selected the University of San Diego School of Law because she didn't want to be away from Wyatt. Conversely, her law school graduation was bittersweet. Everyone in her family attended, while Clarissa refused to come. Although she was disappointed, Hannah experienced a measure of independence for the first time in her life, because it was she, not her mother or her husband, who'd determined her future.

Hannah entered the bedroom, flipping a wall switch, and the blades of the ceiling fan rotated slowly, dispelling the buildup of heat. She unpacked, taking out the dress wrapped in tissue paper she planned to wear to the reunion. After browsing through several Madison Avenue boutiques she'd found the perfect outfit: a black lace long-sleeved sheath dress with a royal blue silk slip ending at the knees. They were the colors of Jackson Memorial High School. A pair of black silk-covered, three-inch pumps completed the chic ensemble.

She looked forward to reconnecting with classmates with whom she'd shared classes, many she hadn't seen in twenty years. When she'd returned to New Orleans for the twentieth reunion she'd attended unaccompanied. Robert had been assigned to an aircraft carrier in the Indian Ocean. Now, two decades later, she would attend alone again, but this time as a widow.

Hannah returned to the parlor after showering and changing into a loose-flowing sundress and sandals. Aside from the kitchen, it was her favorite room in the house; it had become the perfect space in which to begin the day. It was where she and her younger brother had shared breakfast every morning, and on weekends they turned it into their pretend castle, fort, pirate ship, or classroom. There wasn't a day when she didn't miss Jefferson, or Jeffrey, as everyone called him, who died unexpectedly at nine from an undiagnosed bout of meningococcal meningitis. His death affected the entire household, her mother in particular, who'd gone into a period of mourning and depression lasting years.

Paige closed the magazine resting on her lap and smiled at her. "I know they didn't feed you on the plane, so we ordered takeout of your favorite dishes from Chez Toussaints. When was the last time you had authentic Nawlins red beans and rice, chicken-andouille gumbo, and jambalaya?"

"It's been too long since I've eaten anything prepared by Eustace Toussaint," she admitted. "I'll eat later, because I managed to grab a bagel while waiting to board." What Hannah missed most about New Orleans was the cuisine. Whether Creole or Cajun, she never tired of eating the food indigenous to the region, although she was adept in preparing many of the traditional dishes.

LeAnn scrunched up her nose. "I prefer a beignet to a bagel."

"So do I," Hannah said in agreement, "but a bagel is to New York what a beignet is to New Orleans."

"Are you certain you don't mind staying here by yourself while we're away?" Paige asked.

"Of course I don't mind. Remember I was alone here after my mother passed away."

Paige lowered her eyes. "I know she was your mother, but Aunt Clarissa was a little hard to swallow. What bugged the hell out of me was her always putting on airs."

Hannah flashed a half-smile. "What can I tell you? She always wanted to be a DuPont." And marrying a DuPont topped her mother's wish list. "What time are you leaving for the airport?" she asked, deftly changing the topic.

LeAnn glanced at her watch. "The driver should be here in about forty minutes. Once we arrive in New York, we'll have at least four hours before we leave for Germany. That will give us an extra hour to browse the duty-free shops."

"Just make certain you don't come back with more luggage than you leave with," Hannah teased.

"Paige and I decided whatever we buy we'll ship back to the States. I know you like silk kimonos and perfume, so those will certainly be among our must-haves."

A mysterious smile softened her lips at the same time attractive lines fanned out around Hannah's eyes. If she had any weakness, it was the feel of silk against her bare skin and the distinctive scent of Chanel No. 5. The perfume had been her grandmother's favorite, and she'd given all her granddaughters a gift set for their sixteenth birthdays. Throughout the years Hannah experimented with other perfumes, but the signature scent had remained her all-time favorite.

She chatted with her cousins until the call box chimed. Rising to her feet, LeAnn went over to view the call box screen. The house had been updated every generation with the addition of electricity, indoor plumbing, and central heating, air-conditioning, and a sophisticated security system. Intercoms were installed throughout the downstairs and in several bedrooms. The indoor and outdoor kitchens and all the bathrooms were also updated, while the bedrooms had retained the charm of an authentic early nineteenth-century Southern mansion.

"The driver's here," LeAnn announced. She pressed a button, opening the wrought-iron gate protecting the property.

Hannah exchanged hugs with the two women, promising to keep in touch by email. She stood on the porch long after the Town Car drove away, and then went inside. Her yearning to turn the house into an inn grew even stronger as she stared up at the massive crystal chandelier in the great room. The notion of three single middle-aged women in a centuries-old house with more than six thousand square feet of living space was the perfect plot and locale for an author wishing to set his or her period novel in the Crescent City's historic district. It was also perfect for those wishing to relive the past. Hannah didn't want to recreate the past, but to build a new future for the house for ongoing generations of DuPonts.

Ideas tumbled over themselves as she climbed the staircase. An excitement Hannah hadn't felt in a while eddied through her as she walked into her bedroom and exchanged her dress for a nightgown. She lay in bed, staring up at the delicate fabric until Morpheus welcomed her, and she sank into to a deep, dreamless sleep.

CHAPTER 4

Decelerating, Hannah drove along a street leading to the hotel in the warehouse and central business district. It was one of her favorite neighborhoods, especially the narrow streets lined with Victorian warehouses, office buildings, and banks. The commercial area was also home to the headquarters for banking, energy, and oil corporations.

She looked forward to this reunion with the same excitement as she did going to prom. Hannah knew if she still lived in New Orleans, the reunion wouldn't hold as much significance as it did since she had left her hometown. Over the years she'd become more of a tourist than a resident.

The reunion committee had reserved a block of rooms in the hotel for out-of-town alumni. The program included a cocktail hour, sit-down dinner, cash bar, masquerade ball, and a DJ spinning tunes spanning decades. Smiling, she wondered what theme they would come up for the fiftieth.

She maneuvered to the entrance of the hotel, smiling at the valet as he opened the door to the vintage Mercedes-Benz. Her father had purchased the sedan after his appointment to the bench, and with more than two hundred thousand miles on the odometer, it ran as smoothly as the day Judge Lester DuPont drove it out of the dealer's showroom.

Gathering her evening handbag and the envelope with the printed invitation off the passenger seat, she placed her free hand on the valet's extended palm as he eased her gently to stand. "Thank you."

The young man nodded. "You're welcome, ma'am. I'll park your car where it will be safe."

"Thank you again."

The reunion committee had selected an elegant boutique hotel just a block from the French Quarter. The women who sent out quarterly newsletters kept everyone abreast of what had been going on in the lives of their former classmates, and each time the email arrived in her inbox Hannah perused it, reading about birthdays, wedding anniversaries, the birth of grandchildren, and career changes. Unfortunately, a few of her high school classmates had died or lost their spouses because of illness, and others to accidents. She'd been one of those: she had reported Robert's passing from a massive heart attack.

Flashing a polite smile, a liveried doorman held the door for her. "Good evening, ma'am. The class reunion is in the Lafayette Ballroom."

She entered the ballroom, stopping at the reception table and coming face-to-face with her high school nemesis. Julie Anderson lowered her eyes, and then handed her a Mardi Gras feather mask, colorful beads, and a badge attached to a lanyard. "You're assigned to table five. You'll be required to wear the mask during the ball. I'm so glad you could make it, Hannah."

Hannah smiled, the gesture not reaching her eyes. "I'm glad I made it, too," she drawled facetiously.

Julie had made it known she didn't like her because she'd transferred from a private all-girls school to the public high school, believing snobby rich girls should stay in their place. Picking up her name tag, Hannah slipped the lanyard and beads around her neck.

Hannah had forgiven Julie for her adolescent behavior but doubted whether she would ever forget her cruel remarks. She didn't have many close friends in high school; the exception were a few with whom she'd shared AP courses. They usually alternated studying at one another's homes, and every other month they'd meet at a small restaurant in the French Quarter that had become a hangout for students from several nearby schools.

Her smile was still in place when she walked into the gaily decorated ballroom featuring a Mardi Gras theme. Their twentieth reunion had been held on a riverboat replete with gambling tables, dancehall girls, costumed lawmen, and piano players.

An ear-piercing shriek stopped Hannah midstride. Turning on her heel, she stared at one of her former classmates hanging onto St. John McNair's neck. She shook her head in amazement. Time had been more than kind to St. John, with his handsome features in a tawny-brown complexion. Cropped silvered hair, a neatly barbered matching goatee and a tall, slender physique made him as strikingly gorgeous now as he'd been in his youth. Her eyes moved slowly over the tailored navy-blue blazer, buttoned-down white shirt, black and royal blue–striped tie, and sharply creased taupe slacks falling at the correct break over a pair of cognac-hued wingtips.

St. John, pronounced *SIN-jun,* like the character in Charlotte Brontë's *Jane Eyre,* had been voted best-dressed and best-looking boy in their graduating class because of his impeccable sense of style and uncanny resemblance to the late singer-songwriter Marvin Gaye. A number of girls admitted to having a crush on him, knowing he was off-limits. At the time he was dating and eventually married a girl who'd attended a parochial school in another parish.

St. John McNair forcibly removed the arms from around his neck. It was apparent Eileen Miller didn't know her own strength. "It's good seeing you again, Eileen."

Eileen couldn't stop blushing as she picked up a name badge from the stack on the table. "I'm sorry about attacking you, but I can't believe it's been twenty years since we last saw one another. Stan and I moved to Orlando after the last reunion and we only come back to New Orleans for family get-togethers," she continued without taking a breath. She handed him his name badge and a mask. "By the way, you're seated at table five."

St. John took the badge, pinning it on his lapel. His gaze swept over the assembly in the ballroom. There had been two hundred fifty-seven students in his graduating class, and it appeared that many of them and their spouses were in attendance. Dozens of tables covered with white tablecloths were festooned with blue and black helium-filled balloons. Bartenders at opposite facing bars were doing a brisk business. The DJ was spinning popular tunes from their era, and the sound of Queen's "Bohemian Rhapsody" blared from powerful speakers positioned around the ballroom.

A slideshow of photos was displayed on several large screens set up around the room. A few he'd seen before, while many had been unearthed from the school's archives depicting them as far back as freshmen, sophomores, and juniors. St. John groaned inwardly when seeing himself as a freshman with a mouth filled with metal. It'd taken two years before the braces were finally removed, resulting in a set of straight, white teeth.

He'd mentally debated whether to attend this reunion, but then changed his mind when recalling the number of his classmates who'd passed away. He believed they were gone much too soon, which made him more than aware of his own mortality, and he knew if he didn't attend this gathering, he would have to wait another decade for the fiftieth.

Waiters, carrying trays of hors d'oeuvres and champagne, strolled around the ballroom. A waiter stopped in front of him and he took a flute of champagne and remoulade-covered shrimp skewered on a toothpick. He took a sip of the champagne, and then popped the shrimp into his mouth, finding both excellent. It was apparent the committee had listened to the feedback gleaned from the survey of their prior reunion. Their twentieth had been held on a luxurious riverboat; unfortunately, the food choices at the buffet dinner were never able to match the elegance of the venue.

St. John froze when inhaling the scent of a perfume he'd attributed to only one girl at their high school. "Hannah DuPont?" he whispered.

Turning slowly, he stared mutely at Hannah, unable to believe her transformation. Smoky eyeshadow illuminated large green eyes framed by long, charcoal-gray lashes that seemed to not to look at but go through him. Lushness had replaced the youthful waiflike appearance that had been so apparent when he last saw her twenty years before. Enthralled by her mature attractiveness, St. John couldn't pull his gaze away the curves outlined in the body-hugging lace dress.

Vermilion colored lips parted in a sensual moue as Hannah extended her hand. "Either you're a warlock, or you have eyes in the back of your head."

Ignoring the proffered slender hand, he leaned in and kissed her scented cheek. "I knew it was you even before I turned around," he said in her ear.

"How so?" she whispered against his smooth cheek.

"You were the only girl at school who wore that particular perfume." Most girls had chosen Avon or drugstore fragrances, while Hannah preferred the iconic French perfume.

Easing back, she gave him a direct stare. The three-inch heels put her head close to his height of six foot, two inches. "You remembered my perfume?"

He nodded. "There are very few things I don't remember."

St. John wanted to say there were very few things he did not remember about the tall, willowy, natural blonde. He'd found her different from the other girls: It was her poise and sophistication that had set her apart. She hadn't been one of the more popular female students, seemingly preferring to blend in rather than stand out. However, she'd excelled as an above average student, graduating in the top ten percent in their class.

They'd partnered in biology and chemistry labs and shared history and French classes. She didn't go out with any of the boys at their school, making her a subject of gossip as to whether she preferred a same-sex relationship. The gossipers were silenced when she attended prom with a naval officer as her escort.

"Where's Lorna?"

Her question shattered his reverie. "We're no longer together."

"Did she . . . is she —"

"She's alive," he interrupted. "We divorced five years ago." The pronouncement was cold as his marriage had been.

Hannah's eyelids fluttered. "I'm so sorry. Everyone knew how much you loved her."

St. John didn't want to talk about his failed marriage. He'd tried to make a go of it, but after three decades of living a lie in a childless union, he was relieved when it finally ended. They'd just celebrated their thirtieth wedding anniversary when Lorna suddenly announced she wanted out, and the instant he signed the divorce papers making it final, he realized both had wasted too many years in wedlock that had been doomed from the very beginning.

"I read about you losing your husband." As soon as the words were out, St. John stared intently at Hannah as she pressed her lips together, wondering if she, too, had had a less than happy marriage.

"Thankfully, it was quick."

"How long do you plan to stay in New Orleans?" he asked, deftly changing the topic because their conversation was becoming much too personal.

She paused for several seconds. "I'm not sure. I'm not working this summer, so I know for certain I'll be here until Labor Day." Opening her beaded evening purse, Hannah took out her cell phone, handing it to him. "Why don't you program your number and I'll call to invite you to come out to DuPont House so we can catch up on what's been going on in our lives. I'll give you an update about my experience as big city corporate attorney while you can tell me about your students at Barden College."

He took the phone, then reached inside his breast pocket and handed her his. "You do the same. I still have two more weeks at the college before I'm off for the summer, so once I'm free I will call you." St. John entered his cell and home numbers into Hannah's cell's directory and then gave it back to her. He noticed she'd waved away the waiter with flutes of champagne. Cupping her elbow, he steered her toward the bar. "Can I get you something to drink?"

"Yes, please. I'll have white wine."

"Don't you dare give me any money," St. John warned when she opened her purse again.

Hannah smiled. "Okay, but your drink is on me. It's the least I can do for someone who tutored me in history."

"That's not happening, Hannah," St. John countered. "I'm not paying for your drink just so you can reciprocate." A beat passed, and then she nodded.

His aunt had accused him of being a throwback to another generation, because his mother had raised him with her own set of values. Elsie McNair lectured him constantly about using women, whether for sex or monetary gain. She insisted he stand whenever a woman entered or left a room, hold her chair until she was seated, and open doors for her. He'd grown up watching his father do these things for his mother and despite women declaring they were liberated, for St. John old habits were slow to die.

Resting a hand at the small of her back, he led Hannah to one of the two bars. The bartenders were, pouring, shaking and blending drinks for those calling out drink orders. Hannah moved closer to his side, his arm circling her slender waist. She was right about his tutoring her in a subject that had become his livelihood. He'd always loved geography and American history, selecting the latter as his college major; he taught high school and college-level courses, and now headed the history department at Barden College, a small, prestigious private college with a strong concentration in history, political science, and governmental studies.

The bartender gestured to St. John. "Dr. McNair, what can I get you and your lady?"

He and Hannah exchanged a look, his gaze shifting to the jeweled hairpins holding the platinum twist in place behind her left ear. It was apparent the bartender believed they were a couple. "I'll have a Sazerac and *my* lady wants a white wine."

Sazerac had become the official cocktail of New Orleans and this past year he'd grown quite fond of the concoction of rye whiskey, Peychaud's bitters, and sugar served in a rock glass rinsed with absinthe.

"You know the bartender, *Dr. McNair*?"

Hannah whispered.

"He's one of my former students."

"Why did he refer to me as your lady?"

"I suppose he just assumed you're my lady."

"He has to have a reason for assuming, St. John."

"I'm usually not seen out and about with a beautiful woman on my arm." Her lids slipped down over her eyes, and St. John found himself mesmerized by the demure gesture. This was the Hannah he remembered: shy and innocently bashful.

"You don't date?" she asked, seemingly having recovered from his flattering remark.

Smiling, he angled his head. "No, I don't date." He was truthful when he said he didn't see women in the traditional sense. Several times a month he spent the weekend with a forty-something Baton Rouge divorcée. She'd made it known the third time they went out together she didn't want a relationship. What she wanted was sex without any emotional involvement. It had taken St. John a while to agree to her arrangement but he did because he enjoyed her easygoing personality.

Hannah appeared satisfied with his explanation that he didn't date when she said, "You must run into a lot of your students whenever you're out and about."

St. John nodded. "I do. I know I'm getting a little long in the tooth whenever former students tell me their children are now high schoolers."

"How long do you plan to teach?"

"I'll probably put down my red pencil in another ten years. As chair of the history department, I teach two advanced courses."

She froze. "When were you appointed? And why didn't I read about it in the newsletter?"

He took the wineglass, handing it to Hannah. "That's because I didn't report it." The bartender set his glass on the bar and St. John reached into the pocket of his slacks and left a bill on the bar. "Keep the change." The bartender rang up the sale, dropping the remaining bills in the tip jar. Picking up his glass, he touched it to Hannah's. "Here's to a wonderful fortieth, and hopefully new beginnings."

"To new beginnings," she repeated, smiling at him over the rim of her wineglass. Their eyes met as she took a sip.

St. John's free hand rested at her waist as they headed for their table. They were greeted by former classmates who'd also come unaccompanied. Hugs, handshakes, and rough embraces were exchanged as everyone began talking at once.

Matt Johnston tossed back his drink and set it on the table without taking his eyes off Hannah. His staring made her feel uncomfortable. Matt had set the school record for more quarterback sacks in a single season, which still remained unbroken. Homecoming king and nicknamed the Red Dragon because of his long, bright red-orange hair, Matt had been an outstanding athlete.

A lopsided grin tugged at his slack mouth. "For an ice princess you sure turned into one fine-ass woman, Hannah DuPont," he drawled, reaching out and gripping her shoulders.

Hannah forced a smile she didn't feel. His fingers tightened, biting into her flesh as he attempted to kiss her, she turning her face at the last possible moment. "You're hurting me, Matt. Please let me go."

"You heard her," St. John said, as Matt continued to hold onto Hannah. "Take your hands off her."

Matt dropped his hands and looked at St. John. "I'm sorry, man. I didn't know Hannah was your woman," he shouted loudly enough to garner the attention of those at nearby tables.

Hannah wanted to tell everyone St. John

wasn't her man nor she his woman, although she was more than grateful he'd intervened. She handed him her wineglass. "I'm going to the ladies' room."

She felt sorry for Matt, who'd been a local hero, first-round draft pick by the New Orleans Saints, and a role model for young boys looking for a career as a professional athlete. Unfortunately, a high-profile sex scandal and an addiction to drugs and alcohol brought his professional career to an abrupt halt before he'd celebrated his thirtieth birthday.

Hannah remembered that when she'd greeted Matt in the hall during a change of classes or at the restaurant that had become a hangout for students, and not once had he ever smiled, spoke, or acknowledged her with a cursory glance. The flashy defensive end garnered more than his share of female attention, bragging incessantly about his sexual conquests, while rumors were swirling that he'd slept with every girl on the cheerleading team. Even if Matt had come on to her, Hannah would have rejected him, because she was dating a navy midshipman.

She was sixteen when she met Robert for the first time. Their fathers had been college frat brothers, and when the DuPonts and Lowells attended the same fund-raiser,

Hannah basked in the attention of the handsome midshipman who'd appeared as taken with her as she was with him. Whenever possible they were inseparable, which pleased her mother, because for Clarissa an alliance with the Lowells was akin to marrying European royalty. Her mother got her wish when a month following Robert's graduation he presented Hannah with his grandmother's engagement ring.

Pushing open the restroom door, Hannah came face-to-face with a woman she hadn't seen since their high school commencement. Hannah and Daphne Bouie fell into each other's arms, giggling like young schoolgirls.

"I didn't expect to see you here," she said to the career army officer. Daphne earned the distinction of joining the second class to accept women at the U.S. Military Academy at West Point, and over the years rose to the rank of a two-star general.

Daphne's teeth shone whitely in a flawless mahogany-brown complexion. "Once the army pulls you in, they don't let you go."

Hannah stared at the woman who'd been the first to befriend her when she transferred from McGehee to Jackson Memorial. Daphne was one of six children in her family. Her father was a pastor at a small church and her mother was a caterer. Whenever she visited the Bouie home, Hannah found herself in the kitchen watching Mrs. Bouie prepare meals, which she invariably attempted to duplicate. Although palatable, they never matched or exceeded Daphne's mother's scrumptious dishes. Then one day Mrs. Bouie handed her an envelope with the proviso she never tell anyone about its contents.

Nearly overcome with curiosity, Hannah rushed home, locked herself in her bedroom, and opened the envelope to find recipes for Daphne's mother's prize-winning jambalaya, red beans and rice, and seafood gumbo. Even after more than forty years, she had never told anyone about the recipes for traditional New Orleans dishes that had been passed down through several generations of Bouie women.

"I thought you would've had enough of the military after all these years," she teased.

Daphne ran a hand over her short graying twists. "It's in the blood, Hannah. Even though I'm now a civilian, I'm still addicted to all things military and that's why I recently accepted a position at the Pentagon. You should know what I'm talking about because you married a lifer."

"You're right," Hannah confirmed. "Robert claimed he had sea water instead of blood running through his veins. It was Robert who loved it, while I was quite content to live a normal life without moving from base to base. Not to change the subject, but how are your folks?"

"Mama finally hung up her apron, and my daddy has been diagnosed with dementia."

"How often do you get to see them?"

"Not too often," Daphne admitted. "Most in my family don't approve of my gay lifestyle. I had a real dustup with my holicr-than-thou brother when he said I was going to burn in hell for fornicating with a woman. That's when I had to remind him that real men don't go around making babies with different women, and then not take care of them."

Unconsciously, Hannah's brow furrowed. "Deliver us from judgmental hypocrites."

Daphne lowered her eyes, staring at the toes of her low-heeled pumps. "That's one of reasons I decided to retire from active duty after thirty-five years. I got tired of people looking at me sideways because they never saw me with a man. The other is I'd met someone before the 'don't ask, don't tell' rule came into effect. We now share a house in Georgetown with two spoiled Jack

Russell terriers." She waved her hand. "Enough talk about me. Please answer one question for me."

"What's that?"

"When did you hook up with St. John? My sister told me he was the talk of the town once the news got out that he and his wife split up. She said it was hilarious when women started buzzing around him like flies on a meat skin."

Hannah schooled her expression not to reveal what she was feeling at that moment. It was annoyance. Just because people witnessed St. John's arm around her waist, they believed them a couple. "St. John and I are friends."

Daphne gave her an incredulous stare. "If you say so," she countered with a sly grin. She hugged Hannah again. "I better get back to my table before my partner sends out a search party for me."

"I'm going to be here for the summer, so I'll have time to stop in and see your mother."

"I'm certain she'd love that."

Moments after Daphne left, Hannah dusted her face with a small, silver-plated retractable brush filled with loose powder matching her skin tone and reapplied her lipstick. She'd just completed touching up her makeup when the door opened and several women filed in.

"Nice dress, Hannah," Casey Reynolds crooned flippantly without breaking stride.

Hannah flashed a facetious smile. "Thank you, Casey."

They swept past her and went into stalls. Back in the day, they had collectively sought to establish the trend for what they deemed fashionable for girls. One month it would be a headband, and then another it would either be shoes, scarves, or even makeup.

Hannah had grown up with her paternal grandmother preaching that DuPont women were leaders, not followers — something she'd come to believe and practice. She returned to the ballroom, sitting in the chair St. John had pulled out for her. She felt the buildup of heat in her face when he lingered over her longer than necessary. The warmth of his body, the sensual scent of his cologne, and the light touch of his hands resting on her shoulders stirred something within her she hadn't felt in years: passion.

Peering up over her shoulder, she gave him an open smile. Daphne's accusation that she and St. John were somehow romantically connected forced her to think maybe others saw what she couldn't see or didn't want to acknowledge.

Did she want more from St. John than just friendship? What was there about him that reminded her she was a woman who'd denied her femininity for more years than she could remember?

Her right hand covered his resting on her shoulder; she enjoyed the warmth of his fingers against her skin under the lacy fabric. She lowered her eyes seconds after he returned her smile. Hannah stared at the tablecloth, not seeing the seemingly hypnotized stares of those at the table watching the silent interplay between her and St. John.

Something clicked in her mind. She'd come back to New Orleans for the reunion and to map out her future, and nowhere in her plans did it include her becoming involved with a man. Not even one as seemingly perfect as St. John McNair. He definitely was a trifecta: looks, brains, and an innate sensual charm that had her seeing him in a whole new light. If she had a list of criteria for a man with whom she'd want a relationship, then her former classmate would pass with flying colors.

Hannah chided herself for even thinking along those lines. She'd been celibate for ten years and widowed for eight. Perhaps she was getting ahead of herself. She had no way of knowing if she was even St. John's type.

Reaching for her glass, she took a sip of wine, willing her mind blank. She'd come to the reunion to reconnect with former classmates and have fun. And it had been a very long time since she'd experienced anything that resembled fun. *Hell's bells,* Hannah thought. She was fast approaching sixty and if she didn't have fun now, then she doubted if she ever would.

She went completely still when St. John sat next to her, his shoulder pressing against hers. They shared another smile, this one more intimate than the other; a vaguely sensuous light passed between them, while everything within her seemed to be pregnant with waiting for something so foreign it was frightening. Somehow she managed to glance away and the spell was broken, offering a respite from a physical longing she'd never experienced in her life. Not even with her late husband.

CHAPTER 5

The hotel chef had prepared a gastronomical feast beginning with gumbos, bisques, and soups flavored with spices that tantalized the most discerning palate. Entrées included crawfish and shrimp and etouffée, pannéed pork chops with fennel Creole sauce, and strip sirloin steak Bordelaise, along with the ubiquitous side dishes of red beans and rice, dirty rice, and broiled asparagus parmigiana. Dinner ended with desserts ranging from pumpkin and pecan bread pudding, bourbon whiskey sauce bread pudding, crème caramel and crème brûlée with chicory-laced coffee.

Everyone, including Hannah, was more than ready to dance off the calories they'd consumed over the past two hours as the wait staff cleared away the remnants of dinner.

She slipped on her mask. The Bee Gees singing "Jive Talking" boomed from speakers in the adjoining ballroom as hotel staff pushed back the partition dividing the two rooms.

"Do you intend to dance?" Hannah asked St. John when he hadn't put on his mask.

He shook his head. "Not tonight." He extended his hand. "But I will hold your purse." A smile flitted across his handsome features. "Go and enjoy yourself. I'll be right here when you come back."

She handed him the tiny bag, hiding her disappointment behind her mask. "Thank you." She'd hoped to share at least one dance with him.

Hannah did not lack for dancing partners as she found herself caught up in the frivolity, losing track of time, and the number of line dances she recalled and a few she learned for the first time.

There came a lull when the DJ's voice came through the powerful speakers. "I'm going to slow it down a bit because I got a few requests for an album which has stood the test of time. Ladies and gentlemen, here's Fleetwood Mac's *Rumours.*

Hannah sang along with the assembly, recalling all the lyrics from the 1977 Grammy Award winner for album of the year. Classic tunes recorded by the Rolling Stones, Donna Summer, the Commodores, and Queen continued nonstop. A slight aching in her knees and tightness in her calves reminded Hannah that dancing in stilettos hadn't been the wisest choice. Some women had shed their heels, preferring to dance barefoot.

Knowing when enough was enough, she took off her mask. She found St. John where she'd left him, sitting at their assigned table talking with a group of men. Five pairs of eyes were trained on her when he stood with her approach.

"I'm leaving now," she said in a quiet voice.

Reaching for her hand, St. John threaded their fingers. "You owe me one dance."

A slight frown creased her forehead. "For what?" she asked.

"For minding your purse," St. John explained, patting his jacket pocket for emphasis.

Hannah wanted to tell him that she'd had enough dancing for one night, but he took her silence for acquiescence, leading her back into the other ballroom. The upbeat music had segued to romantic ballads.

He turned to face her, bringing them inches apart. "May I have this dance, Miss DuPont?" he whispered in her ear.

Hannah held her breath. St. John was

close, too close. She was forced to exhale when struggling to breathe. "Yes." The single word was barely a whisper.

She saw the amused gleam in his eyes as his right arm went around her waist. His left hand closed over her right at the same time her left hand rested on his shoulder. She felt the whisper of his breath when he pressed his mouth to her hair, a shudder of awareness eddying through her, which she was certain he felt when his breathing deepened. What was it about him that had her trembling like a virgin about to embark on her first sexual encounter?

They'd become one, her body fitting perfectly into the contours of St. John's like puzzle pieces. She turned her head, so caught up in her own emotions that she hadn't realized her mouth was only inches from his. Hannah attempted to read his impassive expression, but nothing in his features indicated anything more than indifference.

"Weekend in New England" by Barry Manilow ended, and she attempted to extricate herself from St. John's embrace. She didn't trust herself to remain in his arms, for she was unable to disguise her body's reaction when dancing with a man who aroused a passion she refused to acknowledge.

"Thank you, St. John. Good night."

Reaching into his jacket pocket, St. John handed her the tiny purse. "I'll walk you to your car."

She flashed a sexy moue. "I don't think that's necessary. I don't believe I'll get lost between here and the parking lot."

"I'll still walk you," he insisted, taking her hand and escorting her out the ballroom.

Hannah ignored the stares as she and St. John strolled across the hotel lobby. She'd gotten over Daphne's remark about them hooking up together, and those seeing them leave would probably add to the speculation that she and St. John were sleeping together. She had matured enough to accept that people were going to think whatever they wanted and any protest would probably prove futile.

The night had been one of enlightenment for her. It was as if she'd suddenly come into her own. She was a middle-aged, independent, unencumbered woman in control of her life and her future. She didn't have a husband, dependent children, debt, nor an employer to which she had to answer. How many people, she thought, were that fortunate? And reuniting with St. John and her unexpected response to him was a reminder that she was a woman — one who'd denied her femininity for far too long.

St. John waited with her in the warm, humid night as the valet brought her car around. He slipped the valet a bill, and then held the door open to the sedan as she slid in behind the wheel.

His eyebrows lifted questioningly as he closed the door. "Have you ever considered selling the judge's car?"

After he'd won the election to sit on the bench in the criminal court, those who knew Lester DuPont simply referred to him as "the judge." "No. Daddy would turn over in his grave if someone other than a DuPont owned his chariot. But I don't think he'd mind if someone other than a DuPont drove it."

Angling his head, St. John leaned down, smiling at her through the open window. "Is that a hint or a tease?"

Hannah stared at the attractive lines fanning out around St. John's eyes. The color of his eyes always reminded her of cognac. "It's definitely a hint. When we get together I'll let you drive it."

Hunkering lower, he kissed her hair. "I'm looking forward to it. Now get home safely."

"Thank you." She smiled. "You get home safely, too."

St. John winked at her. "Thank you."

She drove away from the hotel, taking furtive glances in the rearview mirror until St. John's image faded when she turned a corner and headed in the direction of the Garden District. Hannah noted the time and temperature on a lighted sign outside a local bank. It was exactly twelve midnight and seventy-six degrees. If she'd been Cinderella, then the Mercedes would have turned into a pumpkin, her dress would be nothing more than rags, and the glass slipper would have also disappeared.

She wiggled her toes in the stilettos, knowing if she removed her shoes she would be forced to walk barefoot from the garage into the house. Never had she danced so much, not even at prom or her wedding reception. A sad smile settled into her features when she remembered the good times she'd shared with Robert. He'd become her knight in shining armor, rescuing her from an overbearing, critical mother who couldn't be appeased or satisfied despite a lifestyle that had given her everything she'd always wanted.

Hannah had promised herself as a young girl that she wouldn't grow up into a replica of her mother, who'd found fault and complained about everyone. The exception had been Robert Lowell, and Hannah knew it had everything to do with his family lineage and his role as a midshipman at the United States Naval Academy. Impressed with all things military, Clarissa's great-grandfather several generations removed had attended the U.S. Military Academy at West Point, graduating in the same class as Robert E. Lee. Like Lee, Clarissa's great-grandfather had also joined the Confederate Army during the Civil War with the rank of major general.

Clarissa was happiest when in the presence of the Lowells, and when it came time for her to host a gathering at DuPont House, she planned it with the meticulousness of a White House state dinner. Hannah was impressed with Robert when first meeting him. She'd just celebrated her sixteenth birthday, and he was a first-year midshipman at the academy. She'd laughed at him when he recited the academy's Honor Concept with the seriousness of someone delivering a eulogy. Much to her surprise he also laughed, remarking he'd memorized the concept when he still hadn't memorized his Social Security number.

The more they saw each other, the more she liked him, because with Robert she could be herself and not someone Clarissa wanted her to be. He was her first serious boyfriend and with time had become her first and only lover. During her marriage she'd fantasized how it would be to make love with another man but she had never acted on it. Not even after she'd discovered her husband's infidelity. And it wasn't for the first time that she chided herself for not being more like LeAnn and Paige, who had openly admitted they'd had a number of lovers.

Hannah shook her head as if to banish all notions of sleeping with a man. Not when she was about to embark on a project that was certain to leave her with little or no time for an affair or a relationship. The ideas tumbled over themselves in her mind as she mentally outlined what she had to do convert DuPont House from a private residence to an inn. All of the upstairs bedrooms would have to be fitted for card-keys instead of door locks. The parlor would become the front desk for guests checking in or out. The space that had been designated a ballroom would serve as a gathering place for guests to enjoy evening cordials, confections, and sweets.

Inasmuch as Hannah wanted to be like her unconventional, somewhat rebellious first cousins, she realized she was more of a traditionalist like her parents rather than a baby boomer. She didn't mind change, but not at the expense of throwing away or ignoring what had come before it. Even with the advent of email and social media, which made it so convenient to connect and interact within nanoseconds, she still liked penning Christmas cards and thank-you notes.

A feeling of calm washed over her as she drove slowly along streets she could navigate as if on remote control. She'd returned to New Orleans last Christmas, and every time she left to go back to New York, Hannah felt as if she'd left piece of herself in her place of birth. She experienced an indescribable longing that had her wondering why she continued to live in a city where she felt she never really belonged. Although she had grown fond of her adopted city, it wasn't enough for her to want to spend the rest of her life there.

She accelerated onto St. Charles Avenue toward the Garden District, bounded by Carondelet, Magazine, Josephine, and Delachaise Streets, and located in a National Historic Landmark District. Her familial home sat in a neighborhood with one of the best-preserved collections of historic mansions in the South. Despite experiencing some wind damage from Hurricane Katrina, the property had escaped extensive flooding because the area was on higher ground.

Hannah drove past the Louise S. Mc-Gehee School, the private all-girls' school that she'd attended from kindergarten through junior high. Within months of going into the eighth grade she told her parents she wanted to attend a public high school. It was the first time she challenged her mother, and in the end it was her father who eventually overruled Clarissa. No one was more shocked than Hannah. Lester had allowed his wife to run the household and make decisions, while his focus was law and playing golf at the private, member-owned Metairie Country Club.

Hannah had no way of knowing that she would be faced with resentment rather than acceptance at Jackson Memorial High — especially from the girls. Some insulted her to her face with acerbic remarks that her kind wasn't wanted and that she should stay with the other snobby rich bitches at Mc-Gehee. Hannah sat alone during lunch for two months until Daphne asked if she could share the table. The single incident broke the ice because Daphne was not only one of the more popular girls at Jackson, but also one of the brightest.

Hannah turned down the street leading to DuPont House. She tapped the remote device attached to the visor, activating the electronic gate surrounding the property. Despite the lateness of the hour there were dog walkers, joggers, and those just taking in the night air. She maneuvered onto the winding path to the rear of the house where a nineteenth-century carriage house had been converted into a garage with enough room for four automobiles. She parked the Mercedes next to Paige's late-model Lincoln. Within seconds of cutting off the engine, Hannah did what she'd wanted to do before leaving the hotel. She took off her shoes.

Tiptoeing on bare feet, she made her way to the back door. Lifting the door handle, she punched in the code, deactivating the security system, and pushed open the door leading into the mud/laundry room. Grimacing with every step, she limped up the back staircase to her bedroom and into the bathroom, filling the tub with warm water and two handfuls of lavender bath salts. Hannah realized she wasn't as much out of shape as she was out of condition. Walking on concrete in running shoes or kitten heels could not compare to dancing for hours in stilettos.

She meticulously removed her makeup with a cleanser specially blended for her skin type, and then applied a moisturizer to her bare face. Twenty minutes in the bathtub worked a minor miracle for her aching legs and feet. She lay in bed and willed her mind blank until she fell asleep.

Hannah woke at dawn with the intent to do something she hadn't done since her firing: walk. Clad in a sports bra, yoga tights, an oversized T-shirt, and running shoes and with her cell phone tucked into her waistband, she set out on a walking tour of the Garden District.

Establishing a measured, unhurried pace, while hoping to ease the lingering tightness in her calves, she became a tourist, slowing to glance at the home used in the film *The Curious Case of Benjamin Button.* Hannah continued on St. Charles Avenue, smiling when spying Mardi Gras beads hanging from a tree. The colorful beads were a constant reminder of how many years it had been since she'd taken part in the annual celebration that turned the entire city of New Orleans into party central.

"Hannah! Hannah DuPont!"

She stopped when she heard a woman's voice calling her from across the street. "Letitia Parker," Hannah whispered.

She'd recognized the voice and the face, but not her body. Letitia had always had a problem with her weight, topping the scales at two hundred even before entering high school. Hannah motioned for Letitia to stay where she was, glancing up and down the avenue for oncoming traffic.

Letitia watched Hannah as she jogged across the avenue, a warm smile tilting the corners of her mouth. Resting her hands at her waist, she angled her head. "Well, well, well. Look at you, Hannah DuPont. You haven't changed a bit. Please tell me you found the fountain of youth, because I'd be willing to give up a kidney just for a sip."

Hannah hugged Letitia, and then held her at arm's length. "No, Miss Nashville Songbird, look at you. You're the gorgeous one." Her gaze lingered on stylishly cut raven-black hair, lightly feathered with gray, before moving down to a pair of robin's-egg blue eyes that appeared even lighter in her sun-browned complexion.

An attractive blush glowed under Letitia's tan. "Thank you." She lowered her eyes. "I've sacrificed a lot to get to this stage. It's taken me more than a year to lose ninety pounds and keep it off. I walk every day around the same time, rain or shine."

Hannah gave her a sidelong glance at they continued in an easterly direction along St. Charles Avenue. "When did you come back?"

"I was going to ask you the same thing," Letitia replied, looping arms with Hannah.

"I came back two days ago for my high school's reunion."

"I've got you beat by seven months."

"You're living here now?"

Letitia nodded. As a retired singer, and a divorcée with an adult son and daughter and four grandchildren, she'd sold her Nashville home to return to her childhood home. She'd been a grade ahead of Hannah when they were enrolled at McGehee. Once she graduated and moved away to attend college, she returned to New Orleans several times a year. Her parents told her Hannah had come back to Louisiana to bury her husband, and Letitia had stopped at Du-Pont House to offer her condolences.

"I moved back to take care of my parents because my brother and his wife are moving to Florida to be close to their grand-children."

"What about your grandchildren?"

A beat passed, Letitia dropping Hannah's arm. "I'm trying to convince my son and daughter to move from Nashville to New

Orleans. The house is much too big for three people. My son is seriously considering it, but my daughter-in-law is still balking. She feels if she moves in with her mother-in-law then she wouldn't be woman of her own house. She's been here enough to know that she will have her own apartment and I'll babysit her kids whenever she and TJ need time for themselves."

"There was a time when it was common for several generations to live together under one roof out of necessity."

"You're right," Letitia said in agreement. "My daughter-in-law's a stay-at-home mom even though her kids are in school. I tried to warn my son that she was a lazy heifer even before he married her because she'd complain about having to get up and go to work."

"My heart bleeds for her," Hannah drawled facetiously. "She's blessed because most women, married or single, have to work nowadays just to make ends meet."

"Tell me about it." She paused. "Now that I think about it, maybe it could be a blessing in disguise if she decides not to come, because the last thing I want is to become her personal maid, especially when I have to look after Mama and Daddy. And I'm not the one to bite my tongue if she decides to show her behind."

They continued walking together, each lost in her own thoughts, until they reached Martin Luther King, Jr. Boulevard. As they turned to retrace their steps, Leticia asked Hannah, "How long are you staying?"

Hannah smiled. Everyone she ran into wanted to know how long she'd planned to stay. "I'll be here until the end of the summer."

Letitia's eyes lit up like polished blue topaz. "If that's the case, then we'll have to get together for lunch."

"What about your folks?"

"They're okay because I just hired a live-in home health aide. Daddy's showing signs of dementia, while Mama still has a problem walking after she fell and broke her hip."

Hannah thought about her parents. Neither had lived long enough to experience a marked decline in health. Her mother died in her sleep at the age of seventy-two and her father from an aneurysm a year later. Lester had complained of ongoing headaches but refused to see a doctor no matter how much she pleaded with him.

She listened intently as Letitia told her about the highs and lows she'd experienced as a popular female country singer. Her husband/manager demanded she lose weight, and she went through periods wherein she existed solely on liquid diets. She gave up eating meat for a year and lost half her body weight, only to regain most of it when touring. She'd missed her children and offset the separation by overeating.

"My children saw the nanny more than me because Trent had me touring nonstop. I missed all my children's milestones, and I knew something had to change. I finally took control of my life when I fired Trent as my manager, filed for a divorce, sold the monstrosity of a house, and went on a medically supervised diet and hired a personal trainer."

"Good for you."

"Thanks. I don't regret that I had to rid myself of my children's father in order to find myself. At first I was filled with guilt, but after a lot of therapy, I realized it was what I had to do to grow emotionally."

Hannah stared straight ahead, wondering why women had to sacrifice so much in order to come into their own. Were they so involved or fixated in seeing to the needs or happiness of the men in their lives to the detriment of their own? She may have had an unfaithful husband, but at no time during her marriage had she allowed Robert to control her; after their first explosive argument she sternly reminded him he wasn't her superior officer, and they were equals in the marriage.

Their walk ended on Constance Street in front of the Branford-Parker House. "Walking tomorrow?" Letitia asked.

"Sure," Hannah replied. "But I don't walk in the rain."

"No problem. I've always said I'm part duck," Letitia joked.

"I'll meet you here at six."

"I'll wait fifteen minutes, and if you don't show up by that time, then I'll know you're not coming."

Hannah waited until Letitia opened the cornstalk wrought-iron fence in front of her gingerbread-decorated late Victorian period house, and then headed home. Listening to Letitia talk about her ex reminded her that even though her marriage wasn't perfect she hadn't had to deal with Robert monitoring every phase of her life. He was assigned either to an aircraft carrier or submarine, which kept him away from home for months on end. The downside of his extended absences was her having to step into the dual role as mother *and* father for Wyatt. Whenever Robert came home on leave, Wyatt followed him as if he were the pied piper, hanging onto his every word about all things military, and from an early age it was apparent her son would follow his father with a career in the military.

She quickened her pace, jogging down streets, arms swinging loosely at her sides, until she stopped at DuPont House. The action had increased her heart rate, eliciting a state of euphoria. Meeting Letitia and promising to join her on early morning walks was ideal for starting a new day.

CHAPTER 6

Leaning back in the executive chair, St. John propped his feet on the edge of the desk while speaking quietly into the telephone receiver. "Are you finished blowing out my eardrum?"

There was silence before Alicia Vernon's exhalation of breath came through the earpiece. His sister calling to complain about his niece wasn't how he wanted to end the morning, a morning that was to become his last at the college for the next twelve weeks. Over the past two weeks he'd spent hours in meetings reviewing résumés and discussing possible applicants to fill vacancies in several departments. All he wanted was to go home and kick back and not have to think about anything to do with Barden College until the fall semester.

"I'm sorry about that, St. John, but the girl's working my last nerve. I ground Keisha, take away her cell phone, and she still defies me."

"Have you ever thought that maybe it's not her fault?"

"That's not fair!"

"What's not fair is you didn't establish boundaries for Keisha when she was a child, and now that she's a teenager and goes buck wild, you want to tighten the reins." He paused. "Look, sis, I'm not trying to come down on you when you need my support, but I can't help you with childrearing because I never had children. You and Kenny need to sit down with Keisha and let her know you're responsible for her, not the other way around. Remember Mama used to tell us 'her way or the highway?' "

"There's no way I can forget, because it's branded into my brain. You were away at college when I broke curfew for the third time and she locked me out the house. And that was before cell phones, so I couldn't call any of my friends. That's when I asked Miss Robinson to let me sleep in her spare room until the next day. She told me if she were my mother, she would've let me in and then took a switch off a bush and set fire to my behind. The next day the entire neighborhood knew what had happened. Miss Robinson didn't like Mama, so she couldn't wait to gossip about how she couldn't control her fast-ass daughter."

St. John chuckled, the sound rumbling in his chest. His sister, eight years his junior, had continually tested their parents' patience. His mother had pleaded with Alicia, asking her why she couldn't be more like her brother. Alicia's flippant response was because she wasn't perfect like her brother. What Alicia didn't know was he wasn't perfect. He just followed the rules. It was the reason he'd stayed married for so long. He'd taken an oath to love and protect Lorna in health as well as in good and bad times. Unfortunately, they had more bad times than good, and he hadn't known how sick she'd been until the divorce proceedings. And no amount of pleading from him could convince her to seek counseling.

St. John shook his head as if to rid his mind of the disturbing memories of a marriage that probably shouldn't have happened, when all of the signs were there beforehand that doomed it to fail. "Did it cure you of breaking curfew?"

"Hell, yeah!"

Lowering his feet, St. John stared out the window at a magnolia tree. Barden College with its on-campus housing was set on twenty-five acres of verdant landscaped gardens with ancient oak trees draped in

Spanish moss and flowering magnolia, cherry and weeping willow trees. It had become New Orleans's collegiate jewel in the crown in the University District.

"Today's my last day here and I'm not lecturing this summer, so do you want to send her to New Orleans for the summer?"

"That won't be necessary. I'm sending her to Tucson. Mama says she and Daddy will look after her for the summer."

He wanted to ask his sister if sending her daughter to their octogenarian parents was the best decision for a teenage girl constantly challenging authority. At the age of forty-five, Daniel McNair had relocated from New Orleans to Tucson, Arizona, for health reasons. The elder McNair's career with the New Orleans Police Department ended after he'd sustained a bullet wound to the chest during an armed robbery, resulting in the removal of a portion of his lung.

"I spoke to Kenny before calling you, and we're going to have a family meeting later tonight," Alicia continued. "Kenny has always been hands off where it concerns childrearing because he spends so much time away from home whenever he goes undercover, but I'm certain that's going to change. I just discovered who his sixteen-year-old princess has been hanging out with. The twenty-something weed-smelling piece of garbage had the audacity to ring my bell and ask if Keisha's coming out. I told him to get off my property and if he ever came back he was going to catch a bullet straight between the eyes."

St. John struggled not to laugh aloud at Alicia's depiction of the boy going after her daughter. If what his sister told him was true, then it didn't bode well for his niece's supposed boyfriend. Her father was a federal agent assigned to the DEA's Seattle Field Division office.

"Did he leave?"

"Is the cheetah the fastest land animal?" she said jokingly. "He took off so fast in his hoopty, he left skid marks on the street."

This time St. John did laugh. Alicia had once worked for the FBI as an intelligence analyst. She resigned after an ultrasound indicated she was pregnant with twins. "Let me know one way or the other the outcome of your family meeting. And I'm still open if you want to send her to me. And how are the twins doing?" His sister had gone on about her daughter while neglecting to bring him up to date about his twelve-year-old twin nephews.

"They're good. I've signed them up for

sleepaway baseball camp again. I'll give you an update after we have our family meeting."

He smiled. "Thanks, sis. Love you."

"Love you back, bro."

Within minutes of ending the call, a ringtone from his cell garnered his attention. St. John glanced at the screen. He'd programmed an alert to call Hannah. The reunion had been filled with surprises. His intent was to reconnect with former friends, but when he left it was with countless emails from those wishing to stay in touch. Despite being a New Orleans native, St. John hadn't cultivated a circle of close friends.

He hadn't been among the more popular boys in high school. The jocks were afforded that honor. However, he was neither geek nor nerd, but there had to have been something about him because he'd been accepted and respected by most of his peers. Some of his classmates had approached him to run for senior class president, but he declined. Carrying a full schedule, playing piano for the school's jazz band, stepping in as interim editor for the school's paper after the former editor transferred to another school, and as vice president of the French club, he had no time for school politics. He reached for the phone and scrolled through the directory and tapped Hannah's number, counting off the number of rings until there was a break in the connection.

Hannah stared at birds splashing in the marble birdbath next to a flowering rose bush. It had been a little more than two weeks since she'd returned to New Orleans, and she'd come to enjoy her early morning walks with Letitia. She also liked having the house to herself, because it allowed her to go about her business without talking when she didn't feel like talking. It wasn't that she didn't love her cousins, but since becoming a widow, she had come to appreciate her own company. A smile parted her lips. It had taken nearly fifty years for her to accept that Hannah Claire DuPont-Lowell was now quite comfortable in her own skin.

Pressing her head against the cushioned rocker, she closed her eyes. If she had reservations about attending the reunion unescorted for the second time, they had quickly vanished once dinner was over and the masquerade ball began. She'd forgotten who she'd danced with, and although she was familiar with the steps for the Electric Slide, she learned new ones when following those in line dances for the Cupid and Cha Cha Slide.

The reunion's masquerade ball reminded her that it had been much too long since she had gone out dancing, and she chided herself for not cultivating a group of girl-friends who would occasionally go to a club or have a girlfriends' vacation at an exotic destination. She thought of Nydia, Jasmine, and Tonya, wondering if they were actively looking for new positions or if they were serious about taking the summer off to come down to New Orleans.

Hannah opened her eyes, smiling. Not only would she become their tour guide for the city, but she'd also researched the pos-sibility of them taking a seven-night, eight-day Mississippi River cruise. Exhaling an audible sigh, she had returned her attention to the book on her lap when her cell phone rang. Reaching into the pocket of the oversized man-tailored shirt, she took out the phone and glanced at the screen. The heat in her face had nothing to do with the sultry afternoon temperatures.

"This is Hannah."

St. John smiled. "And this is St. John," he teased.

"How are you?"

"Wonderful." St. John hadn't lied to her. It was his last day of work for the next three months and he'd committed to joining several of his former classmates for an upcoming poker game. "How are you?" he asked, repeating her query.

"I'm good now that I've recovered from the masquerade ball. The pain in my legs and knees was a constant reminder that I'm too old to go clubbing."

Swiveling in the chair, he stared out the window at the campus's professionally manicured lawn. He hadn't danced with any of the unescorted women, but the highlight of the night was when he and Hannah danced to Barry Manilow's "Weekend in New England." Her height made her the perfect dance partner.

"That's probably because you don't dance enough."

"And you do?" Hannah asked.

"Probably more than you," he said cryptically.

"I assume this call means you're off for the summer?"

St. John noticed she hadn't replied to his comment about dancing. "You assume correctly."

"When do you want to come over?" she asked.

"Would you mind if we put that off for another time?"

106

"No. Why?"

"I'd like to take you to dinner, and if you're not ready to go home, then we can go to a little out-of-the way club to listen to jazz."

"That sounds nice," Hannah said after a noticeable pause.

His eyebrows lifted questioningly. "Is that a yes or a no, Hannah?"

"It's a yes."

"Do you have a favorite restaurant?"

She paused again. "Surprise me."

A smile lifted the corners of St. John's mouth. He liked a woman willing to be spontaneous. "Okay, I will. How does this weekend look?"

"I don't have anything scheduled."

"Good. Then I'll pick you up Friday around seven."

"I'll be here."

St. John rang off and continued to stare out the window. He didn't think of sharing dinner with Hannah as a date but rather as former classmates reminiscing about old times.

Hannah gripped the cell phone long after St. John ended the call. The book which she'd read many times over the years lay open on her lap. He'd promised to call her and now that he had, the unwelcomed feelings of uneasiness were back. She still hadn't identified why she was drawn to him when he hadn't said or done anything to indicate he was remotely interested in her other than because they were former classmates.

Maybe, she mused, she'd been without male companionship for much too long. She'd mentally divorced Robert once he revealed his infidelity, and even after he died she still kept all men at a distance, and the two men she'd dated while employed at the law firm quickly lost interest in her.

Hannah had labeled herself emotionless because something in her brain hadn't allowed her to feel passion — until now. The night before she'd had an erotic dream wherein multiple climaxes left her trembling and burying her face in her pillow to keep from screaming from the passionate aftermath. When fully awake, Hannah realized the man in her dream making exquisite love to her was St. John McNair.

Questions had bombarded her as she lay staring up at the sheer material draping the bed, trying to sort out why St. John had been the lover in her dream when she never thought of him in that way. She'd voted for him as best-looking and best-dressed in their graduating class, and even if she hadn't been dating Robert and St. John hadn't been with Lorna, Hannah would not have dated him. Why now, she asked herself. Why now at fifty-eight when she wouldn't have considered it forty years before?

Because you really didn't know what you wanted at eighteen, a silent voice reminded Hannah. And she hadn't. It was at her mother's insistence that she dated and married Robert. Clarissa, the quintessential social climber, claimed she always wanted the best for her children, and if that meant marrying up, then it was by any means necessary. Even when she told Clarissa about Robert cheating on her, her mother said that's what some men do. When she asked if Lester cheated on her, Clarissa had suddenly become mute, leading Hannah to believe that her father also hadn't been faithful.

Hannah liked to believe she was a modern woman, having grown up when women were sexually liberated, yet something wouldn't allow her to tolerate a man cheating on his wife. When she'd broached the subject with Paige and LeAnn, both were of the mind that she had two options: leave Robert or forgive him. Hannah couldn't do either. She couldn't forgive Robert but she couldn't leave him when the attack had weakened his heart, resulting in him resigning his commission, and leaving him a shell of his former self.

She closed her eyes again. Sitting on the porch ruminating about her past didn't lend itself to finding something to wear. It had been years since she'd readied herself for a date with a man, especially one as charismatic as St. John. She opened her eyes and closed the leather-bound French-language version of Alexandre Dumas's *Count of Monte Cristo.* Reading French came much easier for Hannah than her attempts to speak the language.

She went into the house and locked the door, and set the book on the entryway table with a trio of vases filled with freshly cut flowers. The spring flowers were in full bloom, and she had gone into the garden earlier that morning to pick lily-of-the-valley with their delicate bell-shaped white flowers, lovely mauve-pink anemone, and pink-and-white alchemilla, better known as lady's mantle. There had been a time when Du-Pont House was filled with flowers year-round, and it would be again once the inn was operational.

Three days after she'd returned, she made a phone call requesting the status of her license and permits, identifying herself as Hannah DuPont and hoping the name held more clout in New Orleans than Lowell. The clerk apologized profusely, and then launched into a pre-rehearsed dialogue about a backlog in applications because of the revitalization still going on in the city after the devastation left by Hurricane Katrina. The woman recommended she call again in another month.

Perhaps she was in denial, but Hannah wanted to thank those at Wakefield Hamilton Investment for laying her off, because she was finding it easier to negotiate and implement her plans while in New Orleans rather than from New York. Still, she prayed she'd be able to secure the permits and license required for the house, which would be designated as a small hotel having up to nine sleeping rooms, each having a private bathroom, before the end of the summer. The next step would be securing the services of an engineer to inspect and sign off on the occupancy, and then an architectural historian and/or interior designer to authenticate the furnishings.

She climbed the staircase to her bedroom and opened the door to an armoire. The upside of having two residences meant she did not have to transport her clothes from one city to the other.

It took her less than fifteen minutes to select an outfit for Friday's dinner date. It was what she thought of as casual chic: appropriate for fine dining and casual enough to attend an out-of-the way music venue in neighborhoods boasting a marriage of cultures that made the city a vibrant melting pot to eat, drink, and listen to jazz.

Her steps were light as she descended the staircase and walked into the kitchen. It was one of the nicest rooms in the entire house. The coffered ceiling, terracotta flooring, brick walls, and massive brick fireplace, remnants of a bygone era, added character to the space where countless family meals had been prepared for centuries.

State-of-the art stainless-steel appliances had replaced the wood-burning stove and icebox, and the large vent over the eight-burner range eliminated the lingering odors of cooked foods. Large tins of rice, flour, and grits lined an entire shelf in the expansive pantry. Other shelves were filled with canned fruits and vegetables; there was also a freezer chest stocked with packaged, labeled, and dated meat, fish, and poultry. An outdoor kitchen was used whenever it got too hot to cook indoors during the summer months. Aside from dairy and perishables, Hannah had enough food on hand to last her throughout the summer.

Opening the refrigerator, she took out the ingredients she needed to put together a New Orleans–style Cobb salad. The salad would differ from the classic Cobb because the chicken breast would be grilled with blackening seasoning, giving it a bit more bite.

The callbox chimed, and Hannah pushed the button on the monitor set on a small, round table in an alcove. Leticia's face appeared on the screen. "Come on in. The gate is unlocked and the front door is open," she said into the speaker. She'd left the gate open because the cleaning service was expected to arrive within the hour.

She walked out of the kitchen and through the dining and living rooms and the entryway. Hannah opened the front door and waited for Letitia to make her way up the path to the house. "What the . . ." she said under her breath when she saw what her friend cradled to her chest. "Where are you going with that cat?"

"It's a kitten," Letitia corrected. "I'm promised Paige and LeAnn that I would give them one of Queenie's kittens once they were weaned. Smokey is trained to the litter box and he's had all of his shots."

Hannah's mouth opened and closed several times before she said, "LeAnn and Paige aren't here. In fact, they won't be back until the beginning of September."

"Didn't you say you're going to be here throughout the summer?"

She didn't want to believe her cousins had gone away and not told her about their decision to adopt a cat. She couldn't remember the last time there had been a cat, or even a dog, in the house. Hannah combed her fingers through the hair held off her face with an elastic band. Well, she thought, it could've been worse. At least cats were more independent than dogs.

"Yes, I did say that," she admitted. "I guess I'll have to cat-sit until they get back. The cleaning service is expected to arrive a little later, so you're going to have to hold onto him for a little longer. I'll also need to pick up food, a litter box, and a scratching post for Mr. Smokey, because I don't want him scratching up the furniture." The kitten was beautiful with a sooty blue-gray coat and gold eyes. Reaching out, she stroked the kitten behind the ears and was rewarded with a soft meow and an outstretched paw.

"He likes you," Letitia said proudly.

Bending over, Hannah touched her nose to Smokey's. "That's because he knows I'm a sucker for cats and dogs."

"This is Queenie's last litter and your Smokey is one of only two kittens to survive."

She stroked him again and wanted to tell Letitia that he wasn't her Smokey. As the foster parent, she would take care of the kitten until her cousins returned from their overseas travels.

"He's coming to the right house, because there's no doubt he's going to be spoiled rotten."

Letitia dropped a kiss on the kitten's head. "Call me when you want me to bring him back."

Four hours later Hannah maneuvered into a parking space in the shopping mall with a pet supermarket. She walked in, slightly overwhelmed by the different brands of food for dogs, cats, and birds. There was an entire section dedicated to fish and reptiles. Strolling up and down aisles in the cat section, she read the labels on dry and canned food as if shopping for her own groceries, finally deciding on a dry food boasting natural ingredients. In addition to the food, an automatic self-cleaning litter box, and a cat tree scratching post with a dangling pompom, she also purchased a carrier, window cat perch, and two beds: one a cozy cave in which he could hide and a deep bed to cuddle. She spent an inordinate length of time staring at a programmable pet feeder and an automatic watering system, then decided to add both to the ever-expanding list of items in the shopping cart along with cleanup products and odor removers. Her eyebrows lifted slightly when clerk totaled her purchase at the checkout counter.

"New cat?" the young woman asked as Hannah removed a credit card from her bag.

"Yes. How did you know?"

"Whenever someone buys a complete layette for a dog or cat, I assume they're a new pet parent."

"Bingo," Hannah said under her breath. Even though Letitia said Smokey had gotten his shots, she planned to have the feline neutered and microchipped. There were enough missing and feral cats in New Orleans without Smokey adding to the statistics.

Hannah returned home and set up Smokey's litter box, programmed the water and food feeder, and positioned the scratching post in an area of the laundry room. She attached the perch to the windowsill in the sun-filled parlor and put the cat cave in the corner. She placed the remaining bed in

116

her bedroom because she didn't want to exile the cat to a particular part of the house, because cats were known to retaliate in ways she did not want to imagine. After binge-watching *My Cat from Hell* she saw firsthand the havoc rained on cat owners by their out-of-control pets.

Hannah called Letitia to inform her Smokey could move in, and twenty minutes after he explored what would become his new home, he settled down into the cozy cave and went to sleep. Satisfied that Du-Pont House's resident feline had accepted his unfamiliar surroundings, Hannah settled down on the rocker on the back porch with a tall glass of sweet tea. The sun was setting and dusk descended over the countryside like someone pulling down a diaphanous shade, leaving only pinpoints of lights coming through the near-transparent fabric. It was her favorite time of the day, a time when activity slowed in preparation for total relaxation and sleep. The exception was the French Quarter, which never went to sleep, much like New York City's Times Square.

Fireflies lit up the dusk like twinkling stars. Hannah smiled, recalling the time when she caught fireflies and put them in a jar, watching them struggle to escape and then releasing them before they died. A mosquito settled on her arm and she knew it was time to retreat inside before they feasted on her exposed skin.

Smokey sat in the kitchen staring at her with his brilliant gold eyes. He came over to her, brushing against her bare legs. Bending over, Hannah picked him up. "I know you miss your mother. But I promise you're going to love living here. I'm going to spoil you, and Paige and LeAnn will also take turns spoiling you." She continued to talk to the kitten as if he were a little child, asking him if he'd eaten. Setting the kitten on its feet, she followed him to the mudroom, watching and smiling when Smokey ate some of the kibbles in the food dish and then drank from the automatic water fountain.

Smokey became her shadow, following her everywhere, and when she finally went upstairs to shower, he lay on the bathroom tiles watching her. Hannah put him in his bed, and then she slipped into her own bed. She flicked off the bedside lamp, plunging the room into darkness. The plaintive meowing filled the room, then after a while it ended. Like a baby, the kitten had probably cried itself to sleep.

Hannah didn't mind carrying or cuddling a cat or dog, but drew the line when it came to letting them sleep on her bed. That was where she differed from her daughter-in-law. Karen let her dogs and cats sleep with her sons, and occasionally the animals would accidently soil the bedding. Karen, the daughter of a veterinarian, had grown up with a menagerie that included horses, cats, dogs, rabbits, snakes, turtles, frogs, and a variety of birds and didn't mind cleaning up after them.

Hannah missed her grandsons and had hoped to take them to Colonial Williamsburg, Busch Gardens, and Water Country USA. Now she didn't know when that would happen. She'd projected it would take at least a year before the inn was fully operational, which meant she didn't know when she would have time to take them away.

CHAPTER 7

St. John walked into Slappy's Barbershop, nodding to the men sitting in chairs having their hair cut. Those waiting to be serviced focused their attention on the trio of muted wall-mounted televisions tuned to sports channels. Another four, seated at card tables in the rear of the barbershop, were engaged in games of dominos and checkers.

The ninety-year-old, family-owned and -operated business built its reputation on hiring only licensed barbers with the ability to easily adapt to changing hairstyles and trends. Slappy's was renowned in the early 1950s when the Reynards hired the first female barber in Faubourg Tremé to cut black men's hair.

St. John had gone to the same barbershop to have his hair cut for fifty-six years. His father took him to Slappy's for his first haircut at two, and instead of crying like many kids when hearing the buzzing sound from the clippers, he was transfixed by clumps of hair falling on the cape around his shoulders.

Larry Reynard gave St. John a mock salute. "Whatcha having, Professor?" Third-generation owner, Larry shifted on the chair in the reception area, staring at the appointment schedule on the laptop.

St. John had accepted the sobriquet once the locals discovered he taught college courses. "A haircut and shave." He sat on a black leather loveseat next to Johnnie Simmons, a lifelong resident of Faubourg Tremé.

Larry motioned to a barber who'd just finished applying an astringent to his customer's nape. "Red, please take care of the Professor next. He has an appointment."

St. John knew not to walk into Slappy's without first making an appointment. The few times he'd neglected to call, his wait time had been close to two hours. The shop had undergone major changes over the years, the latest following Hurricane Katrina. Larry and his brothers moved into a nearby church offering free cuts and shaves to displaced residents, reopening five months later and setting up a computerized system for appointments and customer reward points to earn free shaves and haircuts.

"Hang tight, Professor, I'll be with you directly," Red said, smiling.

"No problem," St. John acknowledged. Because Red was born with bright-red hair that had darkened to copper as he grew older, most folks had forgotten his parents had named him Jamal. He was rarely seen without a baseball cap — the exception being when he attended church services — whether in or outdoors. Much to his chagrin, Jamal had passed along his fair complexion, red hair, and freckles to his son, whom everyone called RJ or Red Junior. Whether Red or his government name Jamal, St. John wouldn't let anyone but Red cut his hair.

"How's life been treating you, young man?" Johnnie asked St. John.

"Life's good, Mr. Simmons."

"You keeping company with anyone nowadays?"

"No, I'm not," he answered truthfully.

St. John realized old habits or sayings were slow to die. Instead of asking whether he was seeing or dating anyone it was *keeping company,* a phrase he'd heard his grandparents use once he entered adolescence. He hadn't been able to answer in the affirmative until at fifteen when introduced to Lorna Frazier. It was as if he'd been struck by a lightning bolt. She was as beautiful as she was overtly chaste. Everything about her from her demure smile to her furtive glances sent his raging adolescent libido into overdrive. The first and only time he'd attempted to get her to sleep with him, she stated she was saving herself for marriage.

They'd dated throughout high school and college, St. John keeping his promise that they would not sleep together until they were husband and wife. It wasn't until their wedding night he discovered his wife's aversion to intimacy; it took thirty years of marriage for her to develop enough strength to tell him of the trauma that had held her captive and a prisoner of her own fears.

"If that's the case, then I want to hook you up with my grandbaby girl." A pregnant silence descended on the shop following Johnnie's suggestion.

"Why would he want to meet your granddaughter?" called out one of the men playing checkers. "Everyone knows she done had so many husbands and kids that she can't even remember their names."

Johnnie stood up, glaring. "You ain't got no call to talk about her like that."

Larry shook his head. "You men know I

don't tolerate talk like that in here. If you can't be respectable, then find another shop."

St. John silently applauded Larry for defusing what could've become an uncomfortable situation. He didn't want to date Johnnie's *grandbaby girl* even if he'd found himself attracted to her. She was too young and her life was filled with drama — something he sought to avoid at all costs. He planned to enjoy his summer vacation and was looking forward to having dinner with Hannah later that evening.

Red beckoned him. "Professor, I'll take you now."

He stood up and sat in the barber's chair, staring at his reflection in the wall of mirrors as Red covered his neck with a strip before covering his shoulders with a cape. "You can take off the goatee." The year before, he'd grown a beard over the summer, and then replaced it with a goatee at the beginning of the fall term.

"How about the hair?" Red asked.

"Take a little bit off the top and sides." He'd had Red shave his entire head once and regretted it. A bald pate, although convenient, forced him to wear a hat during the summer months to protect his scalp from the sun.

Fifty minutes later, St. John paid for the haircut and hot-towel shave and gave Red a generous tip for his meticulous work. He was always awed by the barber's ability to glide the straight razor over his face and neck without cutting him. Glancing at his watch, he realized he a little more than an hour to shower, dress, and drive from his house in Marigny to arrive at Hannah's at seven.

St. John downshifted, slowing and stopping at the ornamental wrought-iron gate protecting DuPont House from outsiders. Lowering the driver's-side window, he leaned over and pressed the callbox button. The gates opened, smoothly, silently, and he drove slowly up the tree-lined drive to the front of the historic structure. He stared through the windshield at Hannah as she walked off the porch. He cut off the engine, slipped out of the classic two-seater Jaguar, and opened the passenger-side door.

"You look stunning," he said, pressing his cheek to hers, while inhaling her perfume. Hannah's lids slipped down over her eyes, the gesture so wholly demure he couldn't pull his gaze away from her delicate features.

"Thank you."

St. John hadn't lied. She'd paired an olive-green silk blouse with an aubergine linen pencil skirt with a slit running from knee to mid-thigh. Strappy black patent leather wedges matched the wide belt around her slender waist and her wristlet.

Why hadn't he noticed the throaty timbre of Hannah's voice before? He wondered if she was aware of how sensuous her voice sounded. And St. John had to ask himself whether he was seeing Hannah in a whole new light because both were at different phases in their lives. Twenty years before, they were both married, and he never would've asked her out to dinner — even as friends. He waited for her to get into the low-slung vehicle, settle into the leather seat and fasten the seat belt. All of her movements were executed with the grace of a professional dancer.

Rounding the sports car, he got in behind the wheel and started up the engine. Shifting into gear, he executed a U-turn and drove off the property, the gates automatically closing after the tires passed over a metal plate.

Hannah stared at St. John's distinctive profile, committing it to memory. He'd shaved off the goatee, and she didn't know whether she liked seeing him with or without the facial hair. With the exception of his gray hair, nothing had changed. He was still a tall, incredibly handsome man with a perfectly proportioned physique.

Everything about St. John reminded her why he'd been her lover in the erotic dream. He was so inherently male to what made her female — something she hadn't been aware of so many years before. She wanted to forget his pronouncement he didn't date, because tonight she was going to pretend they were. She pulled her gaze away from the pale blue shirt, with French cuffs and monogrammed silver cufflinks, tucked into the waistband of a pair of gray slacks.

"Shame on you, St. John," Hannah chided softly, staring out the windshield.

He took his eyes off the road for a second to glance at her. "For what?"

"For asking me if I'd sell Daddy's car when you have this beauty." The forest green convertible sports car with a tan leather interior, matching soft top, and cherrywood dash was in mint condition.

St. John smiled. "I just happen to like vintage cars."

Her smile matched his. "How old is it?"

"It's a 1953 Jaguar XK 120. And before you ask, I didn't buy it."

"Where did you get it?"

"I inherited it from an aunt who'd become

placée to a wealthy man who'd owned a fleet of fishing boats in Houma. They couldn't marry and they never had any children, and when he died in 1965, he willed her everything. Some of his relatives challenged the will, but in the end it was upheld. She sold the fleet to a consortium of fishermen, sold her home, and moved back to Marigny and bought a Creole cottage. She died two years ago at eighty-six, and in her will she gave me the house and this car."

She'd read about Loving v. Virginia in law school. Before it was argued before the country's highest court, it was a crime for whites and non-whites to marry in fifteen states, including Louisiana. "He died two years too early, because in 1967 the Supreme Court struck down miscegenation laws."

St. John's fingers tightened on the steering wheel. "You're right. Despite New Orleans having a sizeable population of *gens de couleur libres* going back to the late eighteenth century and even before the Emancipation Proclamation, white men were notorious for attending octoroon and quadroon balls to perpetuate the system of plaçage."

"It sounds so hypocritical."

"What does?"

"Women of color could be consorts, bear children, yet they couldn't become the wives of their predators."

St. John gave her a sidelong glance. "You think of these men as predators rather than their saviors or protectors?"

"Please tell me you're playing the devil's advocate," Hannah said, a hint of annoyance creeping into her voice.

"I am," he admitted. "If a wealthy white Creole had a relationship with a female slave and she bore him a child or children, they were sometimes emancipated along with their mixed-race children, who became the nucleus for the *gens de couleur libres*. Some viewed it as the easiest route for freedom for an enslaved woman and her children."

"That's so duplicitous, St. John. Marriage between the races was forbidden, yet interracial sex was condoned. And there's no way as a mother I'd parade my daughter like a show pony among a group of men so she could become *placée* to someone who couldn't marry her."

"That's because we don't live in the eighteenth, nineteenth, or early twentieth centuries and you're not the mother of a "mulatto," "quadroon," or "octoroon" daughter. Those are words and practices we cringe at now, but it was part of New Orleans history — unsettling though it was."

Silence filled the car; the only audible sound was that of the slip-slap of tires on the roadway. Hannah inhaled an audible breath in an attempt to control her rising temper. "I find it a little concerning that you don't see anything wrong with the system of plaçage."

Downshifting into first gear, and then into neutral, St. John stopped at a red light. "I'm a historian, Hannah, and I've accepted what has happened in our country's history, while praying many of the crimes against certain races and against women will never be repeated. Last year I began researching *gens de couleur libres* for a book on the comprehensive history of New Orleans and I've uncovered facts —"

"You're writing a book," she interrupted. The query was a statement.

St. John nodded. "The idea came to me when I reread my unpublished doctoral dissertation."

"How long do you project the research will take?"

"I haven't given myself a deadline."

"Can you tell me what you've uncovered?"

"I'll have to show you. Even if it takes another ten years to complete the research,

130

I don't intend to begin writing until after I retire."

Hannah met his eyes when he turned to look at her. "Did you ever think you'd be talking about retirement forty years ago?"

The light changed and St. John headed for the French Quarter. "No. The day we graduated the only thing I thought about was going to Howard University."

"Did you like Howard?"

He smiled. "I loved it and I loved living in D.C. I spent most of my downtime exploring the city and taking photographs and interviewing people for research papers. How about you? Did you like Vanderbilt?"

"Yes, because I really liked the whole college experience. I wanted to major in pre-law, but caved when my mother insisted I become a teacher. She believed it was a more genteel profession for a woman."

"But you are a lawyer."

"Now I am. But that became a reality only after I was married and a mother." Hannah told St. John about living on base, and her inability to bond with the other officers' wives, so she decided to pursue her dream to become an attorney.

"Good for you. Our mothers were from a generation where they didn't have nor were offered the opportunities women have to-day."

"You're right . . ." Her words trailed off when Hannah noticed St. John had turned onto Rue Conti. "How did you know?"

"Know what?"

"That Broussard's is one of my favorite restaurants."

St. John maneuvered into a parking space close to the restaurant. "I didn't know, but it happens to be a favorite of mine also."

Hannah experienced a shiver of excitement, recalling the first time her parents had taken her to the iconic restaurant for her sixteenth birthday. It had been one of the highlights of her childhood when her father gave her a strand of Tahitian pearls and matching earrings. Years later, she had the baubles appraised for insurance purposes and was completely stunned by their value.

St. John assisted her from the car and then slipped into the suit jacket he'd left behind the seats. She stiffened slightly when his hand rested at the small of her back as they neared the entrance to Broussard's. Relaxing against his fingers, Hannah resisted the urge to move closer to his length. His firm and impersonal touch elicited a longing to relive the closeness when they'd danced together.

She knew for certain she wasn't a horny middle-aged woman looking for sex as much as she was a woman who'd resigned herself to becoming a social recluse. She spoke to Wyatt or Karen every week, visited with them and her grandchildren several weeks during the summer, and returned to New Orleans to share Thanksgiving and Christmas with Paige and LeAnn. Her position in Wakefield Hamilton's legal division provided her with a workplace setting in which she didn't have to combine business with pleasure.

And after Robert passed away, she had no qualms about dining out, attending a play, concert, or even a sporting event unaccompanied. There were a few incidents when men attempted to garner her attention, but once she exhibited indifference, they turned their interest elsewhere. She went through dark moods when she'd experienced a decrease of sexual and personal confidence, while a lingering rage had taken her several years to overcome, all of which added to her subjective feeling that her life partner had violated a rule they'd established before marrying. Robert had promised to be faithful to her because he saw the pain his mother had endured because of his father's adultery.

St. John's hand moved from her back to her waist, his fingers moving up to her rib cage. Unconsciously Hannah leaned into him, and the instant she walked through the doors at Broussard's Restaurant and Courtyard with St. John McNair, Hannah knew she'd turned a corner to repair the psychological damage she'd brought on herself because her expectations in marriage were not met.

"I hope you don't mind that I made a reservation for us to dine in the courtyard."

St. John's voice penetrated her thoughts. She smiled at him. "Not at all. The few times I ate here, the courtyard was off-limits because of a private party or wedding."

The maître d' greeted St. John by name and they were led to a table for two in the garden courtyard of the historic landmark with its French-inspired décor. Everything about the outdoor space was conducive to romantic dining. Hannah stared her dining partner across the small expanse of the table, a smile playing at the corners of her mouth.

St. John pretended interest in the menu rather than stare at Hannah. High school students had referred to her as the ice princess or Miss Southern Belle, and there were occasions when he'd agreed with them. In all the years they shared the same classes or studied together, she rarely exhibited anything other than a calm demeanor. He knew she'd been taunted by fellow students because she was viewed as a spoiled rich girl who'd been driven to school by her family's chauffeur, and not once had she retaliated or felt the need explain why she'd transferred from one of New Orleans' most elite private all-girls institutions to a public school. One hundred percent of the girls who graduated from the McGehee School attended college.

However, when he witnessed her passionate outburst about the once acceptable tradition of plaçage, she'd appeared anything but cold. And St. John wondered if a few of her male ancestors had engaged in the practice or if she identified with the women who were trained and manipulated by their mothers from a very early age to accept their future plight as a *placée.* Had Hannah's mother been like the mothers of beautiful mixed-race daughters when she put so much pressure on her not to go into law that she caved and majored in education? And had Hannah harbored resentment that she'd been forced to marry in order gain independence from a controlling and overbearing mother?

Whenever he thought of family pressure, St. John recalled how his aunt and music teacher had defied her parents when she decided to *shack up* with a man with whom she'd fallen in love and was legally forbidden to marry. Monique Baptiste had endured years of alienation from her devoutly Catholic family, it only ending after her lover died.

His mother had been the exception. Elsie Baptiste-McNair worshipped Monique and made it a practice to drive him and his sister down to Houma to spend several weeks of the summer with her. The year he celebrated his thirteenth birthday, he joined the crew of a fishing boat for the first time, experiencing twin emotions of fear and exhilaration. Once he overcame his fear of drowning, he went out with the crew every summer until the year he entered college.

"Are you angry with me, St. John?"

His head popped up, and he stared at Hannah, attempting read her impassive expression. "No. Why would you ask me that?"

A slight flush suffused her face. "You're studying that menu as if you've never seen

136

it before, and I thought you were angry with me because I called men who take advantage of women predators."

A glint of amusement flickered in St. John's eyes. "Are you a man-hater, Hannah?" His question caught her completely off guard; a slight gasp escaped her parted lips.

"No! Of course not. Why would you ask me that?"

"I just need to know where we stand if we're going to hang out together this summer."

Hannah stared at him, shock freezing her features. "Did we agree to see each other over the summer?"

St. John nodded. "I remember you saying, 'I'll call to invite you to come out to Du-Pont House so we can catch up on what has been going on in our lives over the past two decades.' You also said, 'I'll give you an update about my experience as a big city corporate attorney while you can tell me about your students at Barden College.' And I did promise to show you my research on *gens de couleur libres.*"

Shock after shock assailed Hannah, making it impossible for her to draw a normal breath. He'd repeated her exact words verbatim. "Do you have eidetic memory?"

Throwing back his head, St. John laughed. "Why do you make it sound as if I'm carrying a deadly communicable disease?"

She leaned over the table. "Just answer my question, St. John."

He sobered. "You could say I do."

His mocking tone irritated her. "Is that a yes?"

"Yes it is, counselor."

"Please don't call me that," Hannah retorted. Leaning back in his chair, St. John gave her a long, penetrating look that added to her uneasiness. They'd studied together, were part of a team researching class projects, and not once had he hinted that he had the ability of total recall. Why, she wondered, had he downplayed his intelligence?

"Aren't you are an attorney?"

"I am, but I'm not licensed here." She wasn't licensed to practice in Louisiana because it didn't have an express reciprocity agreement with other states, but would provisionally admit certain lawyers from other jurisdictions under special criteria.

"Where are you licensed?"

"New York and California. New York has reciprocity with nearly thirty states, while California doesn't, but does offer a shorter bar exam for attorneys in good standing, licensed in other states four years prior. I don't want to change the subject, but why are you under the impression we're going to see each other over the summer?"

St. John put up a hand as the waiter approached their table. "Please give us a moment," he said to the young man. He held up a finger. "Firstly it's going to take more than one or two dinners to talk about what's been going on in our lives since we graduated high school." He held up another finger. "And secondly I'd like to ask you if you'd agree to be my dance partner for a three-week course."

Hannah blinked slowly. "Dance partner?"

He smiled and lines fanned out around his luminous, gold-flecked eyes. "Yes. Every summer I take ballroom dancing lessons. I've learned the foxtrot, jive, and samba. This year I'm taking tango lessons, and if you're not too busy I'd like you to partner up with me."

She was too startled by St. John's suggestion to form an immediate reply. And now she knew what he meant when he said maybe she didn't dance enough. Hannah wanted to reject his offer, but there was something about this more mature version of the man she'd met more than forty years ago that intrigued her. Although physically he hadn't changed much, St. John had become someone who was more of a stranger than friend or ex-classmate.

"With the exception of dancing at the reunion, I haven't danced in years. I took ballet lessons from the age of five until thirteen, but that's been it."

"It's like riding a bike, Hannah. You may wobble a bit when you first get on, and then after a while you're better than you ever could've imagined."

His explanation elicited a smile from her. "Ballet and pointe, yes. But I'm not as confident when it comes to dancing with a partner."

Reaching across the table, St. John rested his hand atop Hannah's. "You did just fine when we danced together."

Hannah smiled. "That's because you're a strong lead. Do you mind if I think about it?"

"Of course not."

"When do you need my answer?" she asked.

"I'd like to have it sometime next week."

"How often do you practice?"

"Three times a week for three weeks."

"I'll let you know in plenty of time for you to get another partner if I decide not to take you up on your offer." She still hadn't heard from her former co-workers as to when they would come down, and Hannah didn't want to commit to anything until then. She made a mental note to send Tonya a text message.

St. John nodded. "Thank you."

He signaled the waiter, giving him their beverage order as Hannah focused on the menu. She'd spent less than an hour with St. John and she felt more relaxed with him than she had with any man since her late husband. Not once had he attempted to flirt or come on to her, and for that she was grateful. Never in her life had she had a male friend — someone to talk to when she needed advice to deal with the opposite sex.

A satisfied smile feathered over her face as she peered up at St. John through a fringe of lashes. It had been years since she'd spent the summer in her hometown, and Hannah was looking forward to the next three months with the same excitement she felt when she'd received her acceptance letter from Vanderbilt. Enrolling in an out-of-state college had put some distance between her and her controlling mother, while setting the stage in her quest for independence.

She stared at St. John staring back at her, and as if on cue they shared a smile.

CHAPTER 8

Hannah lost track of time as she and St. John discussed local and national politics, the environment, and the rebuilding still going on in New Orleans a decade after the devastation wrought from the aftermath of Katrina.

St. John touched the corners of his mouth with a napkin. "Did you have a problem with flooding?" he asked her.

"No. But we did have some wind damage. What about your home?"

"We were fortunate because the Tremé neighborhood received minor to moderate flooding. Luckily, the water was not high enough to damage many of the old raised homes."

"Do you still own the house in Tremé?"

St. John paused, seemingly deep in thought, before he said, "Lorna got the house as a part of the divorce settlement. She sold it last year to move in with her elderly aunt and uncle who'd raised her after her parents died in a car accident."

Hannah sensed a change in St. John's mood when he mentioned his ex-wife. What, she wondered, had happened to end a marriage spanning three decades? Whenever Lorna accompanied him at a Jackson High home game, prom, or even at their twentieth reunion, they'd always appeared to be a loving couple.

She forced a smile she didn't quite feel, because she didn't want anything to spoil the evening. She and St. John shared an appetizer of barbecue shrimp followed by entrées of broiled redfish with a rosemary and mustard crust and grilled rack of lamb. Instead of her usual white wine she ordered a hurricane. The very sweet concoction made with dark rum, passion fruit and other juices gave her instant buzz, and she chided herself for not waiting until after she'd consumed the appetizer.

Picking up a cup of coffee liberally laced with chicory, Hannah took a sip while staring over the rim at St. John. "Have you ever thought about moving from New Orleans?"

The St. John she'd come to know and like was back when he laughed softly. "Never," he admitted. "I know it may sound clichéd, but I'd never leave, because my ancestors sacrificed too much for me to abandon the city you see today. My aunt was one of a few Baptistes who are still living in Louisiana, while the Toussaints have no intention of ever leaving New Orleans."

Resting her elbow on the table, Hannah cupped her chin on her hand. "You're a Toussaint?"

"Yes. My grandmother was a Toussaint."

Hannah digested this information. "By the way, are you related to Eustace Toussaint?"

"Yes. He's a cousin."

Her eyebrow shot up. "Really?"

St. John gave her a smile usually reserved for children from their parents. "Really. Why does this surprise you?"

"I thought with the last name McNair you didn't have any Creole ancestry."

"My mother's people are Baptiste and my father's folks are Toussaints. My paternal grandmother was a Toussaint before she married James McNair."

Hannah was intrigued by this disclosure. "How far back do you trace your people?"

"Archival records document the arrival of the first black Toussaint in the Louisiana Territory around 1811, just before Louisiana was granted statehood. The Baptistes came about ten years later."

Hannah grinned like a Cheshire cat. "The

DuPonts have you beat by a decade."

St. John's expression changed as if someone had pulled a shade down, successfully concealing his innermost thoughts. "The difference is the DuPonts didn't arrive enslaved."

Lowering her arm, she sat straight. The muscles in her stomach knotted as she shot St. John a withering glare. "That may be true, but only because my ancestor's mulatto mistress wouldn't leave Haiti with their children unless he freed them. Yes, St. John," she told him when he stared at her with an incredulous look on his face. "Don't let what I look like fool you, because I'm a direct descendant of Etienne DuPont and Margit, who'd been an *affranchise,* and I'm willing to bet that if I were to take an ancestry DNA test, the findings would indicate European, Native American *and* African." She told him about the documents she'd found and subsequently donated to the local historical society.

Leaning back in his chair, St. John crossed his arms over his chest. The seconds ticked as he regarded Hannah with a gleam of interest in his eyes. "Should I also include some of your family members in my research?"

"I'll let you determine that if you're will-

145

ing to go through the archival records."

"So, you're going to make me spend hours reading documents when you can tell me now about the DuPonts' *gens de couleur.*"

"Weren't you the one who decided that we were going to hang out together over the summer?"

St. John nodded. "I think I remember saying that."

Hannah narrowed her eyes. "You think? Don't pretend you don't remember, because you did admit that you have total recall." She angled her head as a half-smile parted her lips. "However, I'm willing to compromise. Before donating my family's diaries, journals, Bibles, and other business records, I created a family tree on my computer with names, dates of births and deaths of everyone sharing Etienne and Margit's bloodline. I'll print out a copy for you."

"Thank you very much." St. John lowered his arms, his expression impassive. "Please answer one question for me, Hannah."

"What do you want to know?"

"Do you always take off work for the summer?"

"No."

She'd told LeAnn, Paige, her son and daughter-in-law, and only a few days ago Letitia that she was unemployed, and now

St. John wanted to know why she was going to spend the next three months in New Orleans. His expression didn't change when she revealed the details behind her former employer's merger and downsizing half the bank's staff.

"Are you actively looking for another position?"

"Why?"

"I can put in a good word for you at the college if you're willing to teach. We need someone for a course on law and government. You'd start as an assistant professor."

Hannah was momentarily speechless. She didn't want to believe St. John was offering her a teaching position at his college. She didn't want to teach. She wanted to be an innkeeper. "Thank you for offering, but I can't see myself returning to the classroom or lecture hall."

"Does your aversion to teaching have anything to do with your mother?"

She detected a hint of censure in his query and chided herself for telling him how Clarissa had coerced her into not following her career path. "No, it doesn't. I had a lot of unresolved issues where it concerned my mother, but after spending more than a year on a therapist's couch I've come to accept that if someone is unwilling or can't change,

147

then it's incumbent on me to change. I loved my mother despite her being controlling and manipulative, because I realized she wanted the best for me, whether it was a career or marriage. She was raised to marry well, and she did when she married my father. Her focus wasn't so much a career as it was being the perfect mother, wife, and hostess."

"Despite what you've revealed about your mother, I think you turned out okay. You have the career you always wanted, and you're blessed to have had a good marriage which gave you your own family."

Hannah had no intention of correcting St. John about her having a good marriage. On the surface she'd believed she had a good marriage, unaware that her husband had had a number of affairs.

"You're right," she drawled, then covered a yawn with her hand. Even if she didn't love Robert when they first married, she'd grown to love him. They rarely argued when he was home on leave, he was a doting father, and he initiated the necessary steps to ensure her financial viability in the event of his death.

"You're not falling asleep on me, are you?" There was a hint of laughter in St. John's tone.

She liked the sound of St. John's voice. It was deep, drawling, and seductive. "No. I'm just a little tipsy."

"You're not much of a drinker, are you?"

"No. Whenever the girls in my dorm went out partying, I was always the designated driver, because they could count on me to get them back to campus without wrapping the car around a pole. I've made it a practice to eat first if I'm going to have anything alcoholic."

St. John laughed again. "I'll make certain to remember that whenever we go out for drinks. The kids at Howard always loaded up on something greasy before drinking. There was a little rib joint not far from campus, and on the weekend the line would be out the door and down the block. There were times when they'd run out of ribs because the neighborhood folks would get there before us and clean it out. Then one of the owners decided to open up a second spot around the corner, which made everyone happy."

"Did they offer sides?"

"Yes. Potato salad, candied sweet potatoes, cole slaw, and the best damn green beans with white potatoes and smoked ham hocks I've ever eaten."

Hannah smiled. It had been years since

she'd eaten Southern-style green beans. "I like living in New York, but the thing I miss most about New Orleans is the food."

"There're a number of restaurants in Harlem and Brooklyn that serve southern cuisine."

"What do you know about Harlem and Brooklyn?"

"I know enough about Harlem and Brooklyn neighborhoods not to get lost. Whenever I'm invited to lecture or teach a summer course at a New York college or university, I make it my business to familiarize myself with different neighborhoods."

"When was the last time you were in New York?" Hannah questioned.

"Two years ago."

"If I'd known you were in town, we could've gotten together."

"Where do you live?" he asked.

"I rent an apartment in the Financial District."

"Maybe the next time I'm in New York I'll let you know." St. John beckoned the waiter, requesting the check. "I'd planned for us to go to a jazz club in Tremé, but since you're yawning I think we'll call it a night."

Hannah yawned again. "I'm sorry if I ruined your —"

"Don't you dare apologize," St. John said, interrupting her. "If you want, we can always go at another time."

She smiled. "I'd like that."

He settled the bill, and holding her hand with his firm grip, St. John led her to where he'd parked the car. The drive back to the Garden District was accomplished in complete silence, Hannah closing her eyes while sinking down into the supple leather seat. She couldn't remember when she'd had a more enjoyable evening when sharing dinner with a man.

She found it so easy to talk to St. John about things she never would've discussed with or revealed to another man. She was more than aware that her experience with the opposite sex was limited to Robert and the other men with whom she'd worked — almost all of whom had related to her on the professional level. Even the few dates she'd had with the lawyers at the Upper East Side firm were more businesslike than personal. It wasn't until they took her home things changed. They wanted to come up to her apartment for a nightcap, and when she refused with the excuse that she had to get up early, or she'd lie and say she had out-of-town guests staying over, they quickly lost interest.

Hannah opened her eyes. "I'd like to return the favor for a most enjoyable evening by inviting you to dinner next Sunday at my place. That is, if you don't have anything planned."

St. John gave her quick glance before returning his attention to the road. "What time should I come?"

"How's three o'clock?"

He nodded. "Three's good for me."

"Do you have any food allergies?"

"No." He paused. "Are you cooking?"

Her jaw dropped slightly. "Of course I'm cooking. Did you think I'd order takeout?"

A low chuckle filled the car. "I've known quite a few women who prefer takeout and reservations to preparing a home-cooked meal."

"Well, I'm not one of those *women.*" And she wasn't. Not only did she know how to cook, but she also enjoyed cooking.

A satisfied smile played at the corners of her mouth as she stared out the side window. All too soon the drive ended and she opened her wristlet and took out her cell phone. She tapped an app, and the gates swung open and St. John drove through.

"Do you always keep the gates locked?" he asked, coming to a complete stop in front the house.

"I lock them at night. I had closed-circuit cameras installed throughout the house several years ago, but that's before the Garden District and French Quarter got their own private police." Crime rates had escalated in New Orleans in the years following Hurricane Katrina and a local businessman, after having his 8,000-square-foot home burglarized, came up with a plan to protect a neighborhood less than one square mile containing the city's most valuable real estate with his own high-tech police force.

"You can't be too careful," St. John said, as he unbuckled his seat belt. He came around the car and opened her door. She placed her palm on his outstretched one, his fingers closing around her hand, as he eased her gently to her feet.

Hannah climbed the porch steps, with him following. Lifting the door handle, she tapped in the code, deactivated the security system and opened the door. She turned around and found herself nearly face-to-face with St. John. He was close enough for her to feel his breath on her forehead.

She stared at his throat. He'd removed his jacket and tie. Her eyes moved up to study his face, noting the nostrils of his straight nose flaring slightly as he exhaled an audible breath.

"Thank you again for a wonderful evening."

St. John lowered his head and brushed a kiss over her cheek. "Thank for you being a most delightful dining partner." Turning on his heel, he walked off the porch.

She watched the taillights of the sports car as St. John drove off the property, the gates closing automatically. Despite feeling the lingering effects the potent drink, she loathed going inside. Folding her body down to a rocker, Hannah scrolled through her cell's directory for Tonya's number, sending her a text message.

Hannah: Do you still plan to come down?

She placed the phone on the chair's cushioned seat and closed her eyes. St. John said he didn't date but she'd been taught whenever a man invited a woman out, it translated into that. But then she had to ask herself if her inviting him to Sunday dinner was also a date. Hannah opened her eyes, sighing. She'd always had a problem over-analyzing any situation. She just couldn't see things as black or white but had to delve deeper to find shades of gray. Her inner voice told her a man and woman with romantic notions courted. A man and a woman who were friends would occasionally get together for an event or congregate with mutual friends.

Hannah didn't need to lie on her therapist's couch to know what she was undergoing emotionally. Her plan to turn DuPont House into an inn was on hold, pending the approval of a license. Although she hadn't spent more than two consecutive months in her city of birth since becoming Mrs. Robert Lowell, this was the first time she felt that she'd truly come home, which added to her ambivalence about whether she wanted to continue to live in New York if the licenses were denied.

And she did not want to consider St. John's offer for her to join the faculty at Barden College. When it came to teaching, her adage was: Been there, done that. Teaching college-level courses meant ongoing lectures, exams, and grading papers.

As a military wife she'd traveled with Robert whenever he was reassigned to another naval base, but her nomad existence ended once their son was accepted into the Air Force Academy. An empty nester at forty, she passed the New York Bar on her first attempt, moving to New York after Robert resigned his commission to accept a position with the Department of Defense. He rented an apartment in D.C., commuting to New York every other weekend. Eight years later everything changed when he returned to New York complaining of chest pain. Once the pain escalated, Hannah called for medical assistance. During the ambulance ride to the hospital, he bared his soul to her about his many infidelities, including sharing the D.C. apartment with a woman. She'd been too numb to react as her marriage vows — *in sickness and in health* — held her captive until Robert was released from the hospital after an eight-day stay.

Robert resigned his position at the Pentagon and to the outside world they presented the perfect couple; yet behind closed doors they slept in separate beds. Two years later he collapsed during a walk along Battery Park. Death was instantaneous. Hannah arranged for his body to be flown to Baton Rouge, where he was buried in his family plot with full military honors. After the reading of Robert's will, Hannah realized he'd kept his promise to ensure she would be financially independent for the rest of her life, and Wyatt would be the recipient of the flag draping his casket.

The ring tone for a text message shattered her musings. Tonya had answered her text.

Tonya: We'll be there in two weeks

Hannah: Wonderful! ☺ Drive safely

Tonya: Thanks!

Her friends were scheduled to arrive mid-June and now she could commit to tango lessons with St. John. If she was going to learn ballroom dancing, then she needed to look the part. Humming a nameless tune, she walked in the house and closed the door. She hadn't taken more than half a dozen steps when she heard a soft mewling. Glancing down, she found Smokey huddled under the table in the entryway.

The kitten backed up when she attempted to reach for him. "What's the matter, baby? You don't like being home alone?" Hannah managed to pick up the kitten and cradle him to her chest. "Let's see if you've eaten all your food."

Fifteen minutes later she climbed the staircase to her bedroom after Smokey retreated to his bed in the parlor.

Sprawled on a lounger in the sunroom, St. John rested his head on folded arms and stared at the steadily falling rain. When he'd gotten up earlier that morning, his intent had been to run a couple of miles before returning to the house to shower and eat breakfast, but the inclement weather had become a deterrent. Although he'd equipped a spare room with a treadmill, rowing machine, and elliptical bicycle, he still preferred running outdoors.

His first reaction when he'd been informed that his aunt Monique had willed him the house was to put it on the market, because he felt it was too big for one person. The classical Southern vernacular farmhouse was designed on the scale of a smaller version of a grand plantation mansion.

Once he moved in, St. John discovered he liked having enough space for a library-office, gym and spa, and a sunroom off the rear of the house where he could relax or entertain regardless of the weather. There were also enough guest bedrooms to put up his sister and her family whenever they came to visit. He'd also bought a piano to replace the one that had been in his family for three generations.

St. John had made it a practice to host two events at his home for department staff and faculty: Christmas and an end of the year gathering. Picking up his cell phone, he tapped the music app and Earth, Wind & Fire's classic hit "That's the Way of the World" filled the space. He'd refined the app to determine where music could be heard in any of the hidden speakers installed throughout the house. He closed his eyes and crossed bare feet at the ankles, humming to the song by a band that topped his list of favorites. His cell vibrated and St. John opened his eyes. He sat up straight. Hannah had sent him a text message.

Hannah: Do you wanna dance and hold my hand?

A slow smile softened his features. She'd sent him the lyrics of Bobby Freeman's rock and roll oldie from the 1950s.

St. John: Do you want to dance?

Hannah: Yes. I bought several outfits and dancing shoes

St. John: Nice! I'll pick you up at your place around 3:30 tomorrow

Hannah: I'll be ready

St. John: See you tomorrow

Hannah: OK

This would be the first year since he'd taken ballroom dancing lessons that he would have the partner of his choice. Over the years he had selected a partner arbitrarily from a number of unaccompanied women. Once he was paired with a woman, he couldn't request another partner for the duration of the course.

St. John had just settled down to enjoy the tunes in the extensive playlist spanning decades when the doorbell chimed throughout the house. Swinging his legs over the lounger, he walked on bare feet to answer the door. It was Sunday and he wasn't expecting anyone. The only person who usually rang his bell was his elderly neighbor who lived across the street; she claimed she had to check on him because he lived alone. He'd wanted to tell Mrs. Chambers he needed to check on her and her husband because both were quickly approaching ninety. However, he did make it a practice to put out their trash and garbage for pickup, mow their lawn whenever the grass grew too high, and do their grocery shopping when necessary. Although they no longer drove, both were still in relatively good health for their age. Their grandchildren had tried unsuccessfully to convince them to sell their home and relocate to Metairie, where they'd made arrangements for them to them to live in a facility for independent living.

Peering through one of the front door's sidelights, he saw a familiar figure. Opening the door, he came face-to-face with Gage Toussaint. "Come on in."

Gage exchanged a rough embrace with St. John. "Sorry about coming by without calling."

St. John stared at his cousin. At forty-five, Gage was in his prime. Tall and slender, the divorced father of a nineteen-year-old college dropout, Gage occasionally helped out in Chez Toussaints when he wasn't sitting in with a local jazz band as their trumpeter. However, it was the blending of his African, Creole, and Cajun ancestry that drew women to him, while making him one of New Orleans's most eligible bachelors.

St. John patted Gage's broad back in a white tee. "What are you doing up so early? I thought musicians don't get out of bed until late afternoon."

Gage ran a hand over cropped straight black hair with flecks of gray. "I promised Eustace I'd help him cater a birthday party in Lakeview."

"Do want something to eat or drink?"

"Nah. I'm good. I'm not going to stay long. I just came by to see if you're all right. You told me you were coming by the club Friday night, and when I didn't see or hear from you I thought something had happened."

St. John met the younger man's gray-green eyes. "I'd planned to stop by, but after dinner I decided to make it an early night."

Gage gave him a sidelong glance. "Who was she?"

A slight frown furrowed St. John's smooth forehead. "What are you talking about?"

"Did you or did you not have dinner with a woman?"

"Yes. Why?"

"If you were going to make it an early evening, then what she was offering had be way better than you sitting in a club listening to some of the best jazz to come out of Nawlins in a very long time."

"The lady in question is not what you think. We hadn't seen each other since our twentieth high school reunion, so the dinner was nothing more than reconnecting." Now that Hannah had agreed to be his dance partner, St. John knew word of them being seen together would generate gossip, but he couldn't care less about what people said or thought about him.

"If you say nothing's going on, then I want you to meet the new female singer who just joined the band."

Placing both hands on his younger cousin's shoulders, St. John steered him toward the door. "How many times do I have to tell you I don't need you to find a woman for me?"

Gage laughed. "Come on, *kezen,* we haven't seen you with a woman since you broke up with Lorna."

"Cela ne signifie pas que je ne vois pas les femmes," St. John replied in French. Most family members spoke French if only to remain fluent in the language, while a few,

including himself, were fluent in Haitian Creole.

"If you've been seeing women, then that means you've been holding out on us."

St. John shook his head. Once it had been made known he and Lorna were no longer together, many of his relatives embarked on a campaign to hook him up with a number of different women despite his protests.

"You've seen me. I'm good, so now go help your big brother before he brings holy hell down on you for slackin' off."

"I keep telling Eustace that he needs to ease up and let his kids run the restaurant, while he can concentrate on the catering end of the business."

"That's like talking to a brick wall."

St. John knew Gage was right. Eustace, the father of three and grandfather of seven, refused to relinquish the day-to-day operation of the restaurant to his daughters. There had been a time when the restaurant was open for business six days a week for lunch and dinner, but Eustace changed the hours of operation from 11:00 a.m. to 2:00 p.m. several years ago because catering orders accounted for more than half the restaurant's revenue.

"When are you coming by the club?" Gage asked as he made his way to the door.

"Either next Friday or Saturday. That's a promise," St. John added when his cousin shot him a questioning look.

"I'm going to hold you to that."

St. John watched Gage as he sprinted to his Audi SUV to avoid being soaked. The rain was now coming down in torrents. His cousin straddled two worlds: music and cooking. As a Julliard graduate, Gage had lived in Europe for a year, where he learned to cook French dishes, and only returned when his father passed away, and then divided his time cooking at Chez Toussaints and sitting in as horn player for a local band. His short-lived marriage resulted in divorce and a son who was the antithesis of what it meant to be a Toussaint.

He closed the door and retreated to the sunroom. It was a rainy Sunday and his plans were stay indoors, listen to music, watch the basketball playoffs, and if he didn't get enough sports, then an encore of an Atlanta Braves or a St. Louis Cardinals baseball game. The fridge was fully stocked and he still had containers of takeout from Chez Toussaints he could reheat within minutes. Although he lived alone, St. John wasn't lonely. He'd had more than thirty years of sharing a roof with a woman who legally was his wife but never his lover.

No, he didn't need anyone's assistance in finding a woman. He had one — even if she was only there for them to satisfy each other's physical needs. He'd committed himself emotionally to one woman once in his life and swore it would never happen again.

And he couldn't even think of Hannah being anything but a friend and former classmate, even though he enjoyed her company. She was intelligent *and* feminine — a combination he'd found missing in some women with whom he'd interacted. They were either one or the other, but rarely both, and he now looked forward to having her as his dance partner.

CHAPTER 9

Hannah was shown into the office of the man whose family had begun monitoring investments for the DuPonts following the Great Depression. Margit's insistence that Etienne free his slaves and employ only free people of color not only saved his fields from being burned to the ground during the Civil War but it also saved future generations from financial ruin. Unfortunately, Jean-Paul DuPont's shipbuilding descendants did not fare as well, and at the end of the war they lost everything and were forced to align themselves with the anti-slavery DuPonts growing and processing sugar cane for European markets.

Cameron Singleton rose to stand, greeting her with a friendly smile that lit up large, bright-blue eyes in a lean, perpetually tanned face with patrician features. There was a hint of gray in his cropped light-brown hair. He extended his hand. "It's always so nice seeing you in person, Hannah. I hate this damn social media because it's so impersonal. What happened to folks picking up the phone to talk instead of communicating with emails, tweets, and text messaging?"

Smiling, she took his hand. "I did call you for this appointment," she said, reminding him that she'd called him earlier that morning. Hannah wanted to agree with Cameron, but felt there were certain advances to using social media.

"Yes, you did," he said. "Please, let's sit over at the table. I always feel disconnected whenever there's a desk between me and my clients. But you're different because I've always thought of you as a friend."

"And I you," she countered. It wasn't vanity that told Hannah the forty-something, never-married bachelor was interested in her. His flirting, although subtle, had not been lost on her. She sat on the chair he'd pulled out for her. "I'd like your advice about a business venture."

Cameron, sitting opposite Hannah, laced his fingers together. "Tell me about it."

She quickly outlined her plan to turn Du-Pont House into an inn if and when the license and permits were approved. "I have the capital for the necessary renovations but I don't want to liquidate some of my investment for salaries until we're up and running."

"Have you thought about investors?" he asked.

Hannah blinked once, her gaze meeting and fusing with the man who'd earned the reputation as a serial dater because he was never seen with the same woman for more a few months. "No, I haven't," she admitted.

Cameron smoothed down the red silk tie, which was knotted with a precise Windsor knot on a spread-collar white shirt. "Investors are the way to go if you don't want to exhaust all your assets. Do you know anyone willing to invest for a share in the business?"

Hannah digested his query. Unfortunately, she couldn't think of anyone who'd be willing to invest in DuPont House. She knew she could always ask her cousins, despite their protests that they didn't want to have anything to do with running an inn.

"I'll have to think about it," she replied.

"Don't forget you can use your property as collateral if you decide to take out a loan."

She nodded. "I've thought of that. But that would be my last resort, even though I could write off the loan as a business expense."

"There you go. Meanwhile, I have no

doubt you'll get your permits approved. I know someone at the mayor's office who can put your application at the top of the pile."

"I would really appreciate that, Cameron. Meanwhile I'm going to think about who I can approach as potential investors." Reaching across the table, she extended her hand. "Thank you, as usual."

He shook the proffered hand. "That's what I'm here for." He glanced at his watch. "Will you join me for lunch?"

Hannah rose to her feet. "I'm sorry, but I have something scheduled this afternoon." Even though it wasn't quite noon, and she didn't have to meet St. John until three-thirty, but that was something she wasn't going to reveal to the financial planner. "Do you mind if we have lunch at another time?"

"Just let me know when and I'll clear my calendar."

"I'm expecting friends to come in from out of town for a few weeks, but after they leave I'll call you and we can set a date."

Her explanation appeared to please Cameron; his smile was wide enough to reveal flawless porcelain incisors and molars. "I'll be expecting your call."

Hannah rode the elevator in the office building on Carondelet Street and walked to the lot where she'd parked LeAnn's Ford Explorer. She'd promised her cousins she would occasionally drive their cars in their absence. Leaving the downtown business district, Hannah headed for Tremé. She'd decided to stop and see Daphne's parents, because she still had time before her dance lesson with St. John.

Her day had begun joining Letitia in their walk, and after returning to the house she saw to Smokey's needs. The kitten, after rolling down the staircase in his first attempt, couldn't stop crying and shaking; now he went up and down the stairs without a hint of fear. Then she'd called Cameron for an appointment to ask for his advice on converting the historic home from a personal residence to a business.

His suggestion she solicit investors for a percentage of ownership had sent her imagination into overdrive. Hannah knew for certain the bedroom suites on the second story would be used for guests, but then there was the question of the two guesthouses. She couldn't use the guesthouses for guests, because the additional space would negate her operating an inn. Both guesthouses contained two bedroom suites, which would increase the number of rooms from nine to thirteen, and if she used them for guests, DuPont House would have to be listed as a hotel rather than an inn, which would require a license for a hotel.

She drummed her fingers on the steering wheel as she turned off onto a local road leading to the Bouie home. Their neighborhood had sustained substantial flooding, many of its residents leaving and not returning once rebuilding began. Hannah had sat in her Manhattan high-rise watching television footage of the devastation laying waste to her hometown. Once she began to cry, she found that she couldn't stop. It wasn't as much the loss of property that saddened her as the needless loss of life. The images of people on the rooftops of their homes and the corpses of human beings and animals floating in the water haunted her for weeks. Once she was able to get a flight, she returned to New Orleans, and when her cousins picked her up at the airport, once again she was overcome with a sadness that lingered for the duration of her stay.

However, unlike the phoenix, Louisianans didn't rise from the ashes but from the floodwaters to reclaim their city and heritage, because while they were still recovering from Katrina, they were faced with another disaster. This time it was the result of the BP oil spill in the Gulf of Mexico where the impact hit the fishing industry the hardest.

She stared through the windshield, her gaze taking in the homes along both sides of the still unpaved road. Newer structures stood alongside older occupied homes and a few that were abandoned and slated for demolition. She'd come back to New Orleans many times since her marriage, but Hannah knew if she opened the inn, it would be her last move. The lease on her New York City apartment was scheduled to expire at the end of September and the timing could not have been more fortuitous.

Packing up everything in the two-bedroom apartment would be accomplished quickly, because she planned to donate all of the furniture and housewares to her favorite charity, one focusing on helping women with children transition out of shelters, and have only her clothes, books, and personal effects shipped to DuPont House.

Ideas as to how to utilize the guesthouses nagged at her relentlessly until she maneuvered into the driveway leading to the house where she and Daphne had spent countless hours listening to records on her stereo when they should have been studying. Daphne always lowered the volume because her father didn't like her playing the "devil's music" in his house. Even then, Hannah had thought it strange that Daphne never talked about boys she liked or who she'd thought cute, but she never questioned her. It wasn't until years later that word circulated that Daphne was gay. The revelation never affected the way Hannah felt about the girl who'd befriended her when others in their school had shunned her. Coming to a complete stop, she cut off the engine and alighted from the SUV. She hadn't taken more than three steps when a woman's voice stopped her.

"They're not home."

Hannah stared at the tall woman who'd come down off the porch of the neighboring house. "Do you know when they'll be back, Miss Addie?"

Adaline Jensen squinted over the half-glasses perched on the end of her nose. "Not until tomorrow. Aren't you the judge's gal?"

Hannah smiled, nodding. "I am."

Miss Addie had earned a reputation as the unofficial neighborhood watch. All she had to do was hear a snippet of a situation and she made it her business to get the whole story. The tall woman with the catlike green and yellowish eyes in a complexion the color of aged parchment always frightened Hannah. Long-time residents whispered among themselves that Miss Addie was a direct descendant of Marie Laveau, also known as the voodoo queen of New Orleans.

Miss Addie patted the coronet of snow-white braids pinned neatly atop her head. "I really miss him. He was a good man and a fair judge, not like some of them now who want to lock up everyone for spitting on the road. Folks wanted him to run for mayor or governor, but he said he liked being a judge."

Hannah smiled. "That's Daddy. Can you tell Mrs. Bouie that Hannah came by and I'll stop again at another time?"

"I sure will." Addie took off her glasses. "I must say you look good, gal. Not like some women who ruin their bodies and faces with fake breasts and all that plastic surgery."

"Thank you, Miss Addie."

She got back into the car and backed out of the driveway. In the past she'd never exchanged a word with the former dress-maker who'd earned her living sewing for local celebrities. Daphne claimed Miss Addie never married because as a psychic she knew what men wanted from her before they opened their mouths. Someone had burglarized her home to steal the supposed

174

stash of money she'd hidden away, but came away empty-handed. The burglar didn't know that, after a few clients refused to pay her, the astute seamstress had her clients deposit money directly into her bank account before she would relinquish their finished garments.

Hannah drove back to the Garden District and was greeted by Smokey as soon as she walked through the door. "I'm glad to see you, too," she crooned as he wound his way through and around her legs. Smokey followed her up the staircase as she walked into her bedroom and slipped out of the pale-blue cotton coatdress and navy-blue patent leather pumps. She still had plenty of time to eat a light lunch, shower, and change into dance attire before St. John arrived.

St. John downshifted, slowing and stopping in front of DuPont House to make certain the woman standing there was Hannah. Like a chameleon she'd changed again, this time into the quintessential Latin dancer, with a black spandex top with capped sleeves and an asymmetrical neckline. The bloodred ruffled skirt ending at the knees and riding low on her hips screamed sensuality. His eyes moved lower to her long bare legs and narrow feet in a pair of black ballet flats. He got out of the car and came around to open the passenger-side door.

"I almost didn't recognize you," he said, staring at her bare face. A lovely blush stained her cheeks, adding color to her fair complexion.

Ducking her head, Hannah slipped onto the seat. "I know I must look like a ghost without makeup," she replied before he closed the door.

Waiting until he seated behind the wheel, St. John focused on her delicate profile. "You look lovely." Hannah turned to look at him. He lifted his eyebrows questioningly. "You don't think of yourself as lovely?" She compressed her lips and averted her eyes, staring at the tote on her lap. Where, he mused, was the confident woman who'd challenged him about the practice of plaçage? She had to know she was blessed with above average looks, and men were certain to give her a second look whenever she entered a room. He'd been no exception when he first noticed her at the reunion.

St. John started up the car, went through the gates of the DuPont House, and then turned off onto St. Charles Avenue and headed in the direction of the Lower Garden District. Although he'd never found himself attracted to blond women, there was something about Hannah that more than piqued his interest, and it wasn't just her revelation that she was a descendant of a free woman of color.

"We're here," he stated, pulling into a space on the street behind the three-story building facing St. Charles Avenue. The short ride was accomplished in complete silence.

Hannah waited for St. John to come around and open her door, chiding herself for appearing gauche because he'd complimented her. She knew she had been at the top of her game when it came to her career, yet she lagged far behind with interpersonal relationships, which she attributed to being involved with only one man for more than half her life. She was engaged at seventeen, slept with Robert for the first time at eighteen, married him at twenty-one, and gave birth to their son at twenty-two. She'd dedicated thirty-four of her fifty-eight years to one man, and now she found herself having to start over.

"Aren't we going in?" she asked when St. John didn't move.

Unbuckling his seat belt, St. John shifted to face her. "Not yet. The last class is still in session." Resting his right arm over the back of her seat, he tugged playfully on the hair she had secured in an elastic band. "Are you uncomfortable being with me?"

Hannah went completely still. If she said no, then she would be lying. But on the other hand, if she told him the truth, then there was a possibility they wouldn't continue to see each other — something she definitely didn't want to happen.

"A little," she admitted. "But it's not what you think," she added quickly.

He gave her a sidelong look. "And what am I thinking?"

"That you're very well known in New Orleans and to be seen with me would generate gossip you don't need."

He gave her a long, penetrating stare and then burst out laughing. "It's too late for that, Hannah."

Her eyelids fluttered wildly. "Why would you say that?"

"After Matt Johnston apologized for manhandling you and then said he didn't know you were my woman, tongues started wagging. While you were dancing in the other ballroom, several of our former classmates asked me if I was dating the judge's daughter."

Hannah held her breath for several seconds. "What did you say?"

A slow, sensual smile spread over his face, an expression she had come to look for because it made him appear both boyish and playful at the same time.

"I told them we were picking up where we'd left off while in school."

Her eyes grew wide. "That's not true, St. John! Both of us were seeing other people at the time."

"I meant as friends, not lovers."

Hannah scrunched up her nose. *Awkward!* St. John's expression changed as he measured her with a steady appraising look. She returned the stare, studying his handsome face feature by feature. His golden-brown eyes darkened as he continued to stare at her. "What are you thinking about?" she asked as the silence inside the sports car swelled until it was deafening.

St. John blinked as if coming out of a trance. "Nothing."

"We're too old, at least I know I am, to play games, St. John. You just didn't spend the past sixty seconds staring at me to say it's nothing."

"What do you want me to say?"

"I want you to tell me the truth. If you've changed your mind about being seen with me because it may cause a problem for you with other women, then just say so."

His fingers curled around her neck, tightening slightly when she attempted to pull away. Hannah didn't have time to react as he slanted his mouth over hers. The kiss lasted seconds but the throbbing in her lower lip continue after he'd pulled away.

"There are no other women, Hannah. Now close your mouth or I'll be forced to kiss you again," he teased. He threw back his head and let out a laugh that reverberated inside the car. A flush darkened Hannah's face as she rolled her eyes at him. St. John caressed her cheek with the back of his hand. "It's time we go in now before we're arrested for public lewdness."

"And if we are arrested I won't be able to defend us, because I'm not licensed here."

"I don't think you'd have to worry about that. After all, you're the daughter one of the most beloved jurists in Louisiana's history."

She frowned. "You're the second person today who referred to me as the judge's daughter."

St. John also sobered. "Does that bother you?"

Hannah paused as she contemplated St. John's query. It wasn't as if she'd practiced law in New Orleans while her father was still alive, and even if she had, she knew she would always be compared to him. "Yes and no. Yes, it bothers me because I'd rather be known as Hannah DuPont rather than the judge's girl. And no, because as a zealous advocate for prison reform, he believed in probation and community service as the deterrent to turning people into hardened criminals."

"Have you thought maybe you'd do well to continue your father's campaign for prison reform?"

She shook her head. "I'd never make it as a politician."

"Why would say that?" St. John asked.

"I have no patience with what I call *polit-tricks*. I'd refuse to be bought by certain interest groups and I'd never make promises on something I know I wouldn't be able to deliver. Politicians have to be willing to sell their souls for money and power. I'm sorry, but mine isn't for sale."

St. John winked at her. "Good for you."

Reaching into the tote, Hannah handed him a folder. "I did promise to print out a copy of the DuPont family tree for you."

"Hold onto it for me. I'll look at it after we finish our lesson."

Hannah and St. John were one of ten couples who'd signed up to take introductory tango. The dance studio, located on the first floor of the office building that had been the headquarters for cotton and sugar cane brokers until the turn of the twentieth century, was owned and operated by a husband-and-wife couple who'd won national and international ballroom dancing championships.

Madame Duarte, a tiny woman in her mid-forties with pale skin, penetrating dark eyes, and spiky black hair which made her complexion appear even whiter, had everyone introduce themselves, she greeting her former students with a barely perceptible nod, and the new ones with a smile.

"For those who are new to Duarte Studios, I'm going to warn you not to overdo it the first week. The barre is here for those who wish to stretch, which is something I recommended you always do before we begin any routine." She paused. "And for you Adonises and ballerinas, please don't spend all your time staring at yourselves in the mirrors." Her remark elicited a smattering of laughter. "And I'd like to recommend you to wear your dance shoes only in the studio." She pressed her palms together. "Are there any questions?"

A young woman with a long red braid raised her hand. "Aside from the lessons, will we be allowed to come in and practice?"

Madame Duarte nodded. "Yes. The studio is open on Sundays from noon to six, and that's when you can come in and practice on your own. Mr. Duarte will put up the schedule as to which room you'll gather for the tango. Right now you'll be assigned to studio C, but that may change. I'm going to give everyone ten minutes to stretch and warm up before we begin."

Hannah, still wearing her ballet flats, was transported back to a time when she'd been a serious dance student. She began stretching at the barre, and then graduated to demi and grand pliés. Holding on to the barre and facing the mirrored wall, she executed first, second, and third positions easily, recalling the time when she'd wanted to be a ballerina. All of her prior training returned as she went through dèveloppés, and tendus. Her dream of a career in dance ended when she'd begun growing at an alarming rate at ten; by the time she celebrated her thirteenth birthday she stood five foot seven in her bare feet. She'd continued to grow throughout high school until she finally stopped at five-nine.

She glanced over at St. John as he executed pliés, admiring his slender physique in a black tee and a pair of slacks in a fabric that allowed him to move freely. She also noticed two women watching him when they should have been concentrating on their own warm-up routines.

Madame Duarte approached Hannah. "You're not new to dance, are you?" she asked, meeting her eyes in the mirror.

Hannah held the demi-plié position. "I'm not new to ballet." She quickly explained why she'd stopped dancing.

Vertical lines appeared between the teacher's eyes. "That's a pity because with your body and elegance, you would've made a magnificent ballerina."

The warm-up period ended and Hannah exchanged her slippers for a pair of women's closed-toe Latin ballroom dance shoes with a suede sole and two-and-three-quarter-inch heels. Madame Duarte waited until everyone had changed into their dance shoes, and then pounded a staff on the floor to get their attention.

"The most important aspect of the tango is the frame, or in laymen's terms it is the way dancers hold their bodies with each other. If you want to remember the basic tango steps, then think of the acronym T-A-N-G-O. The T is slow, and so is A. N and G are quick steps and finally O is slow. O is the most sensual step because it is a slow

dragging of the left foot toward the right."
She set the staff on the floor in front of the
wall of mirrors. "Mr. Duarte and I will
demonstrate. Remember, gentlemen, you
are the lead and your partner is the follow."
Her husband, a slightly built man with a
shaved head, moved with the fluidity of a
dancer across the highly polished wood
floor.

Hannah watched and listened intently as
the couple executed a close dance position,
his right hand on his wife's left shoulder
blade, and his left hand extended to the side
while grasping her right. "The lead will look
to his side toward the left and the follow
toward the right with very straight spines.
Ladies, you should have a slight tilt back to
your partner's head," Madame Duarte in-
structed.

Hannah moved into St. John's close embrace, curbing the urge to look at him to
gauge his reaction. Her upper body was
pressed intimately against his washboard-
flat middle. Even when they'd danced
together at the reunion, there had been a
modicum of space between their bodies.
Now she felt muscle and sinew from chest
to thigh.

She followed St. John as they began with
heel leads wherein the heel of the foot came

down first and not the toe, and within seconds they were moving as if they were one rather than two people. Twenty minutes later Madame Duarte allowed for a five-minute break before demonstrating the second basic step. In between each of the five steps she allowed a break. Her staff kept time with the dancers gliding across the floor. Everything changed when she picked up a remote device and music filled the studio.

Hannah, following St. John's strong lead, made certain to keep her spine straight and her left hand placed midway along his right arm without actually holding on to it, finding the steps passionate and precise. Two hours after they walked into the studio the lesson ended, and she applauded along with the others. Sitting on the bench, she slipped out of the dance shoes and massaged her left calf.

"Let me do that," St. John said, gently pushing Hannah's hands away. Resting her leg over his thigh, he kneaded the tight muscles in her leg.

"Oh-o-o-o. That feels good."

"Do you have anything planned tonight?"

"No. Why?"

"I have the perfect remedy for leg cramps."

"I hope it's not some foul-smelling oint-ment."

Lowering her leg, he pushed his feet into a pair of running shoes. "It's something I'm certain you'll enjoy."

"Can you at least give me a hint?"

After waiting until Hannah changed her shoes, he held her hand and led her to the street. St. John wanted to tell Hannah that he wasn't ready to take her home, that of all of his dance partners, he'd felt her the most accomplished.

"I'm going to drop you back at your house so you can get a change of clothes. Then we're going to my house where you can soak in the Jacuzzi before relaxing in the steam room."

"What are you going to do while I'm tak-ing advantage of your health spa?" she teased.

He winked at her. "I'll be making dinner for my favorite dance partner."

Hannah's smile was dazzling. "I like the sound of that."

St. John started up the car. This was the Hannah he remembered. They'd always enjoyed an easygoing camaraderie. They would meet at her home or the local library to study or work on a project. And he'd kissed her to prove he didn't mind being seen with her.

Everyone had believed he and Lorna had the perfect marriage, while behind closed doors there was no marriage; not when his wife refused to let him make love to her. He'd lain beside the same woman for thirty-two years and each time he attempted to touch her she cried.

After the first year he gave up and looked elsewhere to slake his pent-up frustration. The first time he slept with another woman, the guilt nearly swallowed him whole. He went to confession for the first time since before his marriage. The priest reminded him that he'd committed adultery and therefore had broken one of the ten commandments. St. John left the church and never went back. It was easier the second time he slept with a woman who wasn't his wife, and after his third encounter he'd absolved himself of his own guilt.

He had to admit Lorna played the game well whenever she accompanied him to social events, morphing into her role as the affectionate, adoring wife, but the pretense ended the instant they walked through the door of their home.

Well, he and Hannah didn't have to play a game, because they were friends, and once the summer ended, their friendship would be placed on hold until their next reunion.

CHAPTER 10

Hannah glanced up at St. John's Marigny residence, not knowing what to expect, but it wasn't the brick Southern-style farmhouse. Twin fans were suspended from the ceiling of the second-story veranda, and the portico light fixture matched the two lanterns suspended from stanchions flanking the towering oaks trees shading the front.

"Your house is magnificent."

Cupping her elbow, St. John led her up the porch. "Thank you, but I can't take credit for the house or anything in it because the accolades go to my aunt." He unlocked the front door. "I'd thought about selling this house and moving into a smaller one, but changed my mind once I got used to the spaciousness."

Hannah hoisted the tote with a change of clothes and an ample supply of grooming aids over her shoulder. "How big is it?"

"It's close to three thousand square feet,

which includes the outdoor kitchen."

"Did she put in the kitchen?"

St. John opened the door, stepping aside to let her enter. "No. It was included in the house's original design plans. A Pennsylvania mine owner commissioned it to be built as a winter residence for his family."

"When was that?" Hannah asked.

"It was several years after the Spanish-American War. After a number of strikes which ended in violence, he sold the mine and moved here permanently. He left the property to a grandson who unfortunately had an addiction to gambling and eventually lost it in a poker game. My aunt bought it from a couple who couldn't afford to pay for the upkeep. She updated the interiors, installed central heating and air, and refurbished the exterior and garden."

Hannah's gaze took in the narrow bookcase situated against the wall in the entry and a low-slung leather chair by the door under the sidelight so as not to block the sun. A mahogany console table cradling potted ivy plants matched the banister and newel posts on the curving staircase leading to the upper floor. The paleness of bleached oak flooring in a herringbone design was repeated on walls in the living and formal dining rooms, creating a continuous palette

191

of barely-there color. A gleaming black baby grand piano drew her attention and reminded her that St. John had played piano in the school's jazz band.

Reaching for her hand, St. John led her down a hallway to the rear of the house. "There were three large bedrooms on this floor I knew I'd never use, so I converted one into an office and the other to an in-home gym because I never had the time to drive downtown every morning to work out. Although I have a treadmill, I prefer running outdoors. The last one, which had been the maids' quarters, became a sunroom." He stopped at the entrance to the gym. "It's all yours. I'm going upstairs to shower and change before I start dinner."

The in-home gym contained everything Hannah would find at an upscale health club. Hand weights in various sizes and colors were stacked on a rack against a far wall. A wall-mounted television was positioned for viewing for anyone working out on the treadmill, rowing machine, or bike. There was also a heavy bag and several pairs of boxing gloves hanging from wall hooks.

Setting the tote on a teakwood bench, she walked over to the door labeled "Bath" and opened it. Frosted glass walls let light in, while providing complete privacy from the outside. An enormous black sunken tub with enough room for two was the space's centerpiece. A free-standing shower occupied an entire corner, while the doors to an ultra-modern steam room stood open, beckoning her to come and sweat out her body's impurities. She gathered a towel from an ample supply on a glass-topped, wrought-iron table, placing it on the stool next to the tub.

Hannah turned on the water, adding several capfuls of lavender bath salts. Within minutes the space was filled with the alluring fragrance. Stripping off her clothes, she settled down into the warm water. Closing her eyes, she felt herself succumbing to the sensation of water pulsating against her body. The leisurely soak ended once the water cooled.

Stepping out onto a thick chenille mat, she wrapped the towel around her body and padded barefoot into the steam room. Hannah programmed the thermostat for twenty minutes at ninety degrees, and then lay down to savor the moist heat. A shower followed, where she shampooed her hair and wrapped it in a towel to absorb most of the moisture. It was on a rare occasion that she used a blow dryer because the heat tended to make the strands brittle and flyaway.

An hour after entering the spa, Hannah emerged dressed in a pair of slim-fitting cropped jeans, a man-tailored white shirt, and white deck shoes. She heard music and, following the sound, she found herself at the entrance to the kitchen. St. John stood at the cooking island, chopping herbs with the skill of a professional chef. He'd changed into a sand-colored short-sleeved seersucker shirt, khaki walking shorts, and leather sandals. Without warning, his head popped up and he smiled at her.

"How do you feel?"

She walked into the ultra-modern kitchen with granite countertops, stainless-steel appliances, and a collection of copper-bottom pots suspended from a rack over a commercial cooktop range and grill. It was apparent St. John was quite comfortable in the kitchen, and she wondered if he, like the owners of Chez Toussaints, was skilled in the art of preparing authentic New Orleans dishes.

"Like a new woman. Would you like some help?"

St. John washed his hands in one of the twin sinks, then dried them on the towel he'd thrown over one shoulder. "No, thanks. I have everything under control. Sit down and relax. It's going to be at least twenty minutes before we can eat. Meanwhile, I'll get you something to drink."

Her eyes followed him as he made his way to the built-in refrigerator and took out a pitcher filled with lemon and lime slices in a yellowish bubbly liquid, marveling that St. John had the physique of a man half his age. She sat on one of the three stools at the cooking island. "What's on tonight's menu?"

St. John filled a glass from the pitcher, handing it to her. "I usually try to keep to meatless Mondays, so I decided we'd start with a peach and shrimp ceviche as an appetizer, and follow that with an entrée of Louisiana blue crab–stuffed flounder in a lemon butter sauce with a side of apple-jicama slaw."

St. John didn't know that he'd just gone up several more points on her list of criteria for the perfect man; she was always impressed with men who were able to cook. Unfortunately, her late husband was completely helpless in the kitchen. "That sounds delicious. Do you have a particular menu for the other days of the week?"

He nodded. "For Taco Tuesdays I usually make them with fish instead of beef. Wednesday is wing night. They can be turkey, buffalo, Thai, jerk, or Korean, as long as they are wings."

Hannah swallowed a mouthful of the icy cold carbonated citrus drink. "What about Thursdays?"

"Thursdays is soup night with a side salad."

"What types of soups do you make?"

"Lentil with andouille, split pea or white bean with tasso, and occasionally I'll whip up a pot of gumbo. I always make too much, so I end up freezing the leftovers in single-serve containers. Fridays and the weekends are toss-ups because I usually eat whatever I'm craving on those days. It can vary from boudin balls to grilled oysters or shrimp and grits."

Smiling, she closed her eyes for several seconds. "You're singing my song. You just named all of my favorites. Did your mother teach you to cook?"

St. John shook his head as he carefully cut a radish into paper-thin slices, adding them to a wooden bowl filled with shredded green cabbage and thinly sliced jicama. "No. It was my grandmother. The hospital where my mother worked as a nurse was always short-staffed, which meant her shift changed every three months. My dad always patrolled the most crime-ridden neighborhoods in the city, so whenever both my parents worked nights, me and my sister stayed with my grandmother. Once Grandma's arthritis made it difficult for her to pick up a cast iron frying pan or carry a Dutch oven, she'd sit on a stool and instruct me step-by-step how to prepare dishes that had been passed down from generations of women who perfected their recipes. Designated days are totally forgotten whenever I'm on vacation, because I eat out or order in several days a week. That's when I tend to overeat, which means I have to work out twice as long as I normally would."

"It doesn't show, because you're in incredible shape."

He glanced up at her. "Speak for yourself, Hannah. A lot of the women at the reunion were giving you the stink-eye when you walked in."

She set down the glass. "If they were giving me the stink-eye, it isn't because of how I look. They've always resented me because they felt I didn't belong, that I should've stayed at McGehee with the other snobby rich bitches."

"Why *did* you transfer to Jackson Memorial?"

Hannah mentally struggled how she was going to reveal to St. John something that had haunted her for years and how it

197

changed how she viewed those in the social circle into which she'd been born. "I was fifteen when I was invited to a sleepover. The girl who hosted the sleepover decided to entertain us with photographs her Ku Kluxer grandfather had taken of black men who'd been tortured before they were lynched. Some of the photos were so graphic that I ran into the bathroom and vomited while my so-called classmates laughed and taunted me for weeks. That's when I told my mother I was never going back to McGehee. She tried to convince me the school wasn't at fault, but a bunch of silly girls who were only repeating what they'd heard from their parents.

"It was the first time I challenged my mother. I told her I really didn't give a damn if the girls were parroting their bigoted parents, which caused her to go into histrionics, threatening to take a switch to my behind, when Daddy intervened. He reassured me I didn't have to return to McGehee, and I could either attend a public or a local parochial high school. I chose Jackson Memorial, and the first day Daddy's driver dropped me off in front the school everyone stopped talking to stare at me. It was so quiet you could hear a rat piss on cotton."

St. John burst into laughter, then stopped abruptly when her eyes filled moisture. "I'm sorry about laughing but —"

"Don't apologize," Hannah said, cutting him off. She wanted to cry, but refused to let St. John see her that way. It took a several minutes for her to regain her composure. "If the situation hadn't been so tense, I know I would've laughed. I'd left a private school where girls still carried racial bigotry from past generations to go to a public school where girls carried a different kind of prejudice that had nothing to do with race but social class. They called me every name imaginable, but I never let on how much I cried inside. I don't think I'd be the person I am today if I hadn't gone through the taunts and alienation, because I learned to love myself more than seeking someone's acceptance or approval."

A beat passed, and then St. John said, "I'm sorry you had to go through that. I just thought they were jealous of you."

"Jealous or not, I got over it a long time ago." Her somber expression changed like a snake shedding its skin as a sense of strength replaced the memories of what she'd had to endure while in high school. She took another swallow of the slightly sweet and tart icy concoction. "This is delicious. How did you make it?"

"I substituted club soda for water and agave for sugar. And because you're not much of a drinker I decided to make a fizzy lemon-limeade rather than offer you anything alcoholic that will probably have you fall asleep on me."

"I suppose you'll never let me live that down."

St. John came around the countertop and kissed her damp hair. "I'm not picking on you, sweetheart. I want you to know that whenever we're together, I'll make certain to take care of you."

Turning her head, their noses only inches apart, she stared deeply into his eyes, wondering if St. John calling her sweetheart was a slip of the tongue and whether she actually wanted or needed him to take care of her when she'd been taking care of herself for years. As a military wife, she took care of herself and her son whenever Robert was deployed or on maneuvers. She'd continued to take care of herself even when Robert commuted between New York and D.C., but after he had his first heart attack she'd become his caretaker, monitoring his diet and reminding him to exercise. Hannah had become a caretaker who couldn't bring herself to resume sexual relations with her husband after he was medically cleared by his cardiologist.

Hannah knew she couldn't come down hard on St. John because he'd been raised in the Southern tradition to protect women. He hadn't hesitated to intervene when Matt Johnston had come on too strong. Maybe it was time she let a man take care of her.

"Thank you for offering."

Cradling her face in his hands, he pressed his forehead to hers. "I should be the one thanking you."

"For what?" she whispered.

"For reminding me why I've always liked you."

With wide eyes, Hannah stared at St. John as if she'd never seen him before. What was he talking about? He'd never said he liked her. Yes, they were classmates and friends, but nothing beyond that.

"And I've always liked you . . . as a friend," she added quickly.

St. John's expression did not change. When he'd confessed to Hannah that he liked her, it wasn't the same as when they were teenagers sharing classes. He hadn't slept with so many women that he couldn't remember their names or faces, but as a man quickly approaching sixty he'd come to know St.

John Baptiste McNair quite well. He knew he'd wasted too many years in a sterile marriage he should've annulled within the first year.

He'd always told himself that he was drawn to a certain type, without being able to verbalize what type of woman that was. However, there was something about Hannah that had drawn him to her when both were young adults. Only now as mature, middle-aged adults, he recognized it as her quiet inner strength. He'd observed and overheard the cutting looks and snide remarks directed at her by their female classmates, and not once did she attempt to retaliate either verbally or physically.

During those times St. John wanted to tell Hannah the girls were jealous of her beauty, intelligence, and privileged upbringing. And there were occasions when he suspected she downplayed her intellect, but loathed calling her on it because he knew she'd wanted to fit in with the sons and daughters of poor and working-class parents.

He'd kissed her in the car because unconsciously it was something he'd wanted to do in the hotel parking lot. Dancing with Hannah while listening to Barry Manilow crooning "When Will I See You Again?" echoed his own yearnings as to when he would see her again. He had insisted on dining at a restaurant rather at her home to ascertain whether he wanted to reconnect with Hannah because he craved an open relationship with a woman that had nothing to do with sex.

Holding his head at an angle, St. John continued to stare at Hannah, wondering what it was she was thinking or feeling as she met his eyes. "Are you free this weekend to go with me to listen to jazz?"

Her hands came up to circle his wrists. "Are you asking me out on a date?"

"What if I am?"

Hannah stared at him through her lashes. "I thought you didn't date women."

He smiled. "I don't. But in your case I'm going to make an exception."

The gray lashes shadowing her cheeks flew up. "Lucky me," she drawled. "I haven't dated in a while, so in your case, I'm the one who's going to make an exception. And yes, I'll go out with you."

"Did anyone ever tell you that you have a wicked tongue?"

She flashed a sexy moue. "No. You're the first."

St. John pressed his lips against hers. "I'm going to have to do something about that tongue," he whispered.

Her lips parted under his. "What do you propose?"

A low chuckle rumbled in his chest. "I'll think of something." Suddenly he went completely still. "Is that your stomach making noises?"

"Guilty as charged."

St. John released her. "Don't you eat?"

"I do," Hannah insisted, "but I didn't want to eat too much before our dance lesson."

"I have some melon in the fridge you can have now if you're really hungry."

She slipped off the stool. "I'm not that hungry. Do you mind showing me your home?"

St. John wanted to tell Hannah she could see his home at another time, because he planned to invite her back each time they returned from the dance studio. Lessons were scheduled three times each week for three weeks, which meant he would get to see more of her than he could ever have anticipated.

"We'll begin with upstairs and work our way down."

Hannah followed St. John up the staircase to bedrooms with French doors leading to the veranda. Two of the bedrooms, overlooking the front, claimed en suite baths and two smaller bedrooms overlooked the rear and a flower garden that reminded her of Frances Hodgson Burnett's classic fairy tale *The Secret Garden.* Wrought-iron grates cradled stacks of wood in the bedrooms' working fireplaces.

All of the furnishings were meticulously selected in keeping with the region and climate. Yards of diaphanous white fabric billowed from the many narrow open windows, pooling on the floor like mounds of frothy cream. She was particularly drawn to the window seats covered in fabrics matching or contrasting with the bed dressings. Mahogany plank floors were covered with priceless hand-knotted imported Turkish rugs. It was obvious St. John's aunt had taken particular care in restoring the farmhouse to its original beauty.

"Did your aunt live here alone?" she asked St. John as they descended the rear staircase.

"Yes. She never took up with anyone after her common-law husband died. When I asked her why she bought a house with so many rooms, she said she was used to living in a grand house, and she'd feel claustrophobic in anything smaller."

"Are the furnishings antiques or reproductions?" Hannah asked, because every stick of furniture in DuPont had been appraised and catalogued as antiques. If and when she turned her residence into a business, she knew she had to secure valuable items that could arbitrarily find their way into a guest's luggage.

"They're all reproductions. Why do you ask?"

"I was just thinking about the furnishings in my home." She paused. "I'm contemplating turning DuPont into an inn."

St. John stopped at the bottom of the staircase, turning and staring directly at her. "How long have you thought about it?"

"Almost a year. When I came down last Christmas, I discussed it with my cousins, and even though they don't want to be involved in running an inn, they said to go for it."

His eyebrows lifted questioningly. "You plan to run an inn from New York?"

"That's not possible. Even if my position hadn't been down-sized, I eventually would've had to resign. I just didn't think it would come this soon."

"So, the prodigal daughter has decided to leave the Big Apple for the Big Easy," he teased, grinning. Hannah landed a soft punch to his shoulder, wincing when her hand met solid muscle. "That serves you right for resorting to violence," St. John chided as he picked her up, swung her around, and then set her on her feet. "I like the idea of you going into business for yourself."

"You do?"

"Of course. Homes the size of DuPont House are dinosaurs. Unless you have a large or extended family living there, it becomes a money pit where you're spending tons of money just for the upkeep."

"As soon as the permits and license are approved I plan to meet with an engineer to inspect and sign off on the occupancy, and then an architectural historian and/or interior designer to authenticate the furnishings and to update my homeowner's policy from their last appraisal."

Reaching for her hand, St. John tucked it into the bend of his elbow. "It looks as if you've taken care of everything to become Nawlins's latest innkeeper."

A slight frown furrowed her smooth forehead as she followed St. John into the sunroom. "Not everything. I have two guesthouses on the property, and I'm not certain whether I want to use them for live-in employee housing or have them torn down."

"Can't you use them for an overflow of guests?" St. John asked.

"No." Hannah told him she was limited to nine rooms, and if she were to include the guesthouses, then she would have to start the permit process over because Du-Pont House would be deemed a hotel.

"A couple of years ago I stayed at an inn on the east end of Long Island, and they didn't serve meals in the main house but had turned guest and carriage houses into restaurants where guests of the inn were given priority over the general public."

That's it! St. John had solved her dilemma. "You're a genius, St. John."

He looked at her, totally surprised. "I am?"

"Of course you are. You've just given me the answer to what I can do with the guest-houses." Cameron had suggested she solicit investors and Hannah knew exactly who she was going to approach with the possibility of investing in her future business enter-prise.

"So, you're going to convert them into restaurants?"

"What do you think of me operating one to offer brunch for guests and the other as a supper club with live music for the general public?"

St. John winked at Hannah. "You're the genius. Once you get an idea you really run with it, don't you?"

She felt a warm glow flow through her with his compliment. "I never would've thought of it if you hadn't mentioned it."

"Yeah, you would," he countered, pulling her close and resting his chin on her head. "Hannah DuPont, innkeeper. Who would've thought it all those years ago when those mean girls tried to get the better of you that you would come out victorious?"

Burying her face against his warm throat, she inhaled the lingering scent of soap on his skin. She wanted to tell St. John it wasn't about payback or retaliation. It was more about her coming home and into her own. Perhaps if she hadn't seen the gut-wrenching photographs of burnt and tortured bodies hanging from trees she wouldn't be who she was now. There was no doubt she would've met and married Robert Lowell; however, she was certain her path would not have crossed with St. John McNair's.

And now that she looked back to the sleepover that changed her life, she didn't regret it had happened, because it proved she was blessed with the same grit that Margit used to manipulate the father of her children to grant not only them but all future generations of DuPonts of color emancipation.

Reluctantly she eased out of St. John's embrace, still feeling his warmth and strength. He'd talked about taking care of her, and in that instant she decided that was exactly what she was going to let him do. Exhaling an inaudible sigh, she glanced around the sunroom. It was an oasis of light and color with a trio of dark-green rattan loungers covered in canary-yellow cushions. A number of massive potted planters at opposite ends of the structure, overflowing with ferns and cacti, brought the outdoors inside. A wooden table hewn from a single tree trunk seated six, and a rattan sectional grouping provided seating for an additional six persons, and a flat-screen television and audio components set the stage for relaxed entertaining.

"How often do you entertain outdoors?" she asked, peering through the glass at the pergola covered with English ivy and pink climbing roses growing in wild abandon.

St. John moved behind her, his moist breath feathering over an ear. "It depends on the weather. I usually extend an invitation to my staff and faculty during Christmas and at the end of the school term. It's my turn to host my family's reunion this year, and next month the house, patio, and garden will be will be filled with Toussaints and Baptistes from toddlers to boomers."

Hannah thought about her own family, which had steadily decreased over the years. It had been her father who had kept the DuPonts together, but after he died she lost contact with many of them. And not making New Orleans her primary residence for more than three decades made their connection even more fragile. Except for an occasional exchange of Christmas cards, she wouldn't have known where they were or if they were dead or alive.

"How often do the DuPonts get together for reunions?" St. John asked, seemingly reading her mind.

"Not often enough. I have some distant cousins scattered around the state, but unfortunately I've never met them."

"Maybe now that you're back you'll try to connect with them."

She wanted to tell St. John that tracing her family roots wasn't a priority. Opening the inn topped her wish list. "Speaking of family, I still have to give you the printout of my family tree." Hannah returned to living room, where she'd left the tote on the floor next to an armchair, then retraced her steps and handed him the folder.

St. John set the folder on the edge of a

corner table with a vase of dried hydrangeas. "I'll look at it later. Right now I have to finish making the slaw, broil the fish, and then we'll eat."

CHAPTER 11

Hannah closed her eyes as St. John pressed a light kiss to her forehead. Not only was he an accomplished cook but he'd also been the consummate host. He'd kept her laughing recalling the eccentricities of several teachers: two teachers who wore the same suit for the duration of the school year and another who favored white bucks because he'd once belonged to Pat Boone's fan club. After dinner she'd offered to help him clean up, but he quickly ushered her out of the house to his car, saying he had everything under control.

"Good night," he whispered in her ear, after driving her home.

"Good night, and thank you again for a wonderful evening."

He kissed her again, this time on her cheek. "That goes both ways, Hannah."

She stood there watching as he returned to his car and drove away, the gates protecting the property closing and locking automatically once she tapped the icon on her cell. The warm, fuzzy feeling she'd experienced when spending the afternoon and evening with St. John continued as she checked on Smokey. Hannah tried to spend time with the kitten to avoid it becoming bored and engaging in destructive behavior. Retrieving the teaser cat wand with a feather attachment, she flicked the toy over and over until Smokey tired and retreated to the mudroom to lap up mouthfuls of water.

After placing clean litter in the litter robot, Hannah extinguished overhead lights, leaving on table lamps in the parlor and entryway. Despite the high-tech security system and neighborhood watch, she didn't like plunging the house into complete darkness. She climbed the staircase and tried imagining guests doing the same as they were escorted to their bedroom suites. She was still in a quandary whether to install an elevator to offset having to climb the eighteen stairs between the first and second floors.

When she'd told Cameron she wanted to convert DuPont House into an inn, what had initially been a whim became now more of a reality once he promised to use his influence to fast-track the approval for the permits. St. John's mention of taking his meals in the carriage house when staying at a Long Island inn had sparked another idea as to how she could use the two structures that were once used to accommodate an overflow of guests whenever her parents hosted Thanksgiving and Christmas family dinners, charity functions, or political fund-raisers. She couldn't wait for her former co-workers to arrive so she could talk to Tonya about the possibility of her investing in the DuPont Inn as the owner of a brasserie and/or supper club.

Hannah went through her nightly routine of brushing her teeth and washing her face. She slathered a light layer of moisturizer over her face and neck, and then pulled on a nightgown. Soaking in the Jacuzzi, followed by a stint in the steam room, had eased the tight muscles in her calves. Smiling, she got into bed and reached for the stack of mail on the bedside table. Becoming St. John's dance partner definitely had its perks; his in-home spa among them. Not only did she enjoy being in his home but she also enjoyed the man. It was as if they'd picked up where they'd left off so many years ago, and it was comforting to know they were still friends.

She sorted through several envelopes,

some of which had been forwarded from New York, finding most of it to be junk mail and magazines. There had been a time when she'd become a magazine junkie, subscribing to publications featuring fashion, beauty, travel, and entertainment. Reading the periodicals had become her guilty pleasure before realizing as a newlywed she was bored *and* lonely. Her newly commissioned officer husband was halfway around the world in the South China Sea, while she passed the time reading magazines, cleaning their spotless apartment, and watching daytime and nighttime soap operas whenever she wasn't hovering over the bathroom commode losing the contents of her stomach.

Two months after exchanging vows she discovered she was pregnant, despite Robert using protection. She'd just begun her second trimester when her husband returned home to the news he was going to be a father. Robert's response wasn't what Hannah had expected: He didn't demonstrate the excitement she would have expected from him. It was naïveté on her part when she suspected he was shocked that they would become parents that quickly; because they'd talked about waiting two years.

Unbeknownst to her, the first fissure in her marriage appeared after Robert confessed to his mother-in-law his son was undeniably a Lowell because he'd inherited their dark hair, eyes, and features. Hannah, shocked into silence, was unable to wrap her head around the notion that her husband had believed her unfaithful. Years later she was shocked again once she discovered he'd been the serial adulterer.

Opening a circular from an upscale department store, she found two postcards from her cousins:

Hi Nah. We landed in Budapest & jetlag hit us like a ton of bricks. Boarded the ship and slept like babies. The grand tour will include 4 countries in 15 days. I hope to send you cards from each city rather than email. I'll write again when we get to Vienna. Smooches, Paige

She picked up the other card with a glossy photograph of the Danube River:

Nah, Vienna is like a fairy-tale kingdom with beautiful castles. We went to a Mozart and Strauss concert and it was magical. Paige couldn't stop crying she was so overcome with emotion. I must admit I, too, shed a few tears. Miss you. Wish you were here. LeAnn

Hannah smiled. It was obvious the retired schoolteachers were enjoying themselves. She flipped through the circular, placing it on the table along with the cards, and then perused the cover of *New York Magazine*. She'd flipped open to an article that caught her attention when her cell rang.

Hannah picked it up, smiling when St. John's name and number appeared on the screen. "This is Hannah."

"Hi, sweetheart. I'm sorry to be calling so late —"

"It's not late, St. John," she said, interrupting him, and wondering if he knew it was the second time he'd called her sweetheart.

"What time do you usually go to bed?" he asked.

"Now that I'm among the ranks of the unemployed, I don't have a designated bedtime, even though I usually get up early to run with Letitia Parker."

"I think I heard someone mention that she'd come back to New Orleans. I always thought she should've become a jazz rather than a country singer. But I didn't call you to talk about Letitia. I just got a group text from Madame Duarte that the studio will be closed until further notice."

"What happened?"

"There was an electrical fire in a second floor office, and even though the fire department put it out quickly, the building sustained some water damage. She has to wait for an insurance adjuster to assess the damage to the studio before repairs can begin. She's given all her students the option of having their money refunded or waiting until she can reschedule classes. What do you want to do?"

Hannah wanted to tell him it wasn't her decision to make. After all, he'd paid for the course. "What you want?" she said, repeating his question.

"I'd like to continue, but I don't know what you've planned for the summer, so it would be presumptuous of me to re-register without first checking with you."

"Re-register, St. John."

There came a pause. "I was hoping you'd say that." He paused again. "Are we still on for Friday?"

She smiled. "But of course."

His soft laugh caressed her ear through the earpiece. "I'll let you get back to whatever you were doing and I'll pick you up Friday at nine."

"I'll be ready."

Hannah ended the call and set the phone on the table. She'd been looking forward to dancing with St. John only because it took up the hours that she probably would have spent either in the parlor watching talk shows or reading with Smokey sleeping next to her on the porch rocker.

It'd been years since she hadn't had anything to do. After earning a degree in education, she taught at the base school for two years after Wyatt entered kindergarten. And knowing her heart wasn't in it, she resigned and began studying for the LSAT. Whenever she sat down with her son at the kitchen table to do homework or study, they'd become students together as well as mother and son. And once she received the letter indicating she'd passed the test for admission to law school, her outlook on life changed dramatically. Her father sent her a card congratulating her along with a check for the first year's tuition.

Hannah knew she had to find something to do until her New York friends arrived, but was loath to engage in a project that wouldn't allow her to entertain them. In New York she'd volunteered her free time to an organization geared to helping to get families out of homeless shelters and into permanent housing. Volunteering made her more than aware she'd grown up not only privileged but blessed, and it could take only a single incident for her to lose everything. Some of the organization's clients were living with undiagnosed mental illnesses, while others were victims of domestic violence or drug addiction. And unlike some of the girls with whom she'd attended high school, these women viewed her as their advocate.

Her thoughts wavered again when she made a mental note to apply for an additional permit to convert the guesthouses to eating establishments. The venture, although daunting, wasn't impossible if and when she hired the staff she needed to run and maintain a successful and profitable business. But it wasn't as if she wouldn't have competition. A few of the larger homes in the city were operating as inns or B & Bs or hotels to take advantage of the growing influx of tourists during Mardi Gras and other popular local annual festivals.

It was after midnight when she finally turned off the lamp and closed her eyes. Then it returned. The erotic dream wherein her mysterious lover made her feel things she'd forgotten and others sensations she'd never experienced until she woke in a panic, her heart pumping wildly in her chest. She didn't see her lover's face in this dream, and for that she was grateful; if it had been St. John, then Hannah knew it would mean subconsciously she was physically drawn to him, which would spell disaster for their newly rediscovered friendship.

She sat up, the cotton nightgown sticking to her moist body. *I'm too old for this.* Or was she? Her menstrual cycle had stopped two years ago, but her gynecologist had cautioned her to use protection when engaging in sexual intercourse because there was always the possibility she could get pregnant. He appeared unaffected when she admitted she hadn't had sexual relations with a man in eight years, but still cautioned her if or when she did.

Hannah lay down again, staring up at the fabric draped over the bed. She'd overheard women talking about being horny or needing their itch scratched, and most times she thought they were oversexed. She was far from frigid, although sex hadn't played a major part in her marriage. Perhaps it would have been more frequent if her husband hadn't been away for extended periods of time, or if he hadn't found satisfaction in the arms of other women.

Whenever Robert returned home, he

would make love to her like a man dying of thirst, then when he drank his fill, he didn't want any more and they would go weeks without making love again. Within days after they'd celebrated their fourth wedding anniversary, Hannah realized she'd married a stranger. She hadn't dated him in the traditional sense because as a midshipman in the U.S. Naval Academy he lived in Maryland while she was still in high school in New Orleans. And by the time he'd graduated, he was stationed at a naval base in California while she attended college in Tennessee. And once she became Mrs. Robert Lowell, she found herself a wife in name only. Her elderly grandmother had talked to her about the advantages and disadvantages of being a military wife, but Hannah had insisted she was up for the task.

She knew without a doubt the loneliness wouldn't have been as acute if she'd been able to form friendships with the wives of the other officers. But the memories of rejection and alienation from the girls from her high school hadn't faded enough for her not to be cautious of forming new friendships.

It'd been easier in college because many of the girls shared the same socioeconomic background as hers, but then she discovered they were no different than her high school classmates. They turned their noses up at the girls who'd come to Vanderbilt on either academic or athletic scholarships, deeming them unworthy to join their exclusive circle.

Exhaling an audible sigh, Hannah recalled the few hours she'd spent with Tonya, Nydia, and Jasmine, marveling how quickly she'd felt a kinship with them. It was as if she'd found the sisters she not only needed but always wanted.

Turning over onto her side, she adjusted the pillow under her head and after tossing and turning, she finally went back to sleep. She awoke hours later without the reoccurrence of the disturbing images that reminded her she was a woman who in denying her husband had also denied herself the strong passions within her.

Oppressive humidity, temperatures in the nineties, and off and on thunderstorms for three days reminded Hannah of the time when she and her younger brother would spend hours playing make-believe in the parlor. However, she didn't want to stay indoors to escape the gloomy weather and scheduled an appointment with her local salon for a trim, mani-pedi, and facial. The receptionist was able to fit her in because a client had cancelled, and after three hours of pampering she returned home rejuvenated.

She also filed the necessary paperwork for an occupational license and mayoralty permit for live entertainment zoning to convert the guesthouses into a café and a cocktail lounge. The last errand on her to do list was to meet with an officer at her bank to secure a pre-approved equity loan.

Hannah was optimistic that the licenses and permits would be approved. Pre-planning was essential if she wanted to open for business the following spring. She'd grown up listening to her father preaching that "procrastination is the thief of time," and she didn't want to run out of time because she didn't plan ahead.

She shook hands with the loan officer and had just walked out of his office when she spied St. John standing in a line waiting for a teller. He was dressed for the inclement weather: jeans, running shoes, and a black poncho and matching baseball cap branded with the New Orleans Saints logo.

St. John recognized the tall, willowy, natural blonde striding in his direction. He smiled as she approached him. "Good afternoon, Hannah. How are you enjoying the weather?"

She returned his smile. "It is for ducks."

Dipping his head, St. John kissed her cheek. "Rain is good," he said in her ear, the subtle scent of her perfume wafting to his nostrils.

She lifted her chin, meeting his eyes. "Rain is for sleeping in or lounging around."

He studied her delicate features under the brim of a bucket hat stamped with images of passports and then glanced away before she could detect a longing in his eyes he was helpless to conceal. Hannah stirred emotions that made him want to have something more with her than friendship. He wanted a no-strings relationship wherein he could call her and invite her to accompany him to a restaurant for dinner or a concert or movie.

St. John hadn't lied to Hannah when he'd admitted he didn't date. Even when he and Lorna were waiting for their divorce to be finalized, they'd continued to go out together as a couple. And sleeping with the woman in Baton Rouge didn't fulfill everything he needed and wanted from a woman, despite his agreeing to her mandate they share a sexual liaison without the pretense of commitment.

He didn't want love as much as he wanted

someone with whom he could discuss their views on a movie or concert; a woman whom he could surprise with a special gift even if it wasn't her birthday, Valentine's Day, or Christmas. He wanted to do that and more with his woman.

"You're right about that. Do you have anything planned for this afternoon?"

She stole a glance at the clock over the door of the bank. "I'd planned to drive over to Chez Toussaints and pick up something before they close."

"Wait for me and we'll go together."

A slight frown line appeared between Hannah's eyes. "We have less than fifteen minutes to get there before they close, and if there's traffic, then we're going to be assed out."

St. John flashed a grin. "We're not going to be, as you say, 'assed out' because my cousins will open the door for me."

Her pale eyebrows lifted as she affected a sexy moue, drawing his gaze to linger on her mouth. "Oh, it's like that?"

He leaned closer. "Yes, it's like that. We can pick up lunch before we go back to my house to eat and *lounge* until the rain stops."

Hannah's smile was as bright as rays of sunlight, her clear green eyes sparkling like polished emeralds. "If that's the case, then

I'll meet you there. I'll be waiting in the parking lot."

St. John watched Hannah walk, his gaze lingering on the jeans outlining the curve of her womanly hips. Then, without warning, she glanced over her shoulder and winked at him. He returned it with one of his own, knowing she'd caught him staring. Yes, he thought. He'd made the right decision to ask Hannah to go out with him over the summer because there was no doubt they were going to have a lot of fun together.

Hannah maneuvered into the area set aside for customer parking, finding it empty and the neon sign on the plate glass window to Chez Toussaints flashing CLOSED. Unusually heavy afternoon traffic coupled with a sudden downpour flooding several city streets made the drive longer than expected. She shut off the engine, unbuckled her belt, and waited for St. John. She didn't have long to wait before his white BMW sedan pulled alongside her vehicle, and St. John alighted. She got out of her car before he had a chance to come around and assist her.

Reaching for her hand, St. John said, "I called Eustace to let him know we were on our way."

The door to the restaurant opened and

Eustace stood in the doorway, muscular arms crossed over his wide chest. "You two can spoon later. So get up on here and get your food so I can clean up this place and go home. I've been on my feet since four this morning, and I want to put these dogs up and kick back with an ice-cold beer."

Hannah smiled at the man whose size and speed had made him an outstanding high school athlete. Eustace turned down several scholarships to play college football in order to help his father run their family restaurant. Her eyes were drawn to matching dimples in his round face that always made him appear impish. Opposing team members openly taunted him, calling him Tiny, Smokey the Bear, and the Gingerbread Man because of his reddish-brown complexion, but felt the wrath of his physical prowess when he plowed through their line to average two touchdowns per game. His "family before fame" had become a catch phrase when he was interviewed by the local press after the word got out that he wasn't going to play college football.

Eustace smiled at her. "When did you two start hanging out again?"

Hannah knew Eustace was referring to her and St. John being seen together when they were in high school. "It's going to take a while to catch each other up on what's been happening in our lives over the past forty years."

Eustace stepped aside to let her and St. John enter the small eating establishment, quickly closing and locking the door. "My school's fortieth is coming up next year." He patted his belly through the bibbed apron. "That means I have exactly twelve months to join a gym so I can get back to my fighting weight."

St. John took off his poncho, hanging it on a wall hook. "I told you before that you can work out at my place."

Eustace shook his head. "Instead of working out I'd end up lounging in your sunroom watching ESPN."

Hannah shared a smile when Eustace mentioned lounging before glancing around the restaurant with its capacity to seat thirty at any given time. The restaurant had occupied the same location since opening in 1922, and present-day Toussaints resisted expanding or relocating to a larger space to serve the overflow of customers that formed long lines outside the restaurant during the four hours they were open for business.

"Enough about me becoming a lean, mean, sexy machine," Eustace continued. "What can I get you good folks? I have to

230

warn you that we've sold out most of what's on the board."

St. John moved closer to Hannah, resting his hand on her shoulder in a possessive gesture. "What do you feel like eating?"

She glanced up at the chalkboard listing the day's menu. "Do have any seafood gumbo left?"

Eustace nodded. "I think there's enough left for two portions. If you want I can add a few slices of jalapeño cheese cornbread."

She smiled. "Please."

"What about you, cousin?" Eustace asked St. John as he studied the board.

"I'll have the crab cakes with a side order of red beans and rice."

Eustace nodded. "I'll be right back." Turning on his heel, he disappeared behind a set of café doors.

Waiting until Eustace was out of earshot, Hannah leaned closer to St. John. "Is Eustace now running this place by himself?"

"No. His daughters come in at six in the morning to help him prep and cook, and then they work the front to serve customers. At two on the dot, they lock the front door and head home."

Hannah gave St. John a sidelong glance, still in awe of the masculine beauty to which he always seemed oblivious. It wasn't only his face or body, but his entire bearing that radiated urbane sophistication — something he'd not acquired over time but had been born with. Her classmates hadn't voted him best looking and best dressed as a fluke. They'd known then he was different — a cut above all the other male students. Girls shamelessly flirted with him even though they knew he was dating a beautiful girl attending an all-girls' parochial school.

"Chez Toussaints was very different when we were in school," she said. "I can remember calling and ordering takeout for dinner."

"That's because Eustace wasn't catering like he does now."

"Why doesn't he hire additional help?"

"Anyone he hires has to be a Toussaint because most of the recipes are family secrets.

His brother Gage usually steps up to assist him whenever Eustace has to cater an event."

"I know you told me you and Eustace are cousins, but how are you related?"

"Our grandmothers were sisters."

Eustace returned with two shopping bags filled with plastic containers. "I gave you guys a container of lobster bisque, and whatever was left of the shrimp etouffée."

Reaching into the pocket of her jeans, Hannah took out a large bill, placing it on the counter. "Your money's no good here."

"What are you talking about?" she questioned.

Eustace picked up the bill as if it were a poisonous reptile. "I said your money's no good because you're with family."

Hannah looked at St. John, and then at Eustace. "I don't understand."

Reaching for her hand, Eustace placed the money on her palm. "St. John, please explain to your lady that I'm not charging her."

Her body stiffened in shock and she wanted to tell the cook she wasn't St. John's lady — at least not in that way.

"He is not charging you for the food, Hannah," St. John intoned, enunciating each word as if speaking to a child. He cradled the shopping bags in each hand. "Please get my poncho and unlock the door."

She complied, pushing open the door and walking out behind St. John as Eustace let loose with a stream of Haitian Creole, of which she couldn't understand a single word. They stopped at her car. "What did he say?"

A beat passed. "He knew a long time ago that we'd end up with each other."

Hannah, unable to form a reply, gave St. John a barely perceptible nod, then ducked her head and slipped in behind the wheel, pushing the engine start button and driving out of the parking lot. People had asked when had she hooked up with St. John, and now Eustace believed she was his cousin's lady.

New Orleans claimed a population just fewer than four hundred thousand people, yet news about her and St. John had circulated like a wildfire. Hannah knew if she hadn't been a DuPont — or as she was known, the judge's daughter — most people wouldn't have given her and St. John a second glance. What if she hadn't come back for the reunion? Or if she had come with a stranger, she doubted people would be talking about her.

This isn't all about you. The voice in her head reminded Hannah that St. John was also included in the equation. His family roots — the Baptistes and Toussaints were deeply ingrained in the Crescent City's history, and aside from his leaving to attend college, he'd always lived in New Orleans. Oddly enough, he didn't seem remotely affected by talk of them being a couple, and Hannah decided what was good for the goose was also good for the gander. She planned to enjoy her time with St. John and come the end of summer she would be left with memories of a man who reminded her that although her marriage was over, she could enjoy a normal social life.

Robert had been only a shell of his former self after his first heart attack. Although his body had healed, it was his spirit that appeared to be broken. Hannah knew it was his confession that had swept him under in a tsunami of guilt from which he would never resurface. She never broached the subject of his infidelity again except to inform her husband that she was moving out of their bedroom.

Glancing up at the rearview mirror, she saw St. John following closely behind and smiled. She found it ironic that she had to go back in time to reunite with a former friend in order to move forward to embrace her future. And hopefully, that future included her becoming an innkeeper.

CHAPTER 12

Hannah lay on the lounger in the sunroom, while St. John folded his body down into a matching one.

"Are you all right?" St. John asked after a noticeable silence.

She turned her head, smiling at him. "I'm good."

"You're good, yet you seem a million miles away."

A beat passed. "I was thinking that I have to revise my business plan to include eating establishments." She told St. John everything she needed to convert DuPont House into the DuPont Inn, which now included the venues for serving meals.

Turning on his side, he gave her a long, penetrating stare. "How soon do you project the grand opening?"

"Hopefully before next spring. In fact, I'd like to be up and running before Mardi Gras season."

"I think you're worrying too much. It's not as if you have to gut and restore the house like some folks had to do after Katrina. You may have to make some interior modifications to bring it into compliance with hotel specifications, but I doubt that you won't make your projected deadline."

Hannah knew St. John was right, but the main house wasn't her concern. When she'd contemplated asking Tonya if she'd be willing to relocate to New Orleans to open her own restaurant, she mentally chided herself for expecting a stranger to move to another state just to fulfill her personal dream of becoming an innkeeper.

"You're right. I am worrying too much." She closed her eyes, exhaled an inaudible sigh, and shifted into a more comfortable position. "And it doesn't help that I'm as full as a tick. My brain always seems to shut down whenever I eat too much."

St. John smiled. "I'm with you. I know I definitely ate too much."

"I always overdo it whenever I order from Chez Toussaints. Now, if I could entice your cousin to come and work for me, I'd be in hog heaven."

"That will never happen, Hannah. Eustace wouldn't give up Chez Toussaints even if you offered him ten million dollars. And it's not about money but carrying on a family tradition for his children, grandchildren, and eventually great-grands." St. John sat up. "Speaking of families, I looked over the DuPont family tree and discovered there were a few *placées* and children of plaçages."

"Some of them are the descendants of distant cousins I've never met," Hannah admitted. "It was Grand-mère DuPont who knew most of the family's secrets. When I was a girl I'd sneak downstairs and listen outside the parlor when she'd whisper about mixed-race DuPonts who were fair enough to pass for white, and either left New Orleans for another parish or moved up North to escape Jim Crow. Some of them married into the white race, while there were a few women who gave birth to children of a questionably darker hue and that's when, as they say, the cat was out the bag."

"Do you know what happened to them and their children?"

Hannah nodded. "I recall reading a letter about one couple living in Ohio who told townspeople the baby's mother was part Native American, because there were no laws forbidding whites to marry Native Americans. I came across a diary entry about Elijah DuPont, who gave up his inheritance and moved to Canada with his *placée*. They eventually married and had ten children."

"Do you still have the letters, or did you donate them to the historical society?"

"I donated everything. But whenever you're ready to research the DuPont *gens de couleur libres* I'll contact the archivist at the historical society to allow you access to everything. Just be prepared to spend at least a month reading letters, diaries, Bibles, and legal documents going back more than two centuries."

St. John stared at her under lowered lids. "Now I have to rearrange my roster. I have the families listed alphabetically, which means I'm going to skip over B and C and go directly to D."

"There's a lot to go over. The DuPont men were quite generous when it came to spilling their seed, and their wives and mistresses quite prolific when documenting what was going on in their lives."

A hint of a smile lifted the corners of St. John's mouth. "Back then most white male colonists couldn't marry until they'd accumulated some wealth, so they usually turned to women of color as consorts."

"That still didn't make it right, St. John."

He held up his hands in a gesture of surrender. "I'm not saying it was right. Please, let's not rehash this, because I don't need you going off on me again."

Hannah blinked once. "I had no idea that I'd gone off on you before."

"I'm sorry. Maybe I shouldn't have used that phrase."

She inclined her head, smiling. "I accept your apology."

The last thing she wanted to do was get into a verbal confrontation with St. John; it was only after she'd read the recorded narratives of her family's history that she saw them in a whole new light. She understood why her grandmother didn't want her to know about the scandalous behavior of some of her male ancestors who'd physically and emotionally abused their slaves, wives, mistresses, and *placées.*

St. John swung his legs over the side of the lounger, coming to his feet. Reaching into the rear pocket of his jeans, he took out his cell phone, tapped an icon, and within seconds the melodious tone of a muted trumpet filled the room. He extended his hand to Hannah.

"Please dance with me."

She placed her hand on his palm, and he eased her to a stand, and then swung her into the circle of his arms, her curves molded to the contours of his lean, hard body. Hannah was certain St. John felt the runaway pumping of her heart against his chest as she sank even further into his embrace. A swath of heat swept over her, settling in her chest and then moved lower. Unfamiliar sensations and those she'd forgotten frightened her as she followed St. John's strong lead.

She swallowed back a moan when she felt his warm breath against her hair, wondering if St. John knew what he was doing to her. How dancing with him reminded her of how long it had been since she had experienced any close physical contact with a man. He spun her around in an intricate dance step, her sock-covered feet following his expert lead.

"Very nice, sweetheart." St. John whispered against her ear.

"Do you call all women sweetheart?"

She had to talk, say something if only not to think about how her feelings for St. John deepened each time they were together. Yes, they were friends and she enjoyed his company but she wanted more — much more. Reuniting with him made her aware of her femininity, of the passion she was capable of offering a man, and how wrong she'd been to punish every man who'd expressed an interest in her for her late husband's licentious behavior.

"No. Just the ones I like."

She smiled, easing back slightly to see his expression. "Would it bother you if I call you darling?"

"No." A slow grin revealed a mouth filled with straight, white teeth. "But only if I can be your darling."

Hannah stared at his strong, masculine jaw. "Do you want to be my darling, St. John?"

His lids lowered as he stared at her parted lips. "Yes. But you have to tell me the requisites in order to become your darling, *sweetheart.*"

"We see each other exclusively for the duration of the summer."

He nodded. "I can do that. Is there anything else?" St. John asked when she paused.

She shook her head. "I can't think of anything else." And she couldn't. The only thing she wanted from St. John was not to share him with other women as she unknowingly had done with Robert.

He pulled her closer, resting his chin on the top of her head. "As your darling do I have permission to kiss you?"

Hannah closed her eyes, realizing they were taking their friendship to another level, and although her head told her to say no, it was her body that refused to listen to the dictates of her mind. "Yes," she breathed out.

St. John cradled her face in his hands, lowered his head, and brushed a whisper of a kiss over her mouth. Her hands covered his, and as he deepened the kiss, her lips parted of their own volition. She felt herself drowning in an abyss of newly awakened passion that could only be assuaged with his erection inside her.

Without warning, she was lifted off her feet as St. John's mouth devoured hers in a marauding, smothering kiss that stole the very breath from her lungs. Her arms went around his neck, clinging to him, and she knew if he released her, she would collapse to the floor like a rag doll. She'd agreed to let him kiss her; kisses she knew were a prelude to foreplay. In her erotic dreams she'd fantasized about a man making love to her, and Hannah feared sleeping with St. John would impact their easygoing friendship.

Pushing against his chest, she managed to extricate her mouth, her breasts rising and falling heavily under her favored man-tailored shirt. She closed her eyes and bit down on her lip to keep from begging St.

John to make love to her. The dormant sexuality had awakened and now screamed for release. Hannah realized she was falling for St. John, and falling hard, while not knowing where it would lead.

"Please," she pleaded against his throat.

Burying his face in her hair, St. John breathed a kiss on her scalp. "Please what?"

"I can't do this right now." What she meant was she couldn't allow him to continue to kiss her and not have him make love to her. She was on fire — everywhere.

St. John pressed his mouth against the rapidly beating pulse under Hannah's ear. It wasn't as if he hadn't been aware of a growing physical tension between them whenever they shared the same space, yet he wasn't certain whether she was ready to go from friends to lovers. His promise to see her exclusively meant he would spend his entire summer break in New Orleans rather than spending several weekends in Baton Rouge.

"Does this mean I can't kiss you again?"

"No. I mean yes, you can kiss me again. It's just that it's been a while since a man — a man . . ."

St. John's eyes caught and held hers. "You don't have to explain. I know it can't be easy for you to get involved with another man after being married for so long."

She pressed her lips tightly together. "It has nothing to do with the length of my marriage."

Now he was totally confused. "If it's not that, then what is it?"

"I've only been with one man, and I don't know I can satisfy you if we do happen to sleep together."

Hannah caught him completely off guard, because St. John hadn't expected her to be that straightforward. She had changed from the shy, reticent girl he'd remembered to a direct and very confident woman.

St. John schooled his expression not to reveal his confusion. "Why are you talking about sleeping together when you haven't given me any indication that it's something you want? And if you want the truth, then you should know is it hasn't been easy for me to keep my hands off you."

Her eyelids fluttered wildly. "And you think it's been easy for me?" Hannah admitted.

He was momentarily mute, unable to form a comeback. Not once during their brief encounters had she given him a hint that she was remotely interested in him for anything other than friendship. St. John cradled her face between his palms. "Hannah. Sweetheart. We're not a couple of teenagers debating whether we should or shouldn't sleep together. We're adults — consenting adults who don't have to answer to anyone but ourselves for our actions. I realize this is harder for you than it is for me because you've only slept with one man, but I'm more than willing to give you the lead as to where we're going to take our *friendship.*"

She nodded. "If we do sleep together, then there's no way we can remain friends."

He smiled. "What the expression? We'll be friends with benefits."

"Friends with benefits that are certain to change both of us," she said softly.

A tender glow flowed through Hannah, wrapping her in invisible warmth as she experienced a return of a confidence she hadn't felt in years. Then she'd taken complete control of her life when she told Robert although she wouldn't divorce him, they would never sleep together again.

Fast-forward ten years and now she and St. John had rekindled their friendship, this time as equals. There was one time in the past when she'd thrown a hissy fit because he wouldn't do what she wanted, and he told her to grow up, because he had no time to entertain her childish tantrum.

She had to swallow her pride and apologize; he'd given her a disapproving glare before accepting her apology. Although they'd resumed their friendship, Hannah knew things had changed between them, and it had taken years before she realized her outburst mirrored her mother's behavior whenever she didn't get her way.

Taking her hand, St. John led her to the sectional grouping, sitting and pulling her down beside him. Draping an arm around her shoulders, he pulled her close. "I've never lied to you, and I don't want to start now. When I saw you again at the reunion, it was as if I was seeing you for the first time, because we're not married to other people. And when we were classmates I never allowed myself to think of you other than as a friend."

Hannah rested her head against his shoulder. "Are you saying if I hadn't been dating Robert or you Lorna, you would've asked me out?"

"I doubt it. Not because I didn't find you attractive, but it was that we were going in different directions. Remember, you were engaged and going off to college, while I was planning to attend Howard University with the intent of joining the ROTC. I was discouraged by several of my older cousins who'd fought in Vietnam from enrolling in the program. They talked about killing Vietnamese, not knowing whether they were ally or enemy, because they were following orders. Some of them are still suffering from PTSD, and whenever they hear a helicopter they experience flashbacks."

"Do you regret not following through on a career in the military?" Hannah asked as she draped her denim-covered legs over his thighs.

"No, only because I've learned not to regret any choice I've made of my own free will. Is there anything you've done that you now regret?" The seconds ticked as Hannah appeared to ponder his question.

"I regret I married so young."

"How old were you?" St. John asked.

"Twenty-one. Three weeks after graduating college I became Mrs. Robert Lowell, and we still hadn't celebrated our first anniversary when I gave birth to my son."

"That's very young, by today's statistics. I believe the average is now somewhere around twenty-seven for a woman."

"How old were you when you married Lorna?"

"Twenty-five. We'd agreed to wait until I

finished grad school. Lorna was working as a nurse and still living with her aunt and uncle to save money, and after I got a position teaching at a high school in Kenner, we had enough cash to put a down payment on a house in Tremé."

"You never had children." Hannah's question was a statement.

"Lorna didn't want any."

"Did you know this before you married her?"

"No."

"And you were okay with it?"

He kissed the top of her head. "You don't miss what you've never had. Did you plan to have one child?"

"After I had Wyatt, I waited a few years before trying to give him a brother or sister, but I never got pregnant again. I don't regret it, because he's a wonderful son who has given me two adorable grandbabies."

St. John shifted her body so they lay side-by-side, she savoring his warmth and the sensual scent of his cologne. They lay together, each lost in private thoughts as the distinctive voice of Adele singing "Sweetest Devotion" filled the room.

"That's a good song for a tango," he said offhandedly.

She smiled. "You're right."

Softly falling rain sluiced down the glass as Hannah closed her eyes and succumbed to a peace that made her want to surrender herself to the man holding her in a protective embrace. If possible, she wanted to lie with him until hunger, thirst, or nature forced her to get up.

"Are you falling asleep on me, sweetheart?"

"No. I was just thinking," she admitted, not opening her eyes.

"I hope you're not thinking about your inn."

"No. I realize now worrying and agonizing over something over which I have no control is counterproductive."

"Do you have a backup plan if you don't get approval?" St. John questioned.

"I don't need a backup plan. The lease on my apartment expires at the end of September and because I don't plan to look for another job, I'm not going to renew it."

He traced the outline of her ear with his fingertips. "Are you saying you'll move back here permanently?"

Lifting her head, Hannah gave St. John a direct stare, suddenly elated by her newfound objectivity. She lay in the arms of man with whom she could have an honest relationship without having to change into someone she didn't want to be. And she planned to move back to the city of her birth to do what she'd always wanted to do — practice law. She would study for the Louisiana bar and, once licensed, establish a practice where she'd advocate for and defend marginalized women and their children.

"Yes. Inn or no inn, that's exactly what I'm saying. I'm going to take the Louisiana bar, and after I pass I'm going to open a practice."

"So you're really serious about not teaching?"

Hannah pulled back, putting some distance between her and St. John. Even if she'd thought about teaching a pre-law course, she knew that wasn't going to happen now that she'd found herself personally involved with a department head of the college.

"I can't teach at your college even if I wanted to, because I've made it a practice not to mix business with pleasure."

His expressive eyebrows lifted a fraction. "Are you speaking from experience?"

"Yes. I went out with a junior partner at the firm where I'd worked, and after I refused to sleep with him, he started a rumor that I preferred women to men because he believed he was god's gift to women."

"Pig!" St. John spat out.

Hannah managed a small, tentative smile when she recalled the names she hurled at him, while verbally attacking his manhood minutes before handing in her resignation and walking out. "I left on not too pleasant terms, but managed to find another position four months later with the investment bank and earning more than twice what I'd earned at the other firm."

"What made you decide to move to New York?"

"Once Robert started hinting about retiring from the navy, I began studying for the New York Bar. I passed on my first attempt and told him I wanted to move to New York. He said he wanted to move back to Baton Rouge, so I told him he could live wherever he wanted, because after eighteen years of uprooting my household moving from base to base, it was my turn to determine where we should live. Wyatt had been accepted as a cadet at the Air Force Academy, so as an empty nester that strengthened my resolve. Within a month of Robert of becoming a civilian, a former admiral offered him a position at the Defense Department. After he was granted security clearance, he rented a furnished studio apartment in D.C. and commuted between Washington and New York every other weekend.

"Eight years later everything changed when he returned home and began complaining of chest pains. He said it was probably indigestion or heartburn and went to bed. The next morning I found him on the bathroom floor, struggling to breathe. He'd had a heart attack, which forced him into permanent retirement. Two years later he left to go for his morning walk and never returned. When I got the call, the doctors told me death had been instantaneous. Robert never wanted to be buried at Arlington National Cemetery, so I arranged for him to be interned in the Baton Rouge cemetery with generations of Lowells."

"Do you miss him?" St. John asked after a swollen silence.

A cynical smile twisted her mouth as Hannah stared across the room at the potted cacti sporting tiny red flowers. "It's hard to miss someone I got to see for an extended period of time on average of three times a year. Grand-mère DuPont once asked me if I was up to the task of becoming a military wife, and I was adamant when I said I was. The first time Robert was granted leave and we came back to New Orleans, my grandmother saw my expression, and there was an *'I told you so'* look in her eyes. That's when I knew what she'd been trying to warn me about. Her sister had married a lifer and Grand-mère saw firsthand how the loneliness drove her so mad she had to be institutionalized."

St. John pulled her close to his side once again. "Even though your grandmother wanted to spare you the same fate as her sister, she forgot that you were an educated young woman who probably had many more options than the women from their generation."

Hannah knew her life as a military wife would have been a lot more fulfilling if she hadn't had a problem forming relationships with other women. "You're right," she agreed. She untangled herself from St. John. "It's time I head home. I have to take care of Smokey."

His eyes narrowed suspiciously. "Who the hell is Smokey?"

"Smokey is a kitten. I'm cat-sitting until my cousins get back from their great big European adventure." Hannah's eyes narrowed. "Please don't tell me you thought Smokey was a man."

"No."

"Yes you did," she teased when he

wouldn't meet her eyes. "You don't have to concern yourself with me and other men because I've never been able to emotionally spread myself that thin. Either I'm all in or all out. It was the reason I'd stayed married for so long."

"Are you saying you didn't have a good marriage?"

"The only thing I'm going to say is that I played the hand I was dealt." She forced a smile that didn't reach her eyes. "Thank you again for your hospitality, and if I don't leave now I'll have to deal with a cat from hell. Smokey doesn't like to be let left alone for long periods of time."

St. John walked her to where she'd left her shoes and tote. "Maybe Smokey needs a kitty girlfriend."

Hannah slowly shook her head. "Don't you even go there, St. John. Paige and LeAnn never said they were getting a cat before they went away, and now you want to saddle me with two cats when I wasn't expecting to take care of one."

He draped an arm around her shoulders as he walked her to where she'd parked her car. "Cats require less attention than a dog."

Hannah turned to face him. "I've taken care of cats, dogs, fish, and birds, so I've fulfilled my role as a pet parent."

"Does looking after Smokey make you a grand pet parent?" he teased with a wide grin.

"No. I'm Smokey's auntie."

St. John opened the driver's side door, waiting until she was seated and belted in, then leaned in and kissed her cheek. "Drive carefully."

Hannah wiggled her fingers. "I will." Waiting until he closed the door, she started the car and backed out the driveway.

She hadn't expected when she got out of bed earlier that morning that she would spend time with a man who'd gotten her to open up to talk about her marriage. She knew now she never should have married, but in the end she'd resigned herself to a situation of the choices she'd made.

Hannah knew she never would have opened up to St. John if she hadn't gone into therapy after Robert passed away, where she realized that the decisions she made were of her own choosing and that she couldn't blame others for the outcome. She'd been reluctant to seek counseling but knew she couldn't move forward unless she was willing to reconcile her past.

She took responsibility for leaving Mc-Gehee and enrolling in a public high school once she realized she couldn't change how people viewed the world around them. She accepted responsibility for not forming friendships with other women because of distrust. And she'd stopped blaming her mother for forcing her to marry Robert and herself for staying in a marriage that had become emotionally and physically unfulfilling.

What she did take credit for was raising a son to allow him the freedom to accept responsibility for his actions and instilling in him a sense of independence as an only child. And she was most proud that she hadn't become a meddling mother-in-law, and she was also a loving and affectionate grandmother.

A smile spread across her features when she thought of St. John. She didn't know what to expect, but it wasn't to return to New Orleans to find him as unencumbered as she was. And what amazed her was their ability to pick up their easy-going friendship as if time had not passed.

We're adults — consenting adults who don't have to answer to anyone but ourselves for our actions. Her smile grew wider when she remembered how he regarded their relationship. Yes, she thought, they were adults free to do anything they wanted, and knowing this made her look forward to Friday night, when he'd promised to take her to a jazz club.

CHAPTER 13

St. John arrived at DuPont House Friday night and Smokey engaged him in a stare-down as soon as Hannah opened the door. The tiny gray feline arched his back and hissed at him, communicating he wasn't glad to see him. "You didn't tell me Mr. Smokey was an attack cat."

Hannah opened the door wider. "Please come in. Smokey is harmless."

He gave her a quick glance. Her curves were concealed under baggy sweats. "I know I'm early but —"

"Please don't apologize," Hannah said, interrupting him. "I would've been dressed but I got a phone call and the conversation went on longer than I'd expected. Please rest yourself in the parlor and I'll be right down."

St. John entered the house where he'd spent countless hours studying with Hannah because her mother forbade her to go

259

to a boy's home, since she feared the worst. Little had Mrs. DuPont known that her daughter was safer with him than some of the boys who lived in the Garden District.

He walked into the parlor and sat on a loveseat, stretching out his legs as he stared at framed paintings of Hannah's ancestors in period dress. He'd always found DuPont House more of a museum than a home for a modern family. Its very size had astounded him the first time the uniformed maid opened the door, her eyes reflecting surprise that he would ask for the daughter of the mistress of the house. It was only when he told her his name and that Hannah was expecting him that she acknowledged him with a smile. The woman had ushered him into the parlor, asking if he would like something to drink, then went off to tell her young mistress that her visitor had arrived. Because Hannah had opened the door today, he surmised she no longer had household help.

Although New Orleans had had a long and storied history of race-mixing, the fact was that he'd been born into a region of the country where segregation had been a way of life. St. John had grown up knowing it would take time for the evil practice of apartheid to give way to equality for all citizens.

If Hannah had grown up eavesdropping on her grandmother's conversations about how plaçage was most practiced in New Orleans because a wealthy planter society supported the system, he'd also heard oral histories about women in his own families who'd participated in quadroon balls and how their mixed-race children joined the class of *gens de couleur libres* or free people of color. What had begun in the early eighteenth century continued well into the twentieth century, until the laws against interracial marriage were finally struck down by the U.S. Supreme Court.

St. John's fascination with history had begun at nine when he found his great-great-grandmother's journals. The entries chronicled her life with wealthy Creole planter Claude Pierre Jean Baptiste. He had selected her as his *placée* when her mulatto mother presented her at a quadroon ball. Baptiste set up Marie Louise in a house in Tremé and together they had eleven children, two of whom lived to majority. Baptiste never married, leaving his entire estate to his surviving heirs. When St. John's mother discovered what her son had been reading, she told him it wasn't age appropriate and when he was older she would introduce him to her family's archival records in order for him to know where he'd come from.

A boyhood's curiosity became an obsession when he pored through books on military campaigns and the history of the United States as a colony of Great Britain, coupled with unearthing historical details on the Marigny Baptistes and Tremé Toussaints and many other *gens de couleur libres* in Haiti, formerly called Saint-Domingue and New Orleans. He'd discovered plaçage was also practiced in Natchez and Biloxi, Mississippi, as well as Mobile, Alabama, and in St. Augustine and Pensacola, Florida. His undergraduate research papers, graduate school thesis, and doctoral dissertation documented little-known historical details about the extralegal system in the French and Spanish slave colonies of North American and the Caribbean.

St. John studied each of the rosy-cheeked DuPonts in the paintings, wondering if they'd known the blood of an African woman ran in their veins, and if they did, were they ashamed of it. One thing he knew for certain was that a twenty-first-century blond-haired, green-eyed DuPont woman was proud and flaunted it.

Smokey crept silently into the room, eyeing him as if he were prey. "You look as if you want a piece of me, Mr. Smokey, but that's not happening tonight. I must give it to you," he continued as if the kitten understood what he was saying, "for trying to protect your auntie."

Smokey stopped inches from the toe of St. John's shoe. Leaning over, he held out a forefinger for the kitten to catch his scent. Smokey sniffed his finger and then scooted away.

St. John came slowly to his feet when Hannah walked into the parlor in a bloodred, three-quarter-sleeved silk peplum blouse over a black pencil skirt. His eyes moved lower to her long, slender bare legs and her feet in a pair of strappy black stilettos. The polish on her groomed toes was an exact match to her blouse and lip color. Everything about Hannah screamed sexy, from the tousled pale hair pinned atop her head in sensual disarray to her legs, which seemed to go on forever. She'd gone from a fresh-faced girl-next-door look to a seductive siren in less than twenty minutes.

"Wow!"

Hannah held her arms out at her sides. "I hope you approve."

He closed the space between them, reaching for her hand and dropping a kiss on her knuckle. His gaze lingered on the smoky color on her eyelids, mascara spiking her lashes, a hint of blush on high cheekbones, and the vermilion color on her generously curved lips. A pair of diamond studs sparkled in her pierced lobes.

"I more than approve. I didn't think you'd be able to improve on perfection, but you have."

A smile trembled over Hannah's lips. "You're going to hell in a handbasket, St. John McNair, for telling tales."

He threw back his head and burst out laughing. "Did you really have to use my government name?"

She rested her hands at her waist. "Yes, because I needed to prove a point."

St. John knew when adults called their children by their first, middle, and last name it usually meant they were in trouble about something they'd said or did. He tightened his hold on her hand, cradling it in the bend of his elbow. "Let's go before Smokey comes back and really attacks me for touching his auntie."

Hannah smiled. "He is a little possessive."

His smile matched hers. "You think?" St. John waited as Hannah picked her crossbody bag off the table in the entryway, activated the security system and closed the door, then he led her off the porch.

"Where's the club?"

"It's in Tremé."

"What happened to your Jaguar?"

St. John opened the sedan's passenger-side door for her. "It's being tuned up."

Hannah slid gracefully onto the seat, her skirt rising above her knees and displaying an expanse of firm, smooth thighs. Although he'd closed the door, he still couldn't shut out the image of her perfectly formed dancer's legs.

During the drive to Tremé, St. John tried not to think of the woman who'd unknowingly disrupted his well-planned summer vacation. He'd successfully pushed all thoughts of Hannah out of his mind when spending hours in the office poring over copies of microfiche to complete the research he'd begun on the first family on his list of Saint-Domingue's *gens de couleur libres* until seeing her again.

Whenever they were together, he found it impossible to ignore the husky timbre of her voice and the haunting scent of her perfume, which lingered on his skin long after they'd parted. When he'd asked if he could kiss her, he didn't know what to expect, but it wasn't her response or his reaction when he'd picked her up. It had taken all of his self-control not to carry her up the staircase into his bedroom, strip her naked, and make love to her until ejaculating inside her or passing out — whichever came first.

He hit the brake, coming to a complete stop seconds before the driver in the next lane swerved in front of his car to avoid something in the road. Instinctually, St. John's right arm shot out, his hand pressed to Hannah's breasts as the sudden motion propelled her forward.

"Are you all right?"

With wide eyes, she nodded. "Yes."

St. John lowered his arm and clutched her left hand. She was shaking. He knew if his reaction time had been any slower there was no doubt he would have rear-ended the car that had swerved to avoid driving over a large cardboard box in the middle of the road.

"Are you sure you're all right?"

Hannah nodded again. "I'm okay, St. John."

They arrived in Tremé without further incident, St. John pulling into one of the few remaining parking spots behind the wooden building where those looking to break into the music business signed up months in advance for Friday night's amateur hour. From the hours of ten to eleven four bands were given fifteen minutes each to perform. Occasionally music producers would attend the jam sessions to look for new talent.

St. John assisted Hannah from the car and entered the local music venue known as Jazzes. Those not familiar with the club believed it referred to the genre of music, but longtime residents of Tremé knew it had been named for the original owner's wife: Jasmine.

"How long has this place been here?" she asked as they made their way around to the front.

"I heard it was once a church, but it was never large enough to hold all the people who came to Sunday service, so the congregation decided to move to a larger building on the other side of town. A couple of brothers who were session players bought it about twenty years ago, and Jazzes was born."

"How often do you come here?"

"If you listen to my cousin Gage, he would say not often enough. He usually sits in with the house band on the weekends."

"Is he the cousin who helps out at Chez Toussaints?"

St. John met Hannah's eyes when she

looked at him. With her heels they stood nearly eye-to-eye. He knew she had to be very confident to wear stilettos with her above-average height and pull it off with the aplomb of a runway model. "Yes, he is."

"Will he be here tonight?"

He wanted to tell Hannah that tonight she was just full of questions but held his tongue. After all, she knew practically nothing about his family. "Yes."

"So," she crooned, "he cooks and plays music. Now that's what I call a renaissance man."

"With the Baptistes and Toussaints it's either music or food. Gage is blessed because he's equally proficient with both."

"Gage isn't the only one, St. John. I've heard you play the piano and you're quite skillful in the kitchen."

He opened the door, and the sounds of jazz filled flowed out into the warm late spring night. The hostess greeted him by name. St. John paid the cover charge, slipping two tickets into his jacket pocket.

"Speaking of Gage, I see him." His cousin stood off to the side, trumpet in hand, talking with a young woman who appeared totally entranced by what he was saying to her. "Let me introduce you to him before he goes on stage."

■ ■ ■ ■

Hannah grimaced as she experienced tenderness between her breasts where the seat belt had restrained her when St. John had had to slam on the brakes. He led her through tables with just enough room to navigate without bumping into seated patrons. The wait staff, dressed in white shirts, black slacks, shoes, and red bowties, with trays hoisted on their shoulders, were busy serving drinks and small plates of hot and cold hors d'oeuvres, from which wafted the most tantalizing aromas.

She watched, smiling, as St. John and his cousin exchanged a rough embrace. St. John was handsome while she found Gage almost too beautiful to be a man. The only thing he shared with his brother Eustace was height. Both were several inches above six feet. Large gray-green eyes framed by long black lashes, a palomino-gold complexion, and delicate features, cleft chin, and cropped straight black hair had her staring like a star-struck groupie as St. John made the introductions.

"It's a pleasure to meet you, Mr. Toussaint," she said, recovering her voice and extending her hand.

He took her hand. "It's Gage. And it's definitely a pleasure to meet you, too, Hannah."

My word! she thought. *Why did his voice have to be that resonant?* It was a rich, velvety baritone.

Gage rested a hand on St. John's pale-gray linen suit jacket. "Follow me. I had the boss reserve a table for you and your lady not far from the stage."

She followed Gage and St. John to a table where they had an unobstructed view of the stage. Gage removed the "Reserved" sign from the table for two and walked away as St. John pulled out a chair for her.

Hannah had come to accept the epithet *St. John's lady.* She'd been given a second chance at finding companionship, and she knew if she did sleep with St. John it would be a no-strings-attached relationship. She wasn't looking for marriage and it was apparent neither was he. She met St. John's smile across the table with one of her own.

"The house band is really good." She recognized New Orleans's native Dr. John's classic hit "Right Time, Right Place."

"You're right. They have a phenomenal horn section."

Hannah perused her menu. Jazzes offered a variety of shellfish appetizers along with frog's legs persillés, chicken livers with bacon and pepper jelly, and creole-Italian pot stickers. "Everything looks good."

"Everything is good," St. John confirmed.

"What do you recommend?" she asked,

"I'm partial to the chicken livers and oysters Rockefeller."

She nodded. "I think I'm going to order the pot stickers and shrimp with the red and white rémoulade sauce."

"The cover price includes a complimentary drink," St. John informed her. "The drink menu is on the back."

Hannah looked at him through her lashes. The last time she shared a drink with St. John he'd cancelled their coming to Jazzes because she couldn't keep her eyes open. "I'm definitely not going to order another hurricane," she said teasingly. "And don't you dare say anything," she warned as he chuckled softly.

"Why don't you order a virgin hurricane?"

She scrunched up her nose. "That would be the same as drinking fruit punch."

"Speaking of punch. The bartender happens to make an incredible Jamaican rum punch. It's made with dark rum instead of dark and light rums for the hurricane."

Her expression brightened. "Okay. You can order it for me. But I'm going to warn you that if it has me mumbling and stumbling, then I'm not going to be responsible for any risqué behavior."

St. John winked at her. "Don't worry, sweetheart. I'll take you home and put you to bed before you embarrass yourself." He signaled for the waiter, giving him their order and the tickets for their drinks.

The house band took a break before the first contenders took the stage and prerecorded music blared from powerful speakers set up around the one-story building. A young woman approached the table with their drinks, setting them down on coasters with the club's logo.

St. John tipped her, then raised his glass of Sazerac. "To the most beautiful woman in the room."

Hannah rolled her eyes. "What did I say about you going to hell in a handbasket? Quit lying, St. John."

"You don't believe you're beautiful?"

"It's not about what I look like."

"Then what is it, Hannah? Aren't you used to men complimenting you on your looks?"

She stared at the table. "No."

"Why not?"

She glanced up, giving him a steady look.

"I told you before that I don't have a lot of experience with men."

"I'm not talking about sleeping with them. I'm certain even when you were married men tried hitting on you. And what about when you went out socially? You have to have met men when hanging out with your girlfriends."

"I don't . . . I don't have what you would call close girlfriends. I've sort of bonded with three women I used to work with. They're coming down before the end of the month."

"Sort of bonded?" St. John listened intently as Hannah revealed how she and three of her former coworkers commiserated at her home with mimosas and Bellinis. "It sounds as if you and your friends didn't seem too broken up about being downsized."

"That's because after a while we all realized Wakefield Hamilton was just a slight bump on the road for us to get where we should be."

He shook his head. "I don't know why you're so self-deprecating, Hannah, when you really have it together. You're smart, beautiful, and you're a lot stronger than you believe. There're times when you're so confident that I'm in awe and a little intimidated. Then you tell me I'm going to hell in a handbasket when I tell you something you're not willing to accept. And where's the fire I witnessed when you just about cussed me out when I told you I couldn't study with you because I was on deadline to put out the school newspaper."

Hannah took a sip of her drink, staring at him over the rim. "Do you have to remind me of that?"

"Yes, I do," St. John countered. "Because all the pent-up rage you'd held in when you should've confronted the girls who bullied you was transferred to me." Reaching across the table, he held her hand, tightening his grip when she attempted to pull away. "I know what you went through in high school, and if you hadn't been as strong as you are, you never would've made it through. There were times when I wanted to shake the living shit out of you and tell you to fight back, but I didn't and couldn't.

"I'm eight years older than my sister and I'd always looked out for her, but there came a time when I wasn't there for her, so she knew she had to stand up for herself. She'd call me crying because there was a girl in the neighborhood that used to take Alicia's money. Even though my mother warned us about fighting, I told Alicia the next time the girl approached her she should uppercut her in the nose, and then stand her ground if she came back at her. And if her brother got into it, then I'd drive from D.C. to New Orleans to kick his ass."

"Did she hit the girl?"

St. John smiled. "No. My father heard from someone on the block that this girl was extorting money from younger kids. He approached the girl's father and threatened to arrest her as a juvenile offender if she continued. Dad had earned the reputation as a no-nonsense, take-no-prisoners cop and Mr. Landry promised he would take care of it. My sister went on to become an intelligence analyst for the FBI, and her former tormenter is now a resident at a women's prison where she's serving a life sentence for murder."

Hannah's eyes were large as silver dollars as she stared at St. John. "I'm glad it ended without you getting involved, but I still can't imagine you fighting."

"Why?"

"Because you've always been so genteel."

"Everyone has a dark side. I try not to let folks see it."

She nodded. "You're right. I've been known to drop F-bombs and four-letter words when I get pissed off."

St. John touched his glass to hers. "There you go. Now, what do we toast to?"

Hannah raised her glass, smiling. "I toast the DuPonts, Baptistes, and Toussaints for making us who we are today. Badasses!"

Pressing his fist to his mouth, he closed his eyes. "What in the world have I turned you into?"

Setting down her glass, she flexed her arms. "I am woman. Hear me roar."

This was a side of Hannah St. John had never witnessed, and much to his chagrin he liked seeing her that way. He'd spent more than half his life with a timid woman whose childhood fears held her captive because she'd blamed herself for the deaths of her parents and younger brothers; it wasn't until she finally found the strength to break free and stand on her own that she was able to talk about it. And looking back, he knew he never would have married Lorna if he'd known what she'd had to go through, because he always wanted children; they'd talked about starting a family and she'd been in agreement, but that was before they exchanged vows.

St. John shook his head as if to clear his mind of the painful memories of a time when he should have enjoyed his marriage without having to seek out other women to satisfy the primal human need for sexual fulfillment. His gaze shifted from Hannah to Gage as he approached their table.

"*Kezen,* I have to ask you something, and if you don't want to do it, then just say so."

"What is it, Gage?"

"Our vocalist just told me the keyboard player is in the restroom throwing up, so would you be willing to sit in with us for a couple of numbers when I don't have a horn solo?" he asked in French.

He gave his younger cousin a long, penetrating stare, wanting to tell him he'd come to Jazzes to enjoy Hannah's company, not play with the band. As a professional musician, Gage alternated playing piano and trumpet for the band, and the year before he'd asked him to sit in for the musician for six weeks after the man had nearly cut off the tip of his finger chopping onions.

"I'd love to hear you play," Hannah interjected, earning a frown from him.

Gage's eyes sparkled like semi-precious gems. "You heard the beautiful lady in red. She wants to hear you play."

"*Je ne comprends pas* English," St. John said.

"If you do understand English, then why don't you give your *kezen* an answer," Hannah drawled.

Gage hunkered down beside Hannah. *"Parlez-vous français?"*

"Not as well as I should," she admitted.

"I'm going to warn you that if you're going to hang out with my family, then you'd better brush up on your French. The older folks speak only French to the young kids, and by the time they enter school they're completely fluent in both English and French."

St. John's gaze shifted from Hannah to Gage as waves of annoyance washed over him. He'd invited Hannah to accompany him to Jazzes not for her to hear him play piano; that was something they could do at another time. Even later that evening if she agreed to come home with him.

And Gage was truly annoying him the way he was staring at Hannah. Then suddenly it hit St. John. He was jealous, jealous that his cousin had turned on his legendary charm most women were hopeless to resist. He knew jealousy meant his feelings for Hannah went beyond friendship. Yes, he liked her and was amenable to them becoming friends with benefits. However, he wasn't looking for a declaration of love from her. Both had been married to their respective spouses far too long to expect a lifetime commitment.

"I'll play two sets and not one more." The warning was cold, exacting.

Gage rose, smiling. *"Merci."* He inclined his head to Hannah. "I hope I'll get to see you again."

Hannah stared up at him through her lashes. "But of course."

St. John's expression was a mask of stone. Either Hannah was the consummate actress or an expert liar when she'd admitted she hadn't had a lot of experience with the opposite sex, because the look she gave Gage was one of an accomplished modern-day courtesan.

He studied her under lowered lids, wondering if she was aware of her powers of seduction: her demure smiles, the way she'd look up at him from beneath lowered lids, and her formerly waiflike body to which motherhood and age had added womanly curves in all the right places and best displayed in whatever she chose to wear.

A hint of a smile parted Hannah's lips. "Gage is very charming."

St. John's expression did not change. "Most women think so."

Her smile vanished quickly, replaced with a frown. "I'm not most women, St. John, because I'm not remotely interested in him. He's much too young for me and —"

"And what?" he asked when she didn't complete her statement.

"I like you too much to even consider getting involved with another man."

The sweep hand on his watch made a full revolution before he said, "And I you with other women." The admission flowed off his tongue, and St. John realized he'd broken his own rule. He'd promised they would see each other over the summer but hadn't been planning for anything beyond that time.

He stared over her head at the black-and-white photographs of blues and jazz greats lining the wall. Although he'd vowed not to become emotionally involved with Hannah, he was forced to acknowledge he needed to connect with a woman for more than sex; that he only drove to Baton Rouge a couple of times a month because he craved female physical contact when he could have stayed home and masturbated.

St. John realized Hannah represented more than sex. She was someone with whom he could talk, laugh, dance, and share his dreams. Little had he known when they were assigned as lab partners in biology it would lead to a friendship spanning four decades.

CHAPTER 14

Hannah knew New Orleans was lauded for its food, music, and renowned cocktails, but this was the first time she had experienced all three in one place. The tapas or small plates were phenomenal, the rum punch the best she'd ever tasted, and the talent of the amateur performers had left her in awe.

Cocktail napkins were filled with notes she'd jotted down about each act. The note-taking was essential when it came to hiring a band for the supper club. In Hannah's mind it was no longer *if* she opened the supper club, but *when.*

"Which one do you like best?" St. John asked when she set down the pen.

"Which do you think?" she countered.

A knowing smile deepened the lines fanning out around his eyes as he reached into his suit jacket's breast pocket and took out a pen. "I'm going to write down the names of the groups in order on a napkin, and then we'll compare notes."

Hannah stared at St. John's hand with long, slender fingers, marveling how he was the epitome of masculine grace and refinement. When he'd admitted to having a dark side, she remembered his cold warning to Matt to take his hands off her, and then there was the threat of confronting the brother of the girl who'd been harassing his sister. Although not as powerfully built as Eustace, St. John was undeniably physically fit, and she had no doubt even at his age he would prove formidable in a physical confrontation. The heavy bag and boxing gloves in his home gym bore the evidence of continual use.

She perused the notes on the four napkins. Reaching for her pen, she wrote the bands in order of which she liked best and least. "My number one pick is the band with the singer whose style is similar to Sade Abu. My second choice is the band with the saxophonist who plays incredibly like Nelson Rangell. I happen to like saxophones," she added when St. John gave her an incredulous look. "I'm conflicted about number three because I love the guy's voice. He sounds like someone who's popular now but I can't recall his name. I think of him as a throwback to the records Daddy played."

She frowned. "My mother hated when Daddy played blues and R and B in the house, saying that type of music belonged in a juke joint. Grand-mère had to remind her daughter-in-law that gospel, blues, jazz, and R and B came out of the South, and if she wanted to hear opera, then she should move to Europe."

Smiling, St. John said, "Are you thinking of Anthony Hamilton?"

She stared at him, complete surprise freezing her features. "How did you know it was him?"

"It was a lucky guess."

"Yeah, right," she drawled. "I'm willing to bet you have him on your playlist."

"I have a lot of songs on my playlist. You've named three, so who's your last pick?"

Hannah glanced at the napkin. "I'd have to say the group playing the funk jump blues." Waves of shock rolled over her when St. John pushed his napkin across the table and she saw what he'd written down. His selections had matched hers. "How did you know?" It was the second time within minutes she'd asked him the same question.

"I watched your face to see your reaction to each act."

"So now you think you know me that well?"

St. John winked at her. "Well enough, sweetheart. The minute you took out that pen and started writing, I knew you were thinking of hiring a live act for your supper club."

She nodded. "You're right about that. I don't want to pull in a young crowd; there's enough places in the French Quarter and on Bourbon Street to eat, drink, and listen to jazz."

"What type of clientele do you want to attract?"

"I'd like a forty-something and older clientele."

Resting an elbow on the table, he leaned forward. "I don't think you'll have a problem attracting them, because your inn guests will probably be around that age and would prefer checking into a place where they sleep eat, drink, and listen to live music without calling a taxi or getting into their cars."

"Remember, they can do that in certain hotels," Hannah reminded St. John.

"True, but staying at a hotel is less intimate than sleeping in a historic house in an equally historic neighborhood. There were times when I was a kid and my dad and I would drive past a house and I'd wonder who lived there and what it looked like inside."

Her expression brightened. "That reminds me that I've never given you a tour of Du-Pont House."

"Do you still have live-in help?"

Hannah was slightly taken aback by St. John's question because it was something she would have never anticipating his asking. "No. Why?"

"When I used to come to your house for our study sessions, a maid always opened the door for me."

"As you like to say, that was another time. DuPont House always had live-in help from the time it was built and continued until my father passed away. The terms in my father's will provided generously for long-time employees, and because I was living in New York at the time there was no need to employ them any longer. A few months later I convinced my cousins to move in and that's when I contracted with a cleaning service to come in twice a month for a thorough cleaning, while the family-owned landscaping company who'd maintained the grounds and gardens since I was a girl still come every week during the summer months and twice a month during the other seasons."

"Do you plan to hire resident employees once the inn is up and running?"

"No. If I'm going to live on the premises, I don't want the employees to have access to the entire house. All of the rooms on the second floor will be set aside for guests, and the employees will have a designated area for them on the first floor. I'll also show you the proposed floor plan for the inn."

"How about after we leave here? You can give me the tour and show me the plans."

"Okay." Hannah realized St. John would be the only one, with the exception of her family, who would see what she'd envisioned as her plan to preserve DuPont House for the next generation. Once she revealed her plan to convert the mansion into a business to her son, Wyatt surprised her when he said it was something he could see himself doing once he retired. Knowing another generation of DuPonts would live at the house was comforting because she didn't want groups or a family of strangers living in the historic house once she, LeAnn, and Paige were gone.

A waiter came over to the table. "St. John, you're wanted onstage."

Rising to stand, St. John loosened his tie, and then took off his jacket, handing it to

Hannah. "I'll be right back."

She stared at his slender physique as he mounted the steps to the stage and sat on the piano bench. The label on the pale-gray linen jacket indicated it hadn't come off a department store rack, but had been expressly tailored for him.

The house band had returned. Her gaze shifted to St. John as he studied a page of sheet music at the same time he rolled back his shirt cuffs. He'd played piano for the high school's jazz band, and while she'd taken piano and dance lessons, she'd never been able to master playing the more advanced compositions. The music teacher had her practice over and over, and after a while he gave up.

Gage, dressed entirely in black, moved closer to the mic stand. "You good folks know that on Fridays we take requests from the floor, and tonight we're going to feature a couple of selections from Chris Botti's *Night Sessions* and after that for those who want something a little more upbeat, we're going to entertain you with music from the Soul Rebels."

Thunderous applause went up from the assembly, Hannah included. The New Orleans–based brass ensemble was a favorite of her cousins who saw them perform at

Brad Pitt's Night to Make It Right Foundation charity event hosted by Ellen DeGeneres to raise money to build homes for victims of Hurricane Katrina. Paige had sent her one of their CDs, and after listening to it, Hannah immediately downloaded several others into her smart phone. The horns and percussion elicited a funky partylike mood that never failed to have her dancing around the apartment, followed by the yearning to return to her roots to see them live at Les Bon Temps Roulé, a bar where they still played whenever they weren't touring.

There were so many things she missed about New Orleans: starting the day with coffee and beignets at Café du Monde, riding the St. Charles Avenue streetcar, taking the steamboat *Natchez* dinner cruise, strolling Bourbon Street with its string of bars offering lethal concoctions, topless dancers, drag shows, and visiting Frenchmen Street for eardrum-blasting music. And whenever she saw footage of Mardi Gras celebrations, Hannah would immediately turn off the television because homesickness would sweep over her so strongly it was palpable. That was when she wanted to pack up everything and return home to a city with a history as diverse as its people.

Inhaling, she held her breath, and then let it out in an inaudible exhalation. She didn't know why it had taken her forty years to come to the realization that she should never have left. Even as a newlywed she didn't have to follow Robert from base to base. They could have purchased a house in New Orleans where their son could connect with the DuPonts and the Lowells instead of waiting for funerals to meet relatives who were no more than strangers.

The house lights dimmed, leaving the stage lit as two backup singers and Gage moved closer to their respective microphones. Within seconds the building was filled with the sensually sultry haunting sounds of Latin rhythms, Gage's trumpet, and one of the female vocalists crooning about how all would envy an older man and his beautiful young wife.

Hannah watched St. John. He was playing without reading the sheet music; she wondered if he'd given it a cursory glance and then memorized each note. She smiled. The man with whom she'd found herself enthralled was truly incredible, something she'd only glimpsed when they were in school together. As promised, he played two sets and then left the stage as another trumpeter, percussionist, and sousaphonist joined the band.

St. John returned to the table, leaning over and brushing a light kiss over her mouth. "You were wonderful," she whispered.

He pulled his chair close to hers, smiling. "It did feel nice to perform in public again."

Looping an arm around his neck, Hannah rested her head on his shoulder, her nose nuzzling his ear. She closed her eyes, seemingly sinking into his strength, and marveling she felt so safe and comfortable with St. John, something she'd never experienced with Robert.

She didn't know why she continually compared St. John to her late husband; a man who, when she thought back, was more stranger than husband and partner; a man whom she'd come to know only during the last two years of his life. Although they did not share a bedroom, she and Robert had become a couple for the first time in their lives. Unfortunately, it had come too late for Hannah, because though she did love her husband, she couldn't trust him. And for her, trust was the bedrock on which any relationship was based.

"Are you ready to join the band?" she teased St. John.

"No way. I can't see myself spending the summer rehearsing for hours, playing at night until the sun comes up, and then sleeping away the morning and getting up in the afternoon. I like music, but not enough to want a career as a musician."

All conversations stopped when the band launched into an upbeat sound that blended funk with jazz. Hannah's foot kept time with the driving rhythms, knowing if given the opportunity she would get up and dance.

It was close to midnight when St. John whispered he was ready to leave. She'd wanted to tell him she'd been ready leave after the amateur hour concluded. Although videotaping was prohibited, she'd wanted to film the performers so she could view them again at another time. Hannah knew she would have to return to Jazzes on subsequent Friday nights before she could determine which ones she would audition, and because of her limited musical knowledge, she would solicit St. John and now Gage's input as to the finalists.

Hannah opened the front door and quickly deactivated the security system. Smokey sat at the door to greet them. "Hey, big boy." She stared over her shoulder at St. John. "Come in."

"Are you certain your attack cat isn't going to jump me?"

She took off her shoes, leaving them on a mat near the table, and then removed the pins from her hair, releasing a profusion of silver blond waves that fell around her face and neck. She dropped the pins in a crystal bowl with car fobs and keys.

"Very funny. I overheard you earlier to-night talking smack to him just before I walked into the parlor."

St. John also removed his shoes, placing them next to Hannah's. "That's because he was giving me the stink-eye."

Reaching for his hand, Hannah led him across the great room to the staircase. "He must sense that you're a male, and because of that he has to protect me."

"Who's going to protect me from you?" he asked her in a tone so soft she had to strain her ears to hear.

Hannah stopped on the first step and stared at St. John. "You have nothing to fear from me."

St. John's lids lowered, hiding his in-nermost thoughts from her. "But I do," he said after a comfortable pause, "because it wasn't my intent to like you as much as I do. When I saw you at the reunion, I knew something had changed between us. I knew you were a widow, and because you'd come unescorted, I was hoping you weren't involved with a man. I wanted us to pick up where we left off in high school."

"But we were friends in high school," she reminded him.

"And that's all I wanted from you. Friendship, Hannah. But somehow things changed, and now I want more."

Hannah cradled his face in her hands, feeling the slight stubble of an emerging beard against her palms. "Things didn't change, St. John. We changed. We're not who we were in high school. Both of us have loved, and those we loved are now lost to us. We're now given a second chance, if not to love again, then to enjoy each other. We have memories spanning forty years, and there is the possibility that we can make new memories for the next forty."

A slow smile crinkled the skin around St. John's eyes. "If that's the case, then we'll probably be wearing adult diapers, putting our teeth in a jar at night, and waking up each morning marveling that we're still alive."

Hannah smiled when she had a mental image of them holding on to each other for support when walking. "Speak for yourself, St. John. At ninety-eight I'm willing to bet I'll still be jumping your bones."

"We don't have to wait until we're ninety-eight for you to jump my bones."

His eyes darkened, his stare hot enough to melt the clothes off her body. Hannah wondered if she'd ventured too far out into dangerous waters and whether she would be able to return safely. "What are you implying?"

St. John's hands went around her waist, pulling her close. "After you take me on a tour of the house and while I look over the plans for the inn, I want you to take care of Smokey, and then pack an overnight bag. We're going to spend the night at my place, where we can begin practicing, so after forty years we'll know if we got it right."

Hannah wanted to tell him that she was just joking about jumping his bones, because although she'd found herself physically attracted to St. John, she still wasn't ready to engage in an intimate relationship with him. And due to her age and limited experience with the opposite sex, she still harbored a hang-up about not knowing if she could please her partner.

"By that time I don't think I'll be able to open my legs wide enough for you to poke me," she teased.

"Then I'll just have to take you doggy style. I'll break you down like a shotgun and poke you from the back."

Pressing her mouth to his, Hannah pulled his lower lip between her teeth. "You are so nasty."

St. John's hands moved lower to her hips, pulling her against his groin. "There's nothing wrong with being nasty every once in a while." He patted her bottom. "I'm ready whenever you are to begin the tour."

St. John saw firsthand the magnificence of the rooms in the historic mansion with its original furnishings dating back to the mid to late eighteenth century. The addition of modern conveniences like plumbing, heating, and electricity did not alter the beauty and charm of a structure erected in a time in American history when cotton, sugar, and slaves brought untold wealth to those whose livelihoods depended on these commodities. Hannah boasted that chairs, tables, and beds had been transported from Etienne's plantation home in Saint-Domingue to New Orleans once the construction of DuPont House was completed.

"I noticed on the family tree that Etienne and Margit had one son and three daughters. Why did he commission a house this large to be built when they would've been more than comfortable in one half the size?"

Hannah lifted her shoulders. "I really

don't know. I suppose he was planning for them to have a lot more children, as people did in those days. His son René, who'd been educated in France, married the daughter of a wealthy French merchant and together they had thirteen children, so at one time they were able to occupy all the bedrooms on this floor. Once the boys reached their teens, they were permitted to sleep downstairs."

"What about the girls?"

"They weren't allowed in the company of men unless chaperoned by their father, brothers, or other male relatives. They were quick to protect the virtues of the DuPont women while they were running amuck procreating with either slave or free women of color."

St. John had begun gleaning research on *gen de couleur libres* from public records, old newspapers, reference departments in local libraries, and out-of-print books, yet knew the most factual would come from family archival material, and from someone like Hannah who was well versed in her family's history.

"I'm going to have to replace the wallpaper, repair the rugs, and redo the floors," Hannah stated offhandedly. "Then of course there's painting to be done inside and out. I had the windows replaced three years ago, so that's one project I can cross off my list."

St. John curved an arm around her waist. "This place looks good compared to some of the old houses I've been in. And many of the bedrooms don't have en suite baths, which is not the case with this house."

"The one thing I detested when living in a dorm on campus was the communal bathrooms. It wasn't until my last year that I lived in off-campus housing where I didn't have to share a bathroom. Folks talk about boys being slobs, but the habits of some girls are so nauseating that it would turn your stomach to see what they leave around."

"I think I get the picture," St. John said.

"We'll take the back stairs down to the first floor. I was thinking about putting in an elevator, but that's something I have to discuss with the engineer."

"Why would you need an elevator with a two-story house?"

She gave him a sidelong glance. "What if someone can't walk the stairs or they're in a wheelchair?"

He lifted his eyebrows. "True. Where would you install it?"

"There's a dumbwaiter in an area between the kitchen and what we used as a ballroom that was sealed up years ago. It could be reopened and expanded to accommodate an elevator."

St. John did not want to envision what it would take to convert his home into a B & B. Waiting for approval after filing for the license and permits would test the limits of his patience, and he didn't want to sleep under the same roof as strangers, something that would occur for Hannah once DuPont Inn opened for business. He didn't want to alarm Hannah as to the possibility of the theft of priceless artifacts once her guests checked out. Secreting hotel towels in one's luggage was a minor offense when compared to walking off with a pair of circa eighteenth century sterling candlesticks. She didn't want resident employees, which, as a woman living in a house filled with strangers, left her vulnerable: What about her guests? How was she to know if someone with less than good intentions had checked in and might cause her bodily harm or put her life in danger?

He had asked Hannah, "Who's going to protect me from you?" when he should have asked who was going to protect her. He'd promised to take care of her whenever they were together, and only now had the glibly spoken vow become even more concrete. It was one thing for her to establish a business enterprise to sustain her for her own future and the potential future generations of Du-Ponts, but to risk her well-being was something St. John couldn't fathom.

Walking alongside of her down a narrow hallway, St. John stopped at the entrance to a kitchen larger than some of the sharecropper shacks built along the roads in the cotton-growing region of the state. The kitchen was a blend of ultramodern gourmet and farmhouse country. Stainless-steel double ovens, dishwashers and microwaves, a cooking island with a commercial stovetop and grill, and a French-door refrigerator were totally incongruent with the coffered ceiling, terracotta floor, brick walls, and a massive brick wood-burning fireplace. Granite countertops, a breakfast bar, and three stainless steel sinks provided a professional chef with everything he or she would need to cater a lavish dinner for the host's guests.

"You must do some serious cooking in here."

"Not as much as I should," Hannah said, beckoning him to come in. "There was a time when my grandmother lived with us and we had large family celebrations during the holidays. But that's before I had the kitchen remodeled."

St. John walked over to the round bleached pine and oak table with seating for six, running his fingertips over the smooth surface. "What made you decide to remodel it when the other rooms in the house remain untouched?"

"Convenience," she said in a quiet voice. "The gas burner needed replacement parts that were obsolete, and the plumbing was constantly being repaired."

"You did all of this even though you didn't live here?"

Hannah stared down at her bare feet for several seconds. "I knew someday that I'd come back, even though it came sooner than later."

Crossing his arms over his chest, St. John stared at the hair framing her face, a face that had changed for the better. It was fuller, her jawline more defined, and her eyes seemed more alive than when she was a girl. Then, he'd always glimpsed sadness even when she smiled; he knew she'd been ridiculed by those who were quite vocal because they thought of her as a poor little rich girl, but somehow she'd become the consummate actress who appeared unaffected by their taunts. Her attitude communicated that as a DuPont, she was above them, and therefore whatever they said was of no consequence. The ice princess had turned into an ice queen with just enough fire for him to see her in a whole new light.

"When I come for Sunday dinner, will we eat here or in the dining room?"

"We can eat anywhere you want. Weather permitting, we can even eat outdoors."

His gaze shifted to the table and then an alcove that doubled as an in-home office. A computer sat on a built-in desk along with a printer; cookbooks and magazines lined a hutch with a diffuser and jars of scented candles.

"I think I'd like to eat in here." St. John walked over to the expanse of windows. It was too dark to see outside.

"In the daytime you can see the guesthouses from here. And just beyond them are the gardens with the koi pond." He smiled. She'd read his mind.

Hannah made her way over to the desk. "I did promise to show you the tentative renderings. Now that I'm planning to use the guesthouses, the architect will have to revise them."

St. John watched as she retrieved a leather tube, removed the rolled-up plans, and spread them out on the table, using the candle jars to keep them from rolling up again. She stood close, close enough for their shoulders to touch and close enough for him to detect the flowery scent from her shampoo. There was a time when he'd thought of Hannah as benign because he knew there wouldn't or couldn't be anything remotely romantic between them. That was then and this was now.

Since they'd exchanged phone numbers, which now seemed so long ago when in reality it was a little more than a month, he'd asked himself the same questions over and over. Why had he felt the need to reconnect with Hannah DuPont? Why her and not some other woman with whom he'd attended school? And why was he thinking about engaging in an intimate relationship with her when he knew it would be different from his present arrangement?

His part-time lover had established the rules for their liaison. After he'd gotten over the fact that she wanted to use him solely for sex, he finally acquiesced. He was familiar with a number of men who used women only for sex, but when the tables were turned, St. John realized how it felt to be used.

He didn't think of himself as old as much as he was old school when it came to women. He enjoyed them socially, but it wasn't his style to wine and dine them and then expect them to offer up their bodies as thanks for taking them out. There had been a time in his life when sex was a necessary part of his existence, and although he still enjoyed sleeping with a woman, companionship was now a priority.

Although they'd discussed making love, St. John didn't feel any urgency to make it a reality. Maybe it was because he was aware of Hannah's dearth of experience with men that he was holding back, or the knowledge she would compare him to her deceased husband.

He stared at the renderings depicting the front, back, and sides of the house. "Will your guests use the front door to come and go?"

"Yes, but only during the day. After eleven at night they'll have to use the door near the garage."

"You've named the bedroom suites." The question was a statement.

Hannah nodded. "I decided to name them after presidents. It's easier to assign a guest to the Washington or Obama suite than room three or five."

"What about . . ." St. John's words were drowned by a loud bang that sounded like an explosion, and then suddenly the house went completely dark.

"Blackout," he and Hannah said at the same time. The explosion was no doubt a blown transformer.

Hannah gripped St. John's hand. "I think it's time I get a generator. Don't move. I'm going to try and find a flashlight and then light some candles."

Arms outstretched, she felt her way around the kitchen in an attempt to find the utility closet where canvas storage bins were filled with multi-purpose lighters, flashlights, candles, batteries, twine, and menus from various restaurants around the city.

"Dammit!" she screamed when her bare foot made contact with the leg of one of the stools at the breakfast bar.

"What happened?"

"I stubbed my toe. That's what I get for walking around without my shoes." Hannah located the closet and now faced the challenge of finding which bin held the flashlights. Going on tiptoe, she felt around in the one on the top shelf. She was more than familiar with power failures. Whenever there were hurricanes or tropical storms, they would occasionally lose power. They would revert to another era when candles were used for illumination and the heat from the fireplace cooked their food. She found the flashlight and switched it on. A beam of light threw long and short shadows on objects in the immense space.

She focused the beam on St. John. "Come take this one. There're a few more here." He managed to make it over to her without bumping into anything. Within minutes she had a second flashlight and several large jars of scented candles.

The silence was shattered by a voice coming from a loudspeaker outside the house: *"This is the neighborhood watch. All residents are advised to remain indoors until power is restored for their own safety."*

Hannah found a shopping bag and filled it with candles and fire starters. "It's after midnight and it looks as if we're not going to Marigny until the power returns."

St. John took the shopping bag in his free hand. "And it looks as if I'm going to be your first unofficial guest at the proposed DuPont Inn. You can show me where I can bed down, and because I didn't bring any luggage, I'm going to need a few toiletries."

Hannah was grateful for the darkness because St. John couldn't see her expression of relief. He'd made it easy for her when he didn't suggest he would share her bedroom.

"Follow me and I'll get what you need." Her bare feet were silent as she retreated up the back staircase, stopping at a linen closet at the top. "Please shine your light over here," she told St. John as she opened the door, removing a bath towel, facecloth, and a disposable razor, travel size shaving foam, a tube of toothpaste, and a cellophane-wrapped toothbrush. She could count on LeAnn and Paige to keep a supply of everyday essentials on hand, and that included food staples. They'd learned as young girls that their mother had little aptitude for managing a household and the house would invariably run out of everyday basic necessities, causing them to overcompensate and purchase multiples of everything.

"I'm going to put you in the room across from mine. I'll light one candle for the bedroom and the other for the bathroom. I'll also give you a fire starter." She placed the towel and facecloth on the table near the pedestal basin. "Just knock on my door if you need anything else."

He leaned over and kissed her forehead. "I think I'm good."

She smiled. "Sleep tight."

"And don't let the bedbugs bite," he countered.

Hannah turned and walked into her bedroom, not bothering to close the door. She lit her candles and then turned off the flashlight, leaving it on the bedside table. She cleansed her face of makeup and brushed her teeth, and after exchanging her street clothes for a nightgown, she peered through the window, encountering blackness in the moonless night. A sweep of headlights from a slow-moving vehicle was the only indication of life. She detected light from a house several blocks away before it was extinguished. The Garden District had lost power; she wondered if it had reached as far as the Lower French Quarter and Marigny.

She got into bed, extinguished the candle, and lay atop the sheet. The air conditioning had stopped and the cool air was quickly dissipating. She tried not thinking about the man sleeping less than twenty feet away. Whenever she and St. John shared the same space, she felt desired and protected. Hannah had known he was special years ago, yet she hadn't known just how special he would become at this juncture in her life. She hadn't come back to New Orleans to pick up where she'd left off but to start over, to begin a new career.

Hannah tossed and turned, willing her mind blank, until she fell asleep at the same time Smokey crept into the bedroom and crawled into his bed.

CHAPTER 15

Tapping the icon on Hannah's cell phone, St. John waited for the gates to open before returning it to her purse. He closed the front door and walked off the porch to his car. He'd awoken just before dawn to discover the power had been restored. Dressing quickly, he'd tiptoed into Hannah's bedroom, finding her asleep as Smokey crawled out of his bed to give him the stink-eye. He left her a note indicating he would see her Sunday afternoon.

Pinpoints of light pierced the quickly fading nighttime sky as he left the property, the gates automatically closing behind him. St. John drove slowly through the streets in the Garden District. Although the power had been restored, several members of the neighborhood watch still patrolled the streets. He'd wanted to wait for Hannah to get up, but he promised the Chamberses he would mow their front lawn and shop for groceries, and later that evening he was committed to joining several of his former classmates to play cards. He wasn't much of a gambler and only agreed to join the other men to bond with males other than his colleagues.

There were few cars on the road given the early hour, and he made it to Marigny in record time. The Chamberses were on their porch, holding hands while sitting on matching rockers. St. John did not want to think of one passing away, because he knew the other would be lost without their lifelong partner.

He parked and got out of the car, waving to them. "Good morning. I'll be over as soon as I change my clothes."

"Were you caught in that blackout?" Mrs. Chambers asked as St. John mounted the stairs to the porch. Her dark eyes in an equally dark face were bright, alert, belying her advanced age.

"Yes, ma'am."

"We watched it on the television."

St. John nodded as he opened the front door to his house. It was apparent his neighbor wanted to talk when he wanted and needed a shower. "I'll be back directly, Mrs. Chambers."

He'd discovered within weeks of his moving into his aunt's house that Mrs. Chambers talked enough for herself and her taciturn husband. In the three years since he'd moved to Marigny he couldn't remember the man uttering more than fifty words, and that was to protest when St. John offered to have his landscaper take care of their yard. The elderly man claimed he didn't want charity, which prompted St. John to purchase a mower and do their lawn himself. Thankfully, their property was much smaller than his. He made it a habit to cut the grass early in the morning before it got too hot.

There were times when he saw the Chamberses together that he tried to envision things if they had been different between him and Lorna: Would they have spent their golden years together holding hands and reminiscing about the events in their life? Would they have had children? And would they now be grandparents? He'd revealed to Hannah that he didn't miss what he'd never had, and over time he had come to accept it.

He stripped off his clothes, left them on the bench in the bathroom, and stepped into the shower stall. Icy cold water rained down over his head and body, raising goose bumps, and then he adjusted the water to a lukewarm temperature. If he'd come back to Marigny with Hannah after leaving Jazzes, St. John knew they would have spent the night together, possibly in the same bed, even if they didn't make love.

Inasmuch as she turned him on physically, he didn't want to take advantage of her. It was always in the back of his mind that she'd only slept with one man, which he'd found somewhat surprising and welcome at her age, and that meant he had to be respectful of her feelings. When she'd talked about jumping his bones, he'd detected a slight nervousness in the glib quip, indicating she wasn't as confident as she'd presented herself.

He didn't know if he'd shocked her when he asked in which bedroom he would spend the night, because he wanted first and foremost to let her know his purpose for seeing her was not just to sleep with her. What he wanted from Hannah was a relationship in which they were equals in and out of the bed.

Twenty minutes later, dressed in a tee, shorts, a pair of old running shoes, and with a tattered cap covering his head, St. John weeded the Chamberses' front lawn before mowing the grass, making certain not to cut it too low or the sun would burn it. His clothes were soaked with moisture by the time he finished.

Mrs. Chambers stood up to admire his handiwork. "It looks like a green carpet. You did a good job, St. John. Now come inside and eat breakfast with me and the mister."

St. John ran the back of his hand over his forehead. "Thanks for offering, Mrs. Chambers, but I have to change and go to the supermarket. If you need anything, then let me know."

"I have my list and the money."

"I don't need your money." Most times her list included fruit and dairy; she'd arranged for the local supermarket to deliver less perishable groceries to her house twice a month, and the owner would electronically bill the Chamberses' grandchildren for payment.

"Don't fight with her, son," Mr. Chambers said, "because she will just fight with me."

St. John gave the older man an incredulous stare. *He speaks!* "Okay, sir. I don't want her fighting with you." Mr. Chambers nodded.

He put the mower away in a corner of the garage and went back into the house to shave and shower. The morning and afternoon sped by as St. John stopped to fill up his car before dropping off shirts, suits, and slacks at the dry cleaner, and drove to the supermarket to buy groceries and produce and the few items Mrs. Chambers had put on her list. He returned home, put up several loads of wash, ate a light lunch, then retreated to his office to continue his ongoing research, stopping to answer the phone when he recognized his mother's number on the caller ID.

"Hello, Mom."

"Don't you dare hello me, St. John Baptiste McNair."

Damn, he thought. There was that whole name again. "Now why are you using my government name?"

"Because that's the only way I can get your attention. Do you realize how long it's been since we've talked to each other?"

A slight frown line appeared between his eyes. "What are you talking about? I called you last week and spoke to Dad. He said you were out, and I told him to tell you that I'd called."

There came a pause. "Well, he must be getting senile, because he didn't mention a word to me. I'm sorry."

St. John smiled. "There's no need to apologize. How are you?"

"I'm well. Keisha's here and we're getting

along famously. And because it's been so hot, we've had to stay indoors, so I'm teaching her to cook."

"How's she doing?"

"She loves it. I must say she's a natural. I haven't said anything to her because with teenagers if you tell them go right they'll defy you and go left, but she really should think of going into the culinary arts as a pastry chef."

"She's that good?"

"She's more than good. That girl made a pound cake that literally and figuratively melted in my mouth. Then she decided to make a sweet potato pie that was so delicious I wanted to cry with joy."

"Maybe you should say something to her," St. John urged. "Verbal encouragement may be what she needs to steer her in that direction. Maybe next year Alicia can send her here so she can work with Eustace. He's doing a lot of catering, and I'm certain he'd be more than willing to take her on as an apprentice."

"That's something I'll mention to Alicia when I talk to her. Not to the change the subject, but how are you enjoying your vacation?"

St. John's expression brightened. "I'm

actually enjoying it more than past vacations."

There came another pause, then Elsie said, "Are you seeing someone?"

It was St. John's turn to pause. "Why would you ask me that?"

"Because I hear something in your voice I haven't heard in a very long time."

"What's that?" he asked.

"You sound content. I repeat. Are you seeing anyone?"

He debated whether to skirt the question or be direct with his mother, because although she lived nearly three thousand miles away, word would probably get back to her that he'd been seen out and about with Hannah. After all, his father was a Toussaint and the Toussaints kept in touch with one another no matter how far away they lived.

"Yes, I am."

"Who is she?"

"Hannah DuPont. We reconnected at our reunion and we've been hanging out together."

A beat passed. "Is it serious?"

"What do you mean by serious?"

"Don't be obtuse with me, St. John. I know you two were friends back in high school, but that was a long time ago. What's going on with you and the judge's daughter?"

"We're still friends, Mom. And if you want to know if I've slept with her, then the answer is no. Does that answer your question?"

"Yes, it does. I've always thought she was a nice girl."

St. John wanted to tell his mother that Hannah was now an incredible woman. That he and Hannah had hit it off the instant they were paired together as lab partners. That if circumstances had been different maybe they would have ended up together rather than with other people.

"She's still nice."

"I'm glad, because you deserve to be with someone who can make you happy."

His mother was the only one to whom he'd revealed the reason he and Lorna had decided to end their marriage, swearing her to secrecy. Waves of melancholy washed over him. St. John didn't want to think of the curve life had thrown him, which he did whenever he thought of how trepidation and cowardice hadn't permitted him to walk away from a woman so emotionally scarred. He'd sacrificed his own happiness in an attempt to stabilize her mental stability.

"Thanks, Mom. I'm really enjoying her

company."

"You need to do more than enjoy her company, St. John," Elsie stated emphatically. "If you like her as much as I believe you do, then don't let her get away."

"I'm not going to hold on to someone who's not on the same page as me. Hannah and I have decided to see each other over the summer without making plans beyond that."

"Is she planning to leave New Orleans like she did before?"

St. John quickly tired of his mother's interrogation. Did she not realize he was a grown man who could come and go by his leave, and mature enough to deal with the fallout if he or Hannah decided not to continue to see each other?

"I don't know," he lied smoothly. Lying had never come easy for him.

"Maybe you can convince her not to leave."

Leaning back in the chair, St. John massaged his forehead, chiding himself for answering the phone call. His mother was like a dog with a bone once she got something into her head. "Convince her how?"

"Marry her."

"Good-bye, Mom."

"Don't you dare hang up on me!"

"Good-bye. I'm hanging up now."

That said, he depressed the hook, ending the call. Within seconds the phone rang again, but he refused to pick up the receiver when he saw his mother had called back. The ringing ended and a new voice mail notation popped up on the display. He decided to ignore it. St. John didn't want to remind Elsie that he was in his fifties and he didn't want or need her meddling in his personal life.

Running both hands over his cropped hair, he closed his eyes tightly. First it was Gage offering to set him up with a woman, and now his mother giving him advice about what he should do with Hannah. He wasn't looking to remarry, and he suspected it was the same with her. If her husband hadn't died, there was no doubt they still would be together. She'd spent too many years married to the same man to disregard those memories and begin all over with another man.

St. John opened his eyes, staring at the document he'd pulled up on his computer. Cursing under his breath, he saved it. He was more annoyed with himself than his mother. The phone call had shattered his focus, resulting in his losing valuable time compiling research for his book project.

Despite not having a definitive deadline, he didn't want to spend more time than necessary before he sat down to begin writing.

He left the office and walked into the gym to work out some of his frustration on the heavy bag. Forty minutes later and drenched with sweat, he lay on a towel on the bench in the steam room, and when he emerged he'd successfully pushed the conversation he'd had with his mother to the farthest recesses of his mind. Playing cards later that night was what he needed to help him not to dwell on the women in his life.

Mark Fitzsimmons hosted the poker game in a second-story apartment with a lacy wrought-iron gallery overlooking Bourbon Street. Cases of beer were stacked up in a corner of the living room. All players were required to donate beer, Mark's beverage of choice, and he provided the appetizers and cigars. Table stakes for each game was a virtual one hundred dollars, and once the winner accumulated one thousand virtual dollars, they would begin again. It was more an exercise in skill than winning or losing actual money.

Mark placed his cards facedown on the green felt, and then rested massive arms on the table. "McNair, we're waiting for you."

St. John, biting on the cigar stub clenched between his teeth, stared at the cards he'd been dealt. A pile of colorful chips was stacked next to his left hand. He glanced across the table at the former marine drill sergeant sporting a military haircut. Mark admitted when they sat together at the reunion that he'd moved out of his home and rented the apartment after discovering his wife had been involved in an ongoing affair with their bachelor neighbor.

"I'm trying to figure out my next move."

"No shit," drawled George Pinkney, a high school science teacher.

Mark glared at him with laser-blue eyes. "What you're trying to figure out is how to clean us all the hell out."

Tommy Jensen, a sports reporter for the *Times-Picayune,* blew out a perfect smoke ring and then tossed his cards on the table. "I'm out."

Mark's cards joined Tommy's. "Me, too."

George tossed his cards on the pile with the others. "Same here."

St. John placed the cigar stub in an ashtray, and then fanned his cards. Reaching out, he scooped up the chips. "Thank you very much."

Rising slightly from his chair, George stared at St. John's cards. "Straight flush. I think we made a mistake inviting you to play cards with us."

"You still have a chance to clean me out in the next round," St. John countered, smiling.

The doorbell shrilled loudly throughout the apartment and Mark, pushing back his chair, stood up. "That must be the food."

George wiped his dark brown shaved pate with a napkin. "I think after some sustenance we'll be better in better shape to whip the professor's ass."

Tommy also stood up. "Suck it up, Pinkney. McNair trounced our asses and that's just it."

St. John hid a Cheshire cat grin as he rose and walked over to the open casement window and out onto the balcony. It was Saturday night and Bourbon Street was pulsing with energy from locals and tourists crowding into and spilling out of the many bars and restaurants, all under the watchful eyes of law enforcement. He could see why Mark, as a civilian running his own security company, had chosen to live on the infamous street with strip bars, flashy music clubs, and sex bars. Many of his employees worked undercover at various businesses to protect customers and owners alike during the nighttime debauchery.

Once people discovered St. John was from New Orleans, they usually asked him about open containers of alcohol allowed on the streets; he explained that as long as the alcohol was in a plastic cup and not in a glass it was permissible. He'd made it a practice never to request a "go cup." Image and reputation were always first and foremost, and St. John knew his future tenure at the college was contingent upon a strict moral clause in his contract, which prohibited public lewdness and/or intoxication.

Playing cards with the men with whom he'd shared classes brought back memories of when they were young and believed they were invincible. Mark had grown up in a military family and enlisted in the Marine Corps months before graduating, while he and Tommy worked on the school newspaper together; the boy everyone called Jimmy Olsen covered all the school's sporting events and it was inevitable he would eventually become a sports reporter. There were occasions when Tommy would dress like the iconic Superman co-star to further his image as an aspiring journalist.

He found it ironic the four of them had married the girls they were dating in high school, and now, forty years later, none was with the same woman. George had lost his wife to cancer six years ago and hadn't bothered to remarry. Tommy had married and divorced his high school sweetheart after more than twenty years of marriage, once she found the strength to tell him she was gay. Mark's wife had cheated on him. And although he'd cheated on Lorna, the reason behind his actions was totally different.

St. John had long ago accepted that he'd been an adulterer. His wife's alienation of affection was grounds for an annulment or divorce, yet he'd chosen to remain in the sterile union. He felt as if he'd been released from a prison without bars within minutes of Lorna broaching the subject of divorce. Once she explained why she was leaving him, his relief turned to rage because of her inability to trust or love him enough to tell him of her fears.

"Hey, McNair, come and eat," Mark called out.

He returned inside, awed by the amount of food on the table in the dining area. There were trays of fried chicken, catfish fritters, popcorn shrimp, dirty rice, and boudin balls with accompanying sauces. "Do you guys eat like this every time you get together?"

George patted his rounded belly over his

New Orleans Pelicans tee. "Why do you think I'm carrying this corporation up front?"

"Cut the bullshit, Pinkney," Mark drawled. "You looked like that even before we started playing cards. Give me thirteen weeks and I'll have you looking like Mc-Nair."

The science teacher glared at Mark. "If you'd wanted to continue as a badass drill instructor, then you should've stayed in the Marine Corps."

"Thirty years of active duty and another ten as a reservist is all I have to give to my country."

Tommy picked up a plate and began filling it with rice and catfish. "I'm going to eat while you dudes beat your gums about big waistlines. McNair, are you joining me?"

St. John smiled. "Hell, yeah!" He hadn't eaten since earlier that afternoon, and he had no intention of denying himself the dishes from which wafted the most mouthwatering aromas. He, along with the others, filled their plates, and then sat down at the table with frothy mugs of beer.

Leaning back on his chair, Tommy rubbed his slightly rounded belly. "I think I ate too much. Fitz, you're going to have to schedule these get-togethers further apart or we're all going to have to start working out every day."

"You work out?" Mark asked.

Tommy nodded as he smoothed back several strands of salt-and-pepper hair off his deeply tanned forehead. He was an avid boater, and when he wasn't covering a sporting event, he could be found on his boat sailing and fishing along the Gulf.

"Yes. I started a couple of months ago after I met Nicole."

George set down his mug. "You've been holding out on us."

Smoothing back his hair, which St. John recognized as a nervous gesture from his youth, Tommy said, "I'm not holding out. I just hadn't mentioned her before. She lives in Shreveport. She's a school nurse. Nicole lost her husband to diabetes two years ago, and I suspect she's still in love with him, so I'm not putting any pressure on her to make what we have permanent."

St. John patted his back. "Good for you."

"Are you thinking of marrying again?" George asked Tommy. The reporter nodded. "What about you, McNair? You thinking of tying the knot again?"

St. John shook his head. "No. Once is enough."

Mark stared at St. John over the rim of his

mug. "Not even if that woman is a very attractive widow who just happens to live in the Garden District?"

An expression of incredulity settled into George's features. "Does this widow happen to be one Hannah DuPont?"

"Bingo!" Mark drawled. "I saw our brilliant professor with the lady in question when they were having a very intimate dinner in Broussard's courtyard."

Tommy rested a hand on St. John's shoulder. "Now who's holding out? I thought I was imagining it, but you two did look rather cozy at the reunion."

St. John resisted the urge to fling off Tommy's hand. "Hannah and I are friends."

Removing his hand, Tommy met St. John's steady stare. "You guys were friends back in school."

"We're still friends."

A slight smile parted Mark's lips as he lifted his eyebrows. "Now, that's a friendship I wouldn't mind having, only with benefits. I must admit I once had the hots for Hannah. So much so that I asked her out, but she told me she was seeing someone. I didn't believe her until that naval midshipman showed up at prom with her."

George nodded. "What I could never understand was why she transferred from her hoity-toity school to one across the tracks if not to remind us that she was better born and bred."

"It wasn't that at all," St. John said in defense of Hannah. "Did you ever think she was sick of being with a bunch of spoiled, stuck-up girls who looked down their noses at people like us?" Hannah had confided why she'd left McGehee, and he wasn't going to betray her confidence.

It was Tommy's turn to nod in agreement. "You're right, McNair. I had a few classes with her, and not once did she ever act superior to the rest of us. I see why you two have remained friends."

St. John wanted to tell Tommy he and Hannah were very good friends, friends with the distinct possibility of them becoming lovers. The conversation segued from relationships to sports to local politics. They played another round of poker and Tommy won the pot. Mark recorded the winning totals, promising to contact everyone with several dates after Labor Day.

St. John drove back to Marigny, whistling a nameless tune. If Mark saw him sharing dinner with Hannah, then it was just a matter of time before all who knew them would know they were seeing each other. And dating her openly fulfilled his need to have an ongoing relationship with a woman.

CHAPTER 16

Hannah took a step back, admiring her handiwork. She'd set the table in the kitchen with a hand-crocheted tablecloth over a rose-pink liner. The bone china, painted with tiny rosebuds, was one of eight complete sets purchased by the mistresses of DuPont House over more than two centuries. All told, there were more than a dozen sets, many with missing or broken pieces. Silver, engraved with a bold D in Edwardian script, and crystal water, wine, and cordial glasses and white damask napkins embroidered with DP, along with silver candlesticks, complemented the elegant table set for two.

One of her first tasks as a young girl was learning to set a formal and informal table. She'd come to differentiate between a fish and salad fork, and soup, fish, and demitasse spoons. Her mother said it was necessary, because once she married and ran her own household, she wanted her to be the perfect hostess. At the age of eight Hannah did not want to concern herself with hosting dinner parties when she much preferred to curl up on the window seat in her bedroom reading her mother's collection of Nancy Drew books in addition to *Little Women, The Secret Garden,* and *Little Lord Fauntleroy* to being thrust into adulthood with all that went along with it. However, Jefferson's birth provided a respite for Hannah from her mother's constant scrutiny. Clarissa was over the moon because she'd given her husband a male heir who would carry on the family name.

Hannah made her way over to the sink and misted an assortment of flowers she'd picked from the garden. For as long as she could remember, flowers purchased from a florist had never graced any table in the historic house. The well-maintained garden provided the occupants of DuPont House with whatever they needed year-round. Fruit trees, aromatic herbs, and vegetable beds with tomatoes, peas, a variety of berries, and flowers in varying hues from snow-white to deep purple, succulents and grasses created a riot of harmonious color and continuous bloom for many generations.

After arranging the flowers in a vase, she

set it on the table as a centerpiece, opened the oven to check the internal temperature of the turkey, and then went upstairs to shower and change for dinner. Hannah had revised her menu several times over the past few days until finally deciding to offer an appetizer of stuffed mushrooms; a classic Caesar salad would follow, and then she would serve roast turkey with potato salad and asparagus. Dessert was the traditional Southern strawberry shortcakes. She'd prepared the shortcake dough squares and planned to put them into the oven when St. John arrived. That would give her time to bake and then cool the individual cakes before filling them with chilled strawberries and whipped cream.

She couldn't remember the last time she cooked for someone other than herself. After Robert's heart attack they rarely dined out because of his restricted diet, and when she did prepare meals for him, they were much too bland for her taste.

Hannah glanced at the clock on the microwave, smiling. It was one-fifty. She had more than an hour to shower, shampoo her hair, and dress before St. John arrived. Whenever she thought about him, she felt like a young girl about to embark on a date with a boy she'd loved from afar for years. There were times when she chided herself for thinking of him in that way. Neither of them were teenagers. But in a moment of reflection, Hannah wondered if perhaps she had always been in love with St. John and that was why he'd been in her erotic dream.

Her marriage may not have turned out the way she'd wanted, yet she never regretted marrying Robert, because of Wyatt. Becoming a mother and knowing her son was dependent on her, she had made the best choice she could.

She climbed the back staircase, her steps light as she walked the hallway to her bedroom. The harder she tried to resist the truth, the more it nagged at her. She was in love with St. John. Had been in love with him for more than half her life, because she now recognized there was something so special about him and that fate had brought them together at a time when she needed him most.

The callbox chimed and the image of St. John's car appeared on the security monitor. Hannah swore under her breath. She'd forgotten to open the gates. She tapped the button on the console before walking out of the kitchen to open the front door. Vertical lines appeared between her eyes when she walked onto the porch to find him removing something from behind the driver's seat. Her gaze lingered on his off-white, short-sleeved silk shirt he hadn't bothered to tuck into the waistband of a pair of tan linen slacks. A pair of brown woven leather sandals completed his casual look.

"Oh, how beautiful." St. John had brought a moth orchid plant in a pot painted with delicate Chinese characters.

Mounting the steps, he leaned over and brushed a kiss over her parted lips. "You look and smell delicious."

"So do you," she countered. He was always well groomed and stylishly dressed — traits she admired in a man. "Please come in."

St. John glanced down. "Is it safe?"

"Stop it," Hannah chided. "Smokey won't bother you if you don't bother him."

"I just want to make certain I won't be attacked."

She rolled her eyes at him. "It would serve you right if he did attack you for messin' with him."

St. John walked stepped into the entryway. "By the way, where is he?"

"He's in the parlor sitting on his window perch."

"Where do you want me to put the plant?"

Hannah glanced at him over her shoulder. "Please bring it in the kitchen."

St. John stared at the flowing gauzy fabric of the cobalt-blue sundress floating around Hannah's ankles. Narrow straps crisscrossing her bare back revealed an expanse of lightly tanned skin, indicating she'd spent time in the sun.

His gaze shifted from the ballet flats to the tousled waves grazing the nape of her neck. He wondered if Hannah knew just how sexy she was with little or no effort. Even Mark had admitted he'd had the hots for her back in high school. St. John kept himself deliberately busy so not to think about her. He had not figured out why was drawn to Hannah, other than because he could be himself whenever they were together. He didn't have to censor or edit himself.

"Something smells wonderful."

"I'm roasting a turkey."

He followed Hannah into the kitchen. She'd tuned a countertop radio to his favorite satellite station featuring slow jams. His gaze shifted to the splendid table set for two with china, silver, and crystal. "I'd like you to help me host my family reunion."

Hannah took the plant from him, setting

it on the windowsill alongside a collection of potted herbs. "You're kidding, aren't you?"

"No, I'm not kidding. Besides, you already know Eustace, his daughters, and now Gage, so you'll fit right in."

A look of indecision settled into Hannah's features. "I don't know, St. John. My friends from New York will be here at that time and —"

"They can come, too," he said, cutting her off. "The more the merrier. If this is their first time coming to Nawlins, then *'Laissez les bon temps rouler!'* "

She flashed a sexy moue. "Don't be surprised if they let the good times roll Big Apple style."

St. John shook his head. "There's no comparison, sweetheart. If New York is the city that never sleeps, then New Orleans is the city with a nonstop party. Food, music, and drink are the heart and soul of our illustrious city."

"Don't you mean infamous," Hannah teased.

He nodded, smiling. *"Au dit."*

Hannah opened a drawer under the cooking island. "I need you to tutor me in French because I'm really rusty when it comes to speaking it."

"You understood *au dit*?"

"Yes. It means ditto, or the same. I understand the language, read it, but I hesitate speaking it."

St. John watched Hannah slip on a white bibbed apron. "You're probably thinking in English. The instant someone speaks to me in French or Creole, I automatically think in that language, which makes it easier for me to respond."

"Where did you learn to speak Creole?"

"The Toussaints were brought here from Saint-Domingue and some of them spoke French, their own patois, and English. When they didn't want folks to know what they were talking about, they'd lapse into Creole. The ones who speak only Creole understand French but are unwilling to speak it."

"Will they be at your family reunion?"

"Yes. Do you need help with anything?" he asked as she opened the refrigerator and removed a baking sheet with squares of dough.

"You can carve the turkey once it's done. Thankfully, I have everything under control."

"What are you going to do now?"

"I'm going to bake the shortcakes and let them cool before filling them with strawberries and cream. Meanwhile, I plan for us to start with stuffed mushrooms as an appetizer. Dinner will include Caesar salad; broiled asparagus with garlic, shaved parmesan, and olive oil; turkey, and potato salad." She reached in the drawer again, handing him an apron.

"You're quite the little chef."

Hannah gave him a facetious smile. "And you thought I couldn't cook."

St. John slipped on the apron, looping the ties around his waist. "I must admit I was skeptical."

"Why?"

He lifted his shoulders. "I don't know. I suppose it's because you grew up with household help that I figured you wouldn't be that proficient in the kitchen."

"And I never thought you'd be that narrow-minded," Hannah chided.

"Come on, sweetheart, you know I'm not that far from the truth. You were dropped off and picked up from school by your father's chauffeur. A maid always greeted visitors at the door, and don't forget you were introduced to polite society at a debutante ball."

"That has nothing to do with who I am."

St. John saw spots of color dot Hannah's cheeks. It was apparent he'd insulted her, and that was something he didn't want to do. "You're right. You're the antithesis of your privileged upbringing."

"Maybe it's because I know who I really am. I'm certain you're familiar with the expression *'vous ne pouvez pas savoir où vous allez si vous ne savez pas où vous venez de.'*"

St. John gave her long, penetrating look, and then nodded. He'd given countless lectures, reminding his students that in order to know where they were going they had to know where they've come from. "Just who are you?"

Hannah turned on the lower oven, and then tapped the panel to program the temperature. "Have you ever heard of Madame Mignon Chartres?"

St. John had read about Madame Chartres, who ran the most popular sporting house in Storyville before legalized vice was abolished in 1917. "Yes. What about her?"

"Madame Chartres was my maternal grandmother."

St. John looked at Hannah as if she'd just taken leave of her senses. "No!"

She smiled. "Yes. Mignon was the mistress of a very wealthy banker whose wife was unable to have children, so he paid Mignon to give him a child, and in return he set her up in business. Mignon became pregnant, and after giving birth to a daughter, she handed the baby over to her benefactor, who recorded the infant's birth as his and his wife's. That daughter was my mother. She lived in a grand house overlooking Bayou St. John for the first ten years of her life, until her father sold it and moved his family to a townhouse on Esplanade Avenue. My mother did everything she could to overcome the stigma of being the biological daughter of a prostitute, but there were times when I realized she tried too hard."

"How did she find out that her mother was Mignon?"

"Her adoptive mother was a very bitter woman who taunted Clarissa every day of her life that she was going to turn out like Mignon Chartres. After she married Lester DuPont, Clarissa turned her back on the woman who'd raised her, refusing to see her as she lay dying from tuberculosis. However, she did attend her funeral, and there was talk that she spat on her grave."

"Where was your grandfather during this time?"

"He died from a ruptured appendix several months after moving his family into the townhouse. My uncle handled the estate, giving his sister-in-law a monthly allowance to run her household until her death. My mother as the sole heir inherited everything, which made her quite well off. The only thing she craved was respectability, and she got that as a DuPont." A wry smile twisted Hannah's mouth. "Now you know the whole sordid story about who I am and where I came from. Do you still want to have a relationship with a prostitute's granddaughter?"

Closing the distance between them, St. John pulled Hannah close until their bodies were molded from chest to thigh. "What did I tell you about self-deprecation?"

Tilting her chin, she looked up at him. "I do remember you mentioning that. In fact, I remember a lot of things whenever I'm with you."

He studied her face, noticing a sprinkling of freckles over her nose and cheeks that hadn't been there before. "Like what?"

Hannah blinked once. "Like how long it's been since I've enjoyed being with a man."

St. John buried his face in her hair. They were close, close enough for him to feel the runaway beating of her heart against his chest. "What else, sweetheart?"

"How long it's been since I've shared a bed with a man."

He closed his eyes. "Is that really what you want?"

"Yes." The single word was a whisper.

St. John wanted to confess to Hannah that it had been a long time since he'd slept in the same bed with a woman, only to get up and leave once their lovemaking ended. Not once had he ever spent an entire night with any of the women with whom he'd had sex.

He knew what he was going to say would change them forever. Sleeping with Hannah would differ from sleeping with the other women because they would go to bed together and wake up together. "Do you have a carrier for Smokey?"

"Yes. Why?"

"Pack up everything you need for him and yourself for a couple of days, because the McNair B and B is now open for business."

"Are you certain you want a cat in your house?"

St. John kissed Hannah's forehead, then nuzzled her ear. "We dudes have to bond if I'm going to hang out with his auntie. I'm certain after a few beers we'll have a real bromance."

Hannah landed a soft punch to his shoulder. "You will not turn my cousins' cat into a drunk."

"One of my cousins had a pork rind–eating cat that used to knock over beer cans and lap up the residue. He was so tanked that he couldn't move, even if you threatened to step on him."

"That's cruel and inhumane."

"No, it wasn't. He was meaner than a junkyard dog when sober. That damn cat would spring from the floor and go for your face if you attempted to make eye contact with him."

"Is that why you and Smokey have stare-downs? To see if he's going to attack you?"

"Yep."

"You're incorrigible. I can leave Smokey here unless you really want to bring him, because he has an automatic feeder, watering system, and self-cleaning litter box."

"Hot damn! Mr. Smokey is definitely living the high life." St. John kissed Hannah again, this time on the mouth. "Bring him."

Hannah disentangled herself from his arms. "I have to put the mushrooms in the oven or we'll be eating the appetizer along with dinner."

"Are you certain I can't help you with something?"

"You can take out the pitcher of punch I have in the fridge and pour us a couple of glasses." She placed the baking sheet with the stuffed mushrooms on a shelf in the oven with the shortcakes.

St. John opened the refrigerator and found

the glass pitcher, covered with clear plastic wrap, filled with orange, lemon, cherries, and lime slices in a sparkling amber liquid. His gaze lingered on a glass bowl of potato salad and another bowl with shredded romaine.

"Is this rum punch?"

Hannah filled two double old-fashioned glasses with ice. "It's a combination of rum punch and sangria, and because we're going to have prosecco with dinner, I decided to go light on the rum and red wine."

"Who taught you to cook?"

"My mother, my daddy's mother, and a friend's mother, who will remain nameless, because she secretly gave me her award-winning recipes for seafood gumbo, red beans and rice, and jambalaya."

"Is yours as good as hers?"

"It's good, but my jambalaya is missing *lagniappe.*"

"Are you certain?" Hannah nodded. "Why don't you prepare it and let me judge."

"You'll probably be biased because you wouldn't want to hurt my feelings."

St. John filled the glasses with punch. "I promise to tell the truth, the whole truth —"

"I get the picture," she said, laughing.

He handed Hannah a glass. "What are we

toasting this time?"

Hannah touched her glass to his. "The McNair B and B."

Throwing back his head, St. John let out an unrestrained peal of laughter. He could always count on Hannah to make him laugh — something he hadn't done often enough. "The McNair B and B," he repeated, and then took a sip of the sparkling rum punch, his eyebrows lifting when he detected cherry cola on his tongue. "This is really good." He took a long swallow. "In fact, it's excellent."

"I can't take credit for the recipe. I saw it in a cooking magazine and decided to make it because it reminds me of sangria."

Ten minutes later, Hannah removed the shortcakes and placed them on a wire rack to cool, and then removed the mushrooms. She placed them on a plate along with two forks. She claimed she didn't have *lagniappe,* or something extra, but the deliciousness of her stuffed mushrooms exceeded any St. John had ever eaten. The piquant spices were the perfect complement to the sweet tartness of the punch.

"Damn! These are incredible. How did you make them?"

"I stuffed the mushroom caps with minced parsley, garlic, tasso, lemon juice, and pepper sauce. I used panko instead of using soda crackers or bread crumbs for the topping."

St. John shook his head in amazement. "I think it's the ham that gives it a smoky taste." He pointed to the four remaining mushrooms. "You better eat one before I inhale them all."

Hannah patted his arm. "I'm only going to eat two, so you're welcome to the rest."

St. John knew why Hannah didn't want to eat too much; she wanted to save room for the expertly seasoned, fork-tender turkey, scrumptious potato and Caesar salads, and delicious asparagus. He'd thought himself an above-average cook, but she was exceptional. "You missed your calling."

"Why would you say that?" Hannah asked.

"You should've become a chef."

Hannah dabbed her mouth with the napkin. "I never would've made it because I couldn't see myself standing over a hot stove cooking dish after dish on demand. I defrosted and brined the turkey a couple of days ago, and I made the potato salad and mushrooms yesterday. This morning I made the shortcake dough, mixed the strawberries, put together the punch, seasoned the asparagus, and made the dressing for the salad."

Propping an elbow on the table, St. John rested his fist against his cheek. It was apparent she'd planned the dinner well. "What exactly did you do at the investment bank?"

She paused for several seconds. "I was responsible for international contracts. Most of the clients were from outside the United States, so I had to spend a lot of time researching their banking laws."

"Do you miss it?"

Her lids lowered as she stared up at him from under her lashes. "No. Initially I was a little upset because the layoff was so unexpected. But now that I look back, I know they did me a favor. Although I'd filed for the license and permits to turn this place into an inn, I probably wouldn't have actually become an innkeeper until I retired at sixty-seven. And I don't know if I'd want to start a new venture at that age." She pushed back her chair, coming to her feet. "Please don't get up. I'm going to put on a pot of coffee and make the strawberry shortcakes."

St. John also stood up. "I'm going to clear the table and put some of the food away."

"Leave the china, crystal, and silver on the countertop next to the sink. They don't go in the dishwasher."

Reaching for the apron he'd thrown over a stool, St. John slipped it on again. "I'll wash them."

"You don't have to," Hannah said in protest.

"Why not? You cooked, so I'll help clean up."

Hannah decided not to argue with St. John and spoil what had become a most enjoyable encounter. Dinner was leisurely; it was if she and St. John were in no hurry for it to end. She'd silently applauded herself that each dish had come out better than she'd expected.

She stole a sidelong glance at the man standing at the sink washing and rinsing dishes before placing them on a rack to dry, marveling that he appeared so comfortable, and then she remembered he'd told her how he'd helped his arthritic grandmother in the kitchen.

Not only had she been given a second chance at romance, but it was with a man with whom she never would have believed it would happen when they were classmates. Hannah wondered whether, if they hadn't been involved with other people, would they have become romantically involved, married, and had children together? Her life would have been vastly different; instead of moving from base to base, she would have returned from college to marry and live in New Orleans; and her husband would have come home every night, leaving him little or no time to cheat on her.

She tried to suppress a giggle when she tried imagining her mother's reaction if she'd revealed that she'd fallen in love with St. John and planned to marry him. Clarissa probably would have thrown a hissy fit, while her father would have quietly encouraged her to follow her heart.

"What's so funny?" St. John asked.

"I was thinking about my mother."

"What about her?"

"How she would've reacted if I'd come home and told her I was in love with you and we were planning to marry."

Resting a hip against the countertop, St. John dried his hands on a towel. "How would she have reacted?" he questioned after a pregnant silence.

Hannah smiled. "There's no doubt she would've played the quintessential Southern belle. She'd faint dead away, and then she would have taken to her bed and not left it until she became a grandmother."

He gave her a questioning look. "Becoming a grandmother was that important to her?"

"It was all she ever talked about. That's

why she couldn't wait for me to get married. When I look back, I have to admit she was an incredible grandmother."

St. John moved behind Hannah, resting his hands on her shoulders. "I'm certain if we had married, we would've had a couple of kids who would make us grandparents."

Hannah closed her eyes as he pressed his chest against her back. "Our grandbabies would've been spoiled rotten."

"And I'm certain you would've been the guilty one when it came to spoiling them."

She felt a warmth in her chest, her nipples tightening with a rising passion she'd long forgotten. A slight gasp escaped her parted lips when she felt his growing erection against her buttocks. Her breathing quickened as she bit down on her lip to keep from moaning from the pleasurable throbbing settling between her thighs. Hannah feared climaxing as orgasmic tremors flooded her whole being.

St. John was there, and then he wasn't as he released her; she felt his loss almost immediately. She felt as if she'd been taken to the heights of ecstasy but then let down when he pulled out. And the degree to which she'd responded to his touch, his erection, stunned Hannah, while a part of her reveled in the fact she was able to physically arouse him as he did her.

"Let's make a pledge."

His quiet voice broke into her thoughts. "About what?"

"Let's not talk about our past, because we can't change it."

Hannah nodded. She realized she did spend too much time dwelling on and talking about her past, and it was time she let it go. Because she trusted him, she'd revealed things to St. John she'd never have told another person outside her family.

"You're right." Picking up a fork, she cut a piece of the shortcake, extending it to St. John. "Have a taste." His expression said it all. He liked it. She cut a piece for herself, popping it into her mouth. The natural sweetness of the berries and buttery taste of shortcake created an explosion of flavor on her tongue and palate.

St. John took the fork, breaking off another piece, and fed it to Hannah before repeating the action with himself. Within minutes the shortcake was gone, and they stared at each other. "All gone," he drawled, grinning from ear-to-ear.

Hannah's smile matched his. "Should I make another one?"

He pointed to the remaining shortcakes. "Can you save them until later?" She nodded. "If that's the case, then wrap them up. We can have shortcakes instead of beignets for breakfast."

"Speaking of beignets, it's been a while since I've gone to Café du Monde for beignets and café au lait."

Reaching for a towel, St. John carefully dried the silver. "How about pralines?"

"I can't remember."

"Damn, woman, you need to detox from bagels and lox, Nathan's hot dogs, and those big salty pretzels you buy from the New York street carts."

"Is that what you ate when you were in New York?"

St. John winked at her. "You've got that right. When in Rome, do as the Romans, and it's the same when in New York. I'd heard so much about Nathan's hot dogs that I took a long-ass subway ride from Manhattan to Coney Island to sample one."

"Was it worth the ride?"

He made moaning sounds while closing his eyes. "Oh, my goodness. I thought I'd died and gone to hot dog heaven. I ate three, and then ordered another three to take back with me. Folks on the subway either glared or smiled at me when the smell of the grilled dogs wafted through the greasy bag."

Hannah laughed until her eyes filled with tears. As they put away leftovers and finished cleaning up the kitchen, she told St. John about the number of cities she'd made home. She packed a bag for herself and then gathered everything she needed for Smokey as St. John scooped up the kitten and placed him in his carrier.

The blackout had thwarted their previous plans for her to stay over in Marigny, but tonight it would become a reality. Hannah knew that once she returned to DuPont House she wouldn't be the same as when she'd left.

CHAPTER 17

St. John helped Hannah reprogram the automatic devices for Smokey as the kitten lounged on his bed in the laundry room. She'd also brought along his cat tree scratching post with a dangling pompom to keep him occupied.

"I think you should close the door to keep him from wandering into the kitchen. Smokey has the run of the house, but the kitchen is off limits."

"I don't want to keep him confined in a new space, because I want him to feel comfortable being here." St. John reached for Hannah's hand. "Smokey's in bed, and it's time we also go to bed."

He led her out the laundry room, picking up her bag with his free hand, and up the staircase to his bedroom. St. John was more than aware that whatever they'd had was going to change the instant they got into in bed together. He liked Hannah more than he wanted to, yet he was realistic enough to know he could change his head but not his heart. Back in the day he knew she was special, but at that time he refused to acknowledge just how special she'd become.

He thought about her statement with reference to her mother: "How she would've reacted if I'd come home and told her I was in love with you and we were planning to marry." He'd been slightly taken aback by her words, wondering if she'd fantasized about him when he hadn't consciously fantasized about her. It was the height of hypocrisy that although race-mixing was a part of the city's history, it wasn't until 1960 that New Orleans schools were forcibly desegregated by federal marshals.

It had taken forty years for their friendship to develop into a more mature relationship in which they could relate to each other on a level playing field. Both of them had had marriages spanning decades, so they weren't looking for a commitment or a happily ever after.

St. John set her bag on the low wooden bench in an alcove outside the en suite bath. "You can use this bathroom and I'll use the one across the hall." Turning on his heel, he left her staring at his departing back.

He took his time brushing his teeth and

showering so Hannah could ready herself
for bed. Wrapping a towel around his waist,
he entered the bedroom. Hannah lay on her
side, the lightweight blanket pulled up
around her shoulders. It was apparent the
temperature in the room was too cool for
her. She'd turned off the lamp on her side
of the bed and dimmed his. Dropping the
towel on the carpet, he slipped into bed next
to her. There was enough illumination to
see her smile.

"What took you so long?"

Her husky voice swept over him like the
mist coming off the water. "I wanted to give
you time to get into bed."

"I almost fell asleep," she said around a
yawn.

Draping his arm over her waist, St. John
pulled her close. "We don't have to do
anything tonight."

Hannah placed her hand against his face,
her fingernails trailing over the emerging
stubble. "I didn't wait all these years to get
into bed with a man to fall asleep on him."

He laughed softly. "If that's the case, then
you're going to have get rid of the nightgown."

She pressed her mouth to his; he inhaled
her mint-scented breath. "Take it off me."

His eyebrows lifted. It was apparent Hannah liked a little teasing as a prelude to foreplay. And as much as St. John wanted to be inside her, he didn't want to rush their coming together. She'd admitted to having only one sex partner, and although he knew there was no way he could compete with a dead man, he wanted Hannah to begin this chapter of her life with new and lasting memories.

Sitting up, he opened the drawer in the bedside table and removed a condom, placing it on his pillow. Slowly, as if choreographed beforehand, St. John pushed the blanket off Hannah's body and in one fluid motion grasped the hem of the pale-blue cotton nightgown, relieving her of the offending garment. He could never understand why women went to bed wearing clothes when he'd always found them restricting. He didn't even own a pair of pajamas.

His breath caught in his chest when he finally gazed on the lush body that clothes had artfully concealed. There was just enough fullness in her breasts and hips to keep her from being labeled skinny. He cupped one breast and lowered his head, taking the nipple into his mouth and suckling her until she rose slightly off the mattress. His hand inched its way down her belly to search between her legs and instinctively her body arched toward him. Her breathing changed, coming faster, and he removed his hand and explored the curve of her back and hips.

Hannah felt as if she was having an out-of-body experience. St. John's mouth knew exactly where her erogenous zones were as he trailed kisses along the column of her neck, under her armpits, and over her breasts. She wanted to scream at him to take her and end the erotic torment threatening to shatter her into so many pieces she would never be whole again. She wanted to touch him everywhere, to explore his body as he was exploring hers.

She gasped and then bit on her lip to keep from moaning her pleasure when she felt his erection brush her upper thigh. Everything about the man who was to become her lover seeped into her: his smell, the texture of his skin, and his lean, hard body that belied his age. He sat back on his heels, reaching for the condom on the pillow next to hers. Hannah couldn't pull her eyes away from the semi-erect penis hanging heavily between muscled thighs. St. John opened the packet and slipped the latex sheath over his now fully erect penis. He opened her legs to allow him to lie between them as he supported his greater weight on his fore-arms.

His light-brown eyes appeared almost cat-like in the diffused lamplight. She curved her arms around his neck, bringing his head down. His tongue traced the outline of her mouth as her lips parted, their tongues meeting in a sensual duel for domination. Hannah kissed him with a hunger of some-one deprived of food for long periods of time. And she was more than hungry; she was starving from a long-denied desire for sexual fulfillment.

She gloried in the sensation of his maraud-ing mouth searing a path down her neck, shoulders, breasts, belly, and lower to the down covering her pubis. Hannah screamed when his teeth gently nipped her clitoris, holding it captive as she bucked wildly, her fingernails biting into his biceps.

Hannah knew she was losing control and didn't want to come without St. John inside her. "Please," she pleaded shamelessly; her body was on fire. There was heat, followed by wracking chills, and then more heat. St. John answered her plea; holding his hard length in one hand, he positioned his erec-tion at the entrance to her sex. She moaned in pain as he attempted to penetrate her.

"Relax, baby," he crooned in her ear.

She wanted to tell him she was more than relaxed. Raising her legs until the soles of her feet were flat on the mattress, she opened her legs wider, but each time St. John tried to push into her he met resistance. The tears filling her eyes overflowed down her face and into the hair fanning out on the pillow beneath her head.

"I'm so sorry," she whispered over and over.

St. John reversed their positions, his arms going around her waist. "Don't cry, baby. It's been a long time and you're probably very tense."

"I'm not tense," Hannah countered. "I've dried up."

Rubbing her back in a comforting gesture, he pressed a kiss on her hair. "Stop it, Hannah."

She sniffled. "I'm menopausal and one of the side effects is vaginal dryness. If we're going to have a satisfying sex life, then I'm going to have to see my GYN to give me something to —"

"Enough," St. John chided, this time in a stern voice. "Do you think I'm with you because of sex?"

"I don't know."

He laughed softly. "For a supposedly

360

bright woman, you're a little slow when it comes to interpersonal relationships. I'm not eighteen anymore, where having sex with a woman was a priority. I'm lucky that at fifty-eight I'm still able to get it up without taking a pill for ED. I'm with you not only because I like you, but I also enjoy your company. It's been a long time since I've courted a woman, and I'm blessed because you're that woman."

Raising her head, she stared directly at him. Moisture had spiked her lashes. "You're courting me?"

"Dating, wooing, courting. It's all the same to me."

Hannah smiled as a dreamy look crossed her delicate features. "I'm the one who's blessed, because I get to go out with the best-dressed, best-looking, and one of the brightest boys in our graduating class."

"And I get to escort Jackson Memorial class of '77's Ice Princess around town."

She sobered. "Do you believe in destiny, St. John?"

He hesitated, replaying her question. "Not really. There are some things that are destined to be, but then another set of circumstances can come into play to change the course of history."

"Give me an example."

"During the Battle of Gettysburg campaign, General George Meade's victory was marred by his ineffective pursuit of the Confederate Army during the retreat from Gettysburg. If he'd pursued and defeated Lee's Army of the Potomac, the war would've probably ended in 1863 instead of 1865. Does that answer your question?"

"Yes and no. I asked because I believe we were destined to be together. It may have taken forty years, but here we are."

St. John ruffled her hair. "You're right."

He never would have thought all those years ago when he and Hannah shared classes, studied together, and hung out at the dive where high school kids crowded into after home games, they would end up in bed together.

Hannah sighed. "I've told you things I've never mentioned to anyone outside my family because I trust you not to repeat it."

"Are you referring to your mother's birth?"

"Yes. And you're the only one who knows why I left McGehee."

St. John shifted their bodies until they lay face-to-face. "I promise never to repeat it to a living soul," he said, his lips brushing against hers as he spoke.

"I know you planned for us to spend

tomorrow together, but if I can get an appointment with my gynecologist, I'll need you to drop me off home so I can pick up my car."

"Don't worry about that. I'll drive you."

"Are you sure?"

"Very sure." Reaching down, he removed the condom and dropped it on the towel, and then flicked off the lamp. "Now let's try and get some sleep before we both wake up with bags under our eyes."

"You're right. I've lost track of the number of times I've had to put either cucumber slices or tea bag on my eyes to bring down the puffiness."

St. John dropped an arm over her waist. "That's because you don't get enough sleep. Hang out with me and you'll get your requisite eight hours."

"I can't remember the last time I slept that long."

"That's because you probably think too much. Good night, beautiful."

"You're quite the silver-tongued devil. If you're not careful you're going to give me a swelled head."

St. John's right hand cupped her bare buttock. "I'm the only one in this relationship that's allowed to get a swelled head."

Hannah giggled like a little girl as she

363

snuggled closer. "You're a nasty old man."

"And you like this nasty old man, don't you, old lady?"

"Hell, yeah! Good night, darling."

He smiled. "Good night, sweetheart."

Hannah shrugged out of the dressing gown, dropping it into the bin for used gowns. It had taken five days before she could get an appointment with her local GYN, and only after the receptionist called to say a patient had cancelled.

The past five days had been enlightening for her and Smokey. The kitten had adjusted to his new surroundings as if it were his home. Most times he could be found curled up on St. John's desk, bonding with the man who'd accused the kitten of giving him the stink-eye. Initial curiosity segued into a close bond between man and feline.

The bond between her and the man under whose roof she'd spent the past five nights was also cemented, giving her a glimpse into what their lives would have been like if they had married. As promised, he made certain she got enough sleep.

They went to bed after watching the late night news and didn't get out of bed until seven the following morning, St. John reminding her she didn't have to get up at five to meet Leticia to jog or walk when she didn't have to leave the house to work out.

They took turns preparing meals, and he spoke French to her more than ninety percent of the time. She was still slow in responding, with the excuse she was a work in progress. St. John's library contained a cornucopia of reading material, including best-selling novels, nonfiction books on history and political science, biographies, literary, travel, news magazines, and the classics in the English and French languages.

She spent most of her time in the sunroom reading, watching cooking shows, and listening to music whenever St. John retreated to his office for several hours to work on his research project. The sunroom had also become their ballroom where he taught her the foxtrot, jive, and samba. She became the dance instructor as she guided him through the steps for the waltz.

Inasmuch as Hannah didn't want to compare her relationship with St. John with what she'd shared with Robert, she failed miserably. As a career military officer, her husband had moved from base to base, and as a result he was physically absent. It was something she'd prepared for. However, whenever he returned he was emotionally distant with her, while lavishing all his attention on their son. In the end she'd come to accept the personality trait, which made Commander Robert Lowell a highly regarded and decorated naval officer.

Even when they weren't in the same room, she felt a tangible connection with St. John. And whether sharing a meal, the bed, or dancing together, they were in sync physically and emotionally.

St. John had hinted of her naïveté with men and Hannah had to agree with him. She'd come of age during the sexual revolution; however, it had passed her by. What hadn't passed her by was her achieving her dream of becoming an attorney. When she entered law school as a first-year student, the national average enrollment for women was thirty-nine percent as compared to sixty percent for men.

Once she graduated, she found the task of finding a position more difficult than passing the bar. She finally secured a position with a small San Diego firm handling personal injury cases. It was only after passing the New York State Bar, circulating her résumé, and after three interviews, that she was hired by a prominent law firm to work in their contracts department. And that was where she found her niche.

Hannah was given the responsibility of

reading contracts and identifying inconsistencies on the first pass. The second and third pass turned up more inconsistencies that were hidden in subsequent clauses most attorneys would overlook or were unable to discern. She'd become an expert cryptographer with an uncanny ability to decode legalese cipher. All in all, she was content how her life had unfolded as wife, mother, and attorney.

She finished putting on her street clothes and walked into the doctor's office.

The elderly doctor's head popped up. "Please sit down, Mrs. Lowell."

"Thank you, Dr. Aaronson." All he needed was a beard and he could easily pass for Santa Claus.

He folded heavily veined hands together. "I've examined you and everything looks good. You're not due for another pap and mammogram until the end of the year, so what's bothering you?"

Hannah chewed her inner lip. "I . . . I'm experiencing pain during intercourse."

"Most women by the age of fifty experience some menopausal vaginal dryness. I'm going to give you a couple of samples of a hormone-free cream that will protect your delicate tissue from friction and inflammation. I recommend this one because it doesn't contain alcohol or dyes and is free of fragrances, parabens, and glycerin."

"Do I have to concern myself with it seeping out?"

"No, Mrs. Lowell. It's not runny or sticky. I'm going to caution you to relax before engaging in sex, because emotional factors such as stress and anxiety can inhibit sufficient blood flow to the area." He picked up the phone and spoke quietly into the mouthpiece. "The nurse at the front desk will give you the samples."

Rising to her feet, Hannah shook hands with the doctor. "Thank you. I'll see you in December."

He stood up. "No, you won't. I'm retiring at the end of October. My son and granddaughter will take over the practice."

"I'm going to miss you."

He affected a sad smile. "I'm going to miss all my patients."

Hannah left the office and made her way to the reception desk where a nurse handed her a small plastic shopping bag. She dropped it into her tote. "Thank you."

She rode the elevator to the ground floor parking lot. St. John had promised to wait for her and drive her back to DuPont House so she could open the house for the cleaning service. She would have put off having them come if she wasn't expecting Jasmine, Nydia, Tonya, and her daughter to arrive the following week. St. John drove up, and she got into the car before he could get out and assist her.

Leaning over, he brushed a kiss over her mouth. "How did it go?"

"It was good. The doctor gave me a lubricant and told me to relax."

"Isn't that what I've been telling you?"

"I am relaxed."

"You weren't before you started living with me."

Hannah wanted to deny they were living together. Spending five days at his house didn't translate into living together. Giving up her permanent residence to move in with him meant she would also give up her independence — something she wasn't quite ready to do. She liked having the option of staying or leaving or deciding where she was willing to sleep.

St. John maneuvered out of the parking lot. "I just got a text from Madame Duarte before you came down. The studio will reopen Monday. So don't forget to bring your dancing shoes and that sexy little outfit that shows off your long, incredible legs when you come back home."

Slumping against the leather seat, Hannah

closed her eyes. She was no longer the blushing ingénue whenever he complimented her. "When I checked into the McNair B and B, I thought it would only be for a few days. Are you extending my stay beyond a week?"

"Your stay is open-ended. You can leave whenever you want."

She opened her eyes, unable to see his eyes behind the lenses of a pair of sunglass. "I'll have to leave once my friends arrive."

"How many are you expecting?"

"Four. That includes my friend's daughter."

"There's enough room at the B and B if they want to stay with us."

"Thanks, but no thanks, St. John. I'm not about to flaunt my relationship with you to my friends."

His jaw tightened. "Are you ashamed to be seen with me?"

"No, I am not." Hannah enunciated each word. "And I'm insulted you would even utter those words."

"Then, what is it, sweetheart? Cat got your tongue," St. John taunted when she hesitated.

"No! I just don't want them trying to hit on my man."

St. John's expression mirrored unadulterated innocence. "Am I your man?"

"Why are you testing me? Of course you're my man. If you weren't, do you think I'd allow you to put your face between my legs?"

St. John hadn't penetrated her but had used oral sex to bring her to climax. She was shocked and awed by his response to her performing fellatio on him. She realized the power she yielded over a man for the first time in her life.

He rested a hand on her knee, squeezing it gently. "I like it when you talk dirty."

She smiled. "I'll show you real dirty when I get home tonight."

"I'm scared, baby." St. John removed his hand. "It's Friday and date night. Where do you want to go?"

"Would you mind if we don't leave Marigny Triangle?" St. John's home was located in the trendy area of Faubourg Marigny, and Hannah wanted to spend the night in a neighborhood less spirited than the Upper French Quarter.

"Have you ever been to Three Muses?"

"No."

"I've been there many times, and I'm sure you'd enjoy it."

Hannah had begun to compile of list of venues she wanted to take her former coworkers to. If they were willing to drive more than thirteen hundred miles to visit her, then she had to make certain to show them a rollicking good time.

St. John dropped her off at DuPont House, waiting until she'd unlocked the front door. He held her face between his hands. "What time should I expect you?"

Her gaze lingered on his strong jaw. "Six. I'll change here to save time."

"Dress casually and wear comfortable shoes because I plan on us walking to Frenchmen Street." St. John lowered his head and caressed her mouth with a tender kiss. *"Je te verrai plus tard, chérie."*

"I'll see you later," she replied in English.

Anchoring the straps of the tote over her shoulder, Hannah closed the door and climbed the staircase to her bedroom. It felt odd not to have Smokey greet her at the door. She wanted to call him a traitor before reminding herself Smokey wasn't her cat but Paige and LeAnn's.

She'd just entered her bedroom when her cell phone rang. Searching into the depths of the tote, she retrieved it. "Hello."

"Let me be the first to congratulate you, Miss Innkeeper."

Her body felt weightless as she sank down to the window seat. "You did it, Cameron."

"No, Hannah, you did it. I just made a call to speed up the process. I was told you'd also submitted an application for an eating establishment and they're going to approve that, too. You should receive official notification sometime next week."

Hannah's heart was beating so fast she feared fainting. "How can I thank you?"

"Go out with me."

"Are you talking about celebrating over dinner?"

"We can begin with that, and go from there."

Euphoria was suddenly replaced with uneasiness. Had he used his influence to fast-track the permits and license as an ulterior motive to get her to go out with him? "I'll have dinner with you, but it can't go any further, because I'm involved with someone."

There came a swollen pause before Cameron said, "Does he live in New York?"

"No. He lives here."

"Are you at liberty to divulge the name of my rival for your affections?"

Hannah chewed her lip as she debated whether to tell him that she was seeing St. John. After several seconds she decided to be forthcoming. "St. John McNair."

Cameron paused again. "The professor

over at Barden College?"

"Yes. Does that surprise you?"

"Yes and no. Yes, because I didn't think he would be your type, and no, because I can see why women would be attracted to him."

Hannah's temper flared. "What the hell do you mean by *my type*?"

"Don't get upset, Hannah. I didn't mean it like that."

"Like what, Cameron!?"

"I —"

"Look," she said, cutting him off. "Let's end this topic before we say something we'll both later regret. However, I'm still open to having that celebratory dinner."

"Forget the dinner, Hannah, because I was hoping it would lead to something else."

She smiled for the first time since answering the call. "What you need is to find a woman with whom to settle down and have a couple of babies before you're eligible for Medicare." Soft chuckles caressed her ear.

"I would if I can find that woman. Do you happen to have any lady friends who'd be interested in a slightly used investment banker who'll treat them like a queen?"

"If you're treating them like they are queens, then why aren't you committed to at least one of them?"

"They all wanted to get married."

"And you're not?"

"No. I saw what marriage did to my parents, and I want no part of that."

Hannah paused. "I've never been a match-maker."

"Are you saying you have someone in mind?"

She thought about Jasmine, wondering if the divorcée would be amenable to seeing the attractive investment banker during her stay. "I'm not going to promise anything, but I just might invite you out to the house to meet some of my friends who're coming from out of town. It'll be informal, so leave your handmade Italian suit in the closet."

"Maybe I need to see someone from out of town."

"That's because you've dated so many women that the word's out that Cameron Singleton is a player."

"That's cold, Hannah."

"It's true and you know it. And thanks again for helping me get the approval for the licenses and permits."

"No problem. Talk to you soon."

Hannah ended the call and kicked up her feet as she'd done as child when something made her happy. It had happened. She was going to become an innkeeper. The news couldn't have come at a better time. Now that she knew she going to turn the guesthouses into restaurants, she planned to ask Tonya if she would be willing to run them.

Slipping off the window seat, she danced around the room like a whirling dervish until dizziness forced her to stop. She'd projected that a year from now DuPont House would open for business as the DuPont Inn, offering lodging, dining, and entertainment for locals and out-of-towners. Hannah made a mental note to call the architect for him to draw up plans for the restaurant and supper club, and the engineer to ascertain whether she would be able to install an elevator.

Everything in her life was falling into place. She'd cemented a relationship with a man who made her feel what it meant to be born female, and she was going to embark on a new business venture to which she planned to give one hundred ten percent. Life wasn't just good. It was unbelievably fantastic.

CHAPTER 18

St. John smiled when he saw Hannah get out of her car. Missing was the sophisticated woman dressed to the nines and in its place was an ingénue who reminded him of a high school coed with her hair secured in a ponytail and her bare face with just a hint of lip color. A white man-tailored blouse, white skinny jeans with turned-up cuffs, and blue-and-white pinstriped espadrilles completed her casual look.

She held her arms out at her sides. "Am I casual enough?"

He caught her hands, leaning in and pressing his mouth to the column of her scented neck. "You're perfect. By the way, how many man-tailored blouses do you have?"

"Last count was a dozen. They're my go-to blouse to pair with skirts, slacks, and suits. It looks as if we were both on the same wavelength when choosing our outfits."

St. John nodded. He'd opted to wear a white golf shirt with a pair of matching linen slacks and navy-blue deck shoes. "We look as if we're dressed for sailing."

"Speaking of sailing, I plan to take my friends on a paddleboat dinner cruise."

Tucking her hand into the bend of his elbow, he started walking in the direction of Frenchmen Street. "How long do they plan to stay?"

"I'm not sure. The last text I got from Tonya she said they'll be here through the Fourth."

"Don't forget they're welcome to come to my family reunion."

"I'll let them know. I got good news this afternoon."

He gave her a sidelong glance. Her smile said it all. "You were approved for the inn."

"Yes. The mayor's office approved the permits and licenses for the inn and the restaurants. As soon as I receive the official documents, it's game on."

"You should've called me earlier. We could've celebrated back at the house."

Hannah came to an abrupt stop, causing St. John to stumble before regaining his balance. "Celebrate how?"

"Prepare something on the grill and eat in the garden."

She took a step, bringing them within inches of each other. "We can still do it."

St. John successfully hid a smile behind an impassive expression. He'd suggested going out because they'd spent so much time at home. He'd enjoyed every second they were together preparing meals together, sitting and listening to music, discussing the events of the local and national news, and dancing together.

It was when they retired for bed that he felt most complete: going to sleep with her beside him and waking up to find her next to him. Most times they'd lie together holding hands without talking. It had become their time to communicate without words, each lost in their own private thoughts. Though he didn't want to think about his failed marriage, he found it hard not to make the comparison between Lorna and Hannah.

St. John knew it wasn't fair to his ex-wife to think of how different his life would have been if he hadn't married her. It wasn't fair because of what she'd had to go through as a child, what she had to endure and never talked about. Horrific stories she hadn't been able to reveal until she found the strength to face her demons.

He enjoyed everything there was about

Hannah: her determination, intelligence, and maturity, while despite her revelation that she'd only had one sex partner, he found her open to experimenting with different positions and practices to bring them ultimate satisfaction.

Bringing her left hand to his mouth, he kissed the back of it. "Let's go home."

Lying between St. John's legs on the lounger, Hannah closed her eyes, reveling in the peace she hadn't experienced enough in her life. They'd exchanged their white attire for shorts and tees. A number of multi-wicked citronella candles in glazed ceramic bowls made the garden appear ethereal, reminding her of the illustrations in books of fairy tales she'd read as a child.

The garden had been meticulously designed to provide for optimum privacy from neighbors and/or prying eyes with a solid oak door cut into a wall of ivy, which when opened revealed an expansive pergola covered with cypress, Artemisia, and English ivy. It was the picture-perfect setting for a private party with nature's decoration of shade trees, hedges, and flower beds. Tiny white lights intertwined in tree branches reminded her of the trees lining Fifth Avenue during the Christmas season. She inhaled the refreshing scent of citrus, cassis, and aromatic bamboo lingering in the humid night air.

"Let me know when you're ready to go in."

Hannah opened her eyes. The night was perfect for sleeping under the stars. "We can go inside once the candles burn out."

"That's not going to be for a long time. The candles have a seventy-five-hour burn time."

"That's more than three days."

St. John kissed her ear. "That's why I bought them. Each one is filled with eleven pounds of hand-poured wax."

"That's why they're so heavy." It had taken her more fifteen minutes to light eight seventeen- and twelve-wick candles. "How much do they cost?"

"More than two hundred dollars."

Hannah sat up. "Each?"

St. John wrapped an arm under her breasts, bringing her to lie against him once again. "Yes."

"You spent nearly two thousand dollars on candles?"

"I really don't need you to watch my bank account, Mrs. Lowell."

Pinpoints of heat pricked Hannah's cheeks with his biting comeback. In other words,

St. John had told her to mind her business where it concerned his finances. "Point taken."

St. John buried his face in her hair. "I'm sorry, sweetheart. I didn't mean for it to come out like that."

"It's all right. I was out of line."

He shifted her until she straddled his lap and they faced each other. "Let's not spoil the evening by going for each other's throats. The only thing I'm going to say about my net worth is that I'm not indigent."

The small, private, and prestigious college paid him quite well, and not only had his aunt willed him her house and surrounding property but also half her estate, the remaining half going to his sister. His music teacher aunt had held out selling her benefactor's fishing business until someone met her price. In the end it took four fishermen to form a consortium to give her the astronomical figure she sought.

Hannah leaned into him and then brushed a kiss over his mouth. "You're right. The weather, the dinner, and the man I'm beginning to like a little too much are all perfect."

St. John had to agree with her. He'd used the outdoor kitchen to grill chicken, which he'd topped with a corn and black bean salsa. Hannah continued to amaze him with her cooking skills when she made a batch of fried green tomatoes and bananas foster for dessert.

"Have you thought that maybe this man is more than fond of a certain woman who continually shows me up with her cooking skills?"

"Is that what you think, St. John? That I'm competing with you in the kitchen?"

A teasing smile tilted the corners of his mouth. "I do."

"Well, I'm not. I like to cook. And now that I don't have a day job, I try experimenting with different dishes."

"I still say you missed your calling. You're a natural in the kitchen."

Hannah rested her head on his shoulder. "You're so good for a woman's ego."

"I don't compliment you to boost your ego, babe." He splayed his hands over her back. "I only speak the truth."

"I do remember you saying you'll never lie to me."

He nodded. "Never have and never will."

Hannah trailed light kisses along the side of his neck at the same time she moved her hips back and forth over his groin. St. John breathed out an audible gasp when he hardened so quickly he suddenly felt light-headed.

"Shit!" The curse had exploded from his mouth.

She went completely still. "Did I hurt you?"

St. John's hands slipped under her tee and covered her breasts. "You tease!" he rasped in her ear. "You knew exactly what you were doing."

Hannah's hands were just as busy as his when she lifted her hips to undo the button on the waistband of St. John's shorts. "What's the matter, darling? You've never had a lap dance?"

Throwing back his head, he swallowed a groan. Pushing her hands away, he unzipped his fly to release his erection. Everything became a blur when he relieved Hannah of her shorts and underwear. Pressing her down to the lounger, he held his penis in one hand and slowly eased himself inside her, not meeting the unyielding resistance that had prevented him from penetrating her before. Mindful of how long it had been since she'd slept with a man, he didn't want to do anything that would cause her pain and lingering discomfort.

Her gasps, one overlapping the other, escalated as her tight flesh stretched to accommodate his sex. St. John froze. He was only in halfway. "Do you want me to stop?" He asked Hannah the question, though it was the last thing he wanted to do. Her feminine heat, the lingering scent of her perfume, and her tight vagina made him feel as if he were losing his mind.

Hannah shook her head because it was impossible for her to speak. She'd used the lubricant, and although it made it easier for St. John to penetrate her, there was still some resistance. Taking deep breaths, she forced herself to relax, and within seconds the pain eased, replaced by pleasure. "No," she finally breathed when she'd regained her voice.

She surrendered to his touch as his hands traced a sensual path down her ribs and hips. He didn't rush, taking his time arousing her until she writhed in an age-old rhythm she didn't have to be taught. The passion and love she felt for St. John pounded the blood through her head and heart. He quickened his thrusts, Hannah following his lead. Heat surged through her like an electric current, and then it happened. Waves of ecstasy washed over her with the first orgasm; it was quickly followed by another and then another until she gasped for air when she felt her lungs exploding.

A deep, abiding feeling of peace entered her being as St. John collapsed heavily on her body. She welcomed his weight. Hannah closed her eyes, smiling. She was now able to acknowledge what she'd denied for years: She was and always had been in love with St. John. The feeling of euphoria was suddenly replaced with fear. They'd just made love without using protection, and Hannah couldn't even begin to imagine herself pregnant at fifty-eight. She wanted him to get off her but loathed him pulling out, because she wanted to revel in their oneness as long as possible.

"St. John?"

"What is it, sweetheart?"

"Even though I'm menopausal, there is still the possibility of my getting pregnant."

"That's not going to happen."

"It's not going to happen because you say so?" she asked.

"It's impossible because I've had a vasectomy. When Lorna said she didn't want children, I underwent the procedure to make certain not to get her pregnant."

Hannah did not want to believe St. John loved his wife so much he would give up all hope of fathering a child. If Lorna didn't want children, then why hadn't she undergone a tubal ligation?

"Now I know what you meant you said you don't miss what you've never had."

St. John pressed a kiss under Hannah's ear. He hadn't lied to her. Once Lorna revealed she didn't want children, he decided if he had the procedure, then she would allow him to make love to her. But it didn't happen, and he didn't blame her but himself for the realization that nothing he could do or say would permit them to live together as a normal couple.

The first time he slept with another woman, he moved out of their bedroom and subsequently moved back after he heard her crying because she believed he'd abandoned her. They continued to share the same bed, he holding her in his arms every night until she fell asleep. He'd sinned, repented, and was now redeemed. The woman in whose scented embrace he lay had come to him when he hadn't known whether he would ever have a normal relationship with a woman.

Burying his face in the area between Hannah's neck and shoulder, he planted a kiss there. "You're a wicked woman who should be rated X."

She giggled. "Why?"

"You have me out here with my shorts down around my ankles making love to you where anyone flying low enough can see my naked ass."

She ran a hand over his hair. "It's too dark for anyone to see anything, and don't forget that I'm also butt-naked."

He nuzzled her ear with his nose. "I think we'd better go in now or we'll end up sleeping out here." Hannah issued a moan of protest when he pulled out of her warmth. He slipped off the lounger and pulled up his shorts. "I'll go in after I put out the candles."

Making love with her had been more than pleasurable. St. John never had to guess whether she'd faked her responses because he'd been with enough women to know when they were feigning passion. And the emotion he experienced penetrating her without the barrier of latex was indescribable.

Hannah slipped into her panties, and then her shorts. "Are you certain I can't help you?"

Resting his hands at her waist, St. John kissed her forehead. "Yes." He patted her backside. "I'll be in later."

"I'm going to shower and then go to bed."

He watched the gentle sway of her hips as

she walked along a flagstone path in the garden that led past the outdoor kitchen to a side door to the house. He never could have imagined when he exchanged cell phone numbers with Hannah that they would rekindle their friendship and become lovers.

St. John knew the more time he spent with Hannah, the more he wanted to spend with her. She'd hinted that her friends were arriving soon, which would allow him the space he needed to assess where his life with her was headed. His thoughts lingered on the woman whose spontaneity sparked uninhibitedness of which he hadn't believed himself capable.

He smiled as he extinguished all the candles, and then flipped several switches on an electrical outlet inside the door to turn off the tiny lights threaded through tree branches, plunging the garden into total darkness.

Smokey greeted him, rubbing against his legs as he walked into the laundry room. Whenever he sat at his computer, the cat would jump up and curled into a ball on the corner of the workstation and go to sleep as sun poured in through the window. The one time Smokey sprang up on the bed, Hannah issued an ultimatum: her or the cat. He'd accused her of being overdramatic until she revealed her son's wife's propensity for allowing their menagerie to share their sons' beds. However, he did get her to compromise. If Smokey soiled the bed, then he would be banished for life. Smokey hadn't soiled the bed, but was content to curl up at the foot and sleep until dawn.

He scratched the cat behind his ears. "As soon I take a shower, you can come to bed." Smokey meowed as if he understood what he was saying, following him up the staircase and into his bedroom, where he sprang up to the foot of the bed. Hannah stirred but didn't wake up.

St. John stripped off his clothes, leaving them in a wicker hamper, and then stepped into the shower stall. Ten minutes later he turned off the lamp and slipped into bed. Resting his head on folded arms, he closed his eyes. He didn't want to think about how quickly he'd become accustomed to having Hannah sleep beside him and how much he loved making love with her. What he refused to allow himself was to confuse sex with love. Sex was something he could get from other women, while sleeping with Hannah was different from other women.

Lowering his arms, he turned on his side

and pressed his chest to Hannah's back. They lay like spoons, his breathing deepening until he finally fell asleep.

Hannah came down off the porch as the gleaming white Denali pulled up in front of the house. It had taken her friends two days to drive from New York to New Orleans. They'd called to report they were spending Monday night in Louisville, Kentucky, before starting out for the second leg of their trip.

She'd spent the entire weekend with St. John, not returning home until earlier that morning. They'd resumed their dance lessons; she told him that her friends could entertain themselves for the couple of hours while they were at the studio. St. John compromised only if she agreed not to take Smokey back to DuPont House. It was her turn to give Smokey the stink-eye for being a defector. It had taken the cat exactly one week to transfer his loyalty from her to St. John.

They made love again — this time without any resistance or pain. Never had she experienced such an overwhelming feeling of complete satisfaction as she did from St. John's raw sensuality. The multiple orgasms she experienced with him took her beyond herself. It had been ten years since she'd shared her body with a man, and Hannah was glad she'd waited for him. The soft-spoken, quiet, intelligent boy had matured into a soft-spoken, sexy man whom she could not get enough of. She'd denied being in love with him at eighteen, but if anyone were to ask her at fifty-eight how she felt about him, she would hard-pressed to deny being in love with him.

There were occasions when she'd wanted to blurt out she was in love with him, yet she couldn't get up the courage to make the passionate confession. Hannah knew St. John liked her, enjoyed being with her, but he hadn't given any indication he wanted to take their current relationship further. They had committed to seeing each other over the summer but nothing beyond that. St. John would return to the college, while her involvement in transforming her personal residence into a place of business would take up most of her waking hours. Her projected date for the grand opening was late January or early February — two weeks before the start of Mardi Gras.

She no longer agonized whether the licenses and permits would be approved, which had lessened most of her stress. Now she could relax and become the consummate hostess for her out-of-town guests. Unknowingly, they were to become the untested subjects for whether she had the wherewithal to own and operate an inn.

The doors to the SUV opened and Jasmine, Tonya, Nydia, and a young woman whom Hannah assumed was Tonya's daughter got out. Arms outstretched, she hugged each woman. "I'm Hannah," she said, introducing herself to Tonya's daughter, who was a younger, slimmer version, sans the dimples, of her mother.

"I'm Samara. Thank you for inviting me to your beautiful home."

Hannah smiled over Samara's shoulder at Tonya. "You're welcome to come any time you want."

Tonya ran a hand over her forehead. "Watch what you say, because it may come to bite you on the behind. My daughter just might take you up on your invitation and descend on you with a hoard of friends who'll eat you out of house and home."

Hannah shook her head. "That will never happen, because we keep enough food on hand to feed several football teams. Speaking of food, I've prepared dinner, but I know you're going to want to freshen up before we sit down to eat. Bring your bags in and I'll show you to your rooms. Jasmine, please give me your key fob and I'll drive your truck around to the garage." Searching in her bag, Jasmine handed her the fob.

"The Big Easy agrees with you, Hannah," Tonya said, smiling. "You're like the girl from Ipanema: 'tall and tan.' "

Hannah patted her hips over a pair of cropped jeans. "Bless you for not mentioning I've put on a few pounds."

Jasmine waved her hand in dismissal. "It's about time you got some booty. Why should you be any different from the rest of us?"

Nydia ran a hand through her curly hair. "I can't believe the size of this place. It's like freakin' *Gone with the Wind.*"

"Word," whispered Samara, as she took her bag out of the cargo area.

Once everyone had their bags, Hannah led the way up the porch. "You're welcome to use the washer and dryer if you run out of clean clothes."

Jasmine stopped in the entryway. "Holy shit!"

Hannah turned. "What's the matter?"

"Are these chairs really antiques, or are they incredible reproductions?"

"They're antiques." She smiled. "I forgot you were an interior decorator in your former life."

Jasmine returned Hannah's smile. "If I

don't get another position as a human resources specialist, then I'm going back to decorating."

"Don't do anything until I talk to you. After dinner I'd like to talk to all of you about something."

Tonya lifted her eyebrows. "Why are you being so mysterious?"

Hannah debated whether to wait or tell them her good news now. She decided to tell them. "I'm going to turn this house into an inn."

"Don't you mean a B and B?" Jasmine asked.

"It won't actually be a bed-and-breakfast. I'll explain everything over dinner. Now come so I can show you your bedrooms."

Hannah stood outside a bedroom suite on the first floor. "Tonya, you are here, and Samara, you're across the hall from your mother." She stopped at the next suite. "Jasmine, you're here and Nydia is across the hall. Each of you will have your own bathroom. In the event you've forgotten something, you'll find a supply of toiletries in wicker baskets on a shelf under the table." She glanced at her watch. It was ten minutes after five. "Will everyone be ready to eat at six?"

"Yes!" they all chorused.

Turning on her heel, Hannah left to drive the massive SUV around to the back of the house near the garages. Now she knew why Jasmine's ex had fought so hard to keep the SUV. It was a dream to drive.

She returned to the house through the side door and made her way into the kitchen. She'd decided to prepare traditional Southern and New Orleans dishes as a celebratory welcome to the Big Easy. Preparing meals with St. John had resurrected her urge to go through several binders filled with recipes passed down through the generations. She'd rewritten Mrs. Bouie's recipes for jambalaya, red beans and rice, and seafood gumbo on index cards in the tin box she kept in a desk drawer in the kitchen alcove.

She'd just finished setting the table when Tonya walked in. She'd changed into a cotton sundress that showed off her toned arms. In that instant Hannah envied the chef's flawless henna-brown complexion, wondering if she'd ever had a pimple or blackhead. Her curly twists were long enough to graze her jawline.

Tonya smiled, twin dimples flashing in her cheeks. "It's amazing what a shower can do to rejuvenate one's mind and body." She glanced around the kitchen. "I'm with

Nydia. This house does remind me of Tara from *Gone with the Wind*. And I could do serious cooking in this kitchen. It's about half the size of my apartment."

Hannah grasped Tonya's hand, leading her to sit on the stools at the cooking island. "Please sit down, because I have to talk to you before the others get here."

Tonya blinked slowly, her dark brown eyes meeting Hannah's. "What about?"

"You already know I'm going to turn this house into an inn. There are two guesthouses on the property. One will eventually become a café exclusively for inn guests and the other a small supper club open to the public. I want to know if you'd be amenable to becoming an investor."

"What do I get out of it if I decide to invest?"

"After you recoup your initial investment, I'm willing to offer you twenty-five percent of all proceeds from the entire business, and that include fees from room rates. Hypothetically if we clear three hundred thousand at the end of a fiscal year, then you'd get seventy-five thousand."

Tonya appeared deep in thought. "What about a salary?"

"You'll be paid a nominal salary that will increase in increments of ten percent each year until you earn back your investment. After that we'll negotiate a salary commensurate with your experience."

"I don't know, Hannah. It sounds nice, but I'm not ready to move from New York."

Hannah wanted to ask her if there was something or someone preventing her from relocating. "I know you can make a lot more money as a chef in New York, but if you do decide to move here, you'll live here, which offsets your having to sell a kidney to rent a halfway decent apartment in New York City."

"Tell me about it," Tonya whispered. "I don't want to tell you what I'm paying to rent a two-bedroom in a renovated East Harlem walk-up."

"Girl, please," Hannah drawled. "You don't have to tell me. Even before I moved to New York ten years ago the rents were prohibitive."

Throwing back her head, Tonya laughed. "You sounded like a sister-girl when you said, 'girl, please.'"

A slight frown appeared between Hannah's eyes. "Maybe that's because there are sister-girls in my family tree."

Tonya sobered. "Really?"

She nodded. "Yes. The first DuPont woman who was the mistress of this house was a Haitian mulatto."

"No shit!"

Hannah smiled. "Yes shit! I'll tell you later about the illustrious and colorful DuPonts."

"Are you going to invite Nydia and Jasmine to come in with you?"

"I plan to broach the subject with them. If they agree, then Nydia can handle all finances and Jasmine will be responsible for hiring and background checks. Jasmine will also assist me with all things that pertain to personnel." Hannah stood up. "Where are my manners? I've been running off at the mouth and you're probably thirsty."

"Do you need help with anything?" Tonya asked.

"No thanks. Is your daughter over twenty-one?"

"Yes. She turned twenty-one last month. Why?"

"I'm going to make one of New Orleans's signature cocktails. I can only have a hurricane if I'm at home because it makes me very sleepy."

Tonya stood up. "Something smells good. What are you cooking?"

"Red beans. We usually serve them over rice with fried chicken, grilled ham, or oysters en brochette. I prefer chaurice, which is a Creole hot sausage grilled to order and placed atop the beans."

"If I'm going to run your café and supper club, then I have to familiarize myself with Creole and Cajun cuisine."

Hannah successfully bit back a grin. Tonya had voiced the possibility of running the inn's eating establishments. "It's all in the seasonings, Tonya."

"What's on tonight's menu?"

Opening the refrigerator, Hannah removed several limes from the vegetable drawer. "I decided on a buffet: red beans and rice, tasso shrimp, chicken livers with bacon and pepper jelly, fried green tomatoes, and hot garlic filet mignon for those who want red meat."

"It sounds as if you've gone through a lot of work."

"Not really," Hannah admitted. "I've prepped everything beforehand. The only task left is frying the tomatoes and grilling the shrimp, chicken livers, and steak."

"What if I step in as your sous chef?" Tonya asked. "I can't stand around and watch other folks cook without getting involved."

Hannah knew if she could get Tonya interested in learning to cook the regional dishes, then perhaps she would consider coming to work for her. "Okay." She handed her an apron from a stack in a drawer under the countertop, and then took one for herself. "You can fry the tomatoes, while I grill the shrimp, livers, and steak. But first let me get the ingredients for the hurricane." Opening an overhead cabinet, she took out bottles of light and dark rum and passion fruit syrup.

"Hey-y-y-y," Nydia crooned as she walked into the kitchen. "This place is so big I got lost trying to find the kitchen."

"What are we drinking?" Jasmine asked. She was several steps behind Nydia.

"Hurricanes." Hannah turned on the radio on the countertop and the kitchen was filled with slow jams from the nineties.

Samara rushed into the kitchen. Like Nydia and Jasmine, she'd changed out of her jeans into a tank top, shorts, and flip-flops. "What did I miss?"

"Nothing, Miss Slow Poke," Tonya said to her daughter.

Samara rolled her eyes upward. "Are you cooking, Mom?"

"No. I'm helping Hannah."

Samara sniffed the air. "Wow! Something smells good."

"That's Hannah's red beans."

"I know I'm going to gain at least ten pounds before we leave here," Jasmine said.

"What's the city motto?"

"Laissez le bon temps rouler!" Hannah said in French. "Let the good times roll!"

Jasmine smiled. "That's it. I intend to party so hard I'll have to go to one of those retreats in the desert to recover."

Hannah slipped on her apron. "I have a few places I'd like to take you while you're here. I didn't plan anything for this coming Saturday because we're invited to a friend's family reunion."

Nydia gave Hannah a questioning look. "Why are we invited?"

"Because you're my guests."

"Hush up, Nydia," Tonya chastised, "and try to be gracious.

Hannah quickly measured the ingredients for a hurricane into a cocktail shaker with cracked ice. She gave it a vigorous shake, strained it into a chilled glass, and then handed it to Nydia. "This will definitely put you in a mellow mood." She repeated the action another four times until everyone held a glass.

"What are we toasting?" Nydia asked when Hannah raised her glass.

She smiled at the young accountant. "To new beginnings." Hannah took a sip of the chilled cocktail, meeting Tonya's eyes over the rim.

Jasmine's eyelids fluttered. "What are we starting?"

"I'll tell you after we sit down to eat."

CHAPTER 19

Hannah waited until everyone had eaten before she told them more about her new venture as an innkeeper and her hope they'd become investors. And judging from the expressions on Nydia and Jasmine's faces, she saw their indecision.

"You know this means we'll have to live here?" Nydia questioned.

She nodded. "What I need you to do can't be accomplished if you live in New York."

Jasmine drained her glass. "I'm with Nydia. I'm going to have to think about it." She stared at Tonya. "What about you, Tonya? You haven't said a word."

"I haven't said a word because I'm still thinking."

"What about Darius, Mom?" Samara asked.

Tonya glared at her daughter. "What about him? We're not married, nor are we joined at the hip."

Jasmine gave Tonya a sidelong glance. "You're involved with someone?"

Tonya exhaled an audible breath. "I'm not involved; I am just seeing someone. I'm thinking about Hannah's offer because I've always wanted to run my own restaurant. I don't want to be in the position again where I'm called in the owner's or boss's office and told they're letting me go. And whenever I find a new position, I always have to start at the bottom. At my age I'm sick and tired of starting at the bottom. So, if y'all want to know, the answer is yes, I'm seriously thinking about it."

Samara applauded. "Good for you, Mom. And if you move to New Orleans, then we can get to see each other more often. I could drive here in about eight hours."

"What about your apartment?" Nydia asked Tonya.

"My lease is up at the end of January. I have to make a decision and let my landlord know at least sixty days before it expires. If you want to rent my apartment, then I'll tell the landlord you're my cousin and he would be getting a good tenant."

Nydia chewed her lower lip. "How many bedrooms do you have?"

"Two."

She scrunched up her nose. "I don't need

two bedrooms. But if the rent isn't through the roof, then I'll consider it."

Hannah took personal delight listening to the interchange between Nydia and Tonya. She understood Tonya's stance when it came to wanting to run her own business, because she was no different. As women in their fifties they'd earned enough life and work experience not to start over again like entry-level high school or college graduates. And even with a law degree she would be prohibited from practicing law in the state of Louisiana until she passed the state's bar.

"Does anyone want another round of drinks?"

Jasmine raised her glass. "What the hell. We're not going anywhere tonight."

"I hear you," Samara chimed in. "I studied so hard this past year that I thought my brain was going to explode. I'm more than ready to hit a few clubs while we're here."

Hannah rose to her feet. "It's all right if you sleep in late tomorrow. I figure you'd want to hang around the house for a day so you can become acclimated, because we're having an unusually hot summer. I've made reservations for us to take a cruise on the steamboat *Natchez* for dinner and live jazz music one day next week. Thursday night we're going to eat at one of my favorite restaurants. Y'all have to let me know what you want to do Friday night. We can begin with some of the more popular jazz clubs before visiting those that feature Cajun and zydeco, brass bands, and bounce and hip-hop."

"What do you know about hip-hop, Miss Magnolia Queen?" Nydia teased.

She laughed. "More than you know."

Hannah sat on the screened-in back porch with Tonya. Everyone had pitched in to clean up the kitchen after their second round of cocktails before retreating to their rooms to retire for the night. She and Tonya had spent the past forty minutes talking about what she'd envisioned for the Du-Pont Inn. They'd negotiated a figure Tonya would invest for a twenty-five percent share of the company.

"Do you think Nydia and Jasmine will come around?" The two younger women appeared reluctant to go in with her and Tonya. Instead of twenty-five percent, Hannah had offered each a ten-percent share.

Tonya shifted until she found a comfortable position on the cushioned rocker. "I hope they do. They probably don't want the responsibility of running a company when they'd rather work for that company. There's a certain mindset of people who're content being the worker bees when someone tells them what to do."

"I don't believe that's true for Jasmine. After all, she did have her own interior decorating firm."

"Remember, Hannah, she gave it over to her husband to run."

Hannah nodded. "You're right. She has an expert eye when it comes to appraising an antique, and she's also a very good HR specialist."

"She's multitalented and misdirected."

"I think you're being too hard on her, Tonya."

"You learn a lot about folks when you spend hours with them in a car. I'm not saying Jasmine isn't intelligent, but I think that ex-husband of hers really did a number on her self-esteem. She kept complaining about his cheating her out of becoming a mother."

"At the age of forty-two she still can become a mother. With the advances in modern medicine, some women are having their first child at forty."

"Would you have considered having a child at that age?" Tonya asked.

"No. Only because when I was forty, my son was entering the Air Force Academy, and there was no way I was going back to changing diapers and walking the floor with a colicky baby."

"I have one more year before Samara graduates. I told her I'd pay her undergraduate tuition, but if she wants to go to grad school, then she has to apply for student loans."

"Is she planning to go to grad school?"

"She's been hinting."

"What's her major?"

"Economics with a minor in political science."

Hannah grimaced. "That's heavy." A beat passed. "She seemed rather upset that you were going to leave your boyfriend."

"My daughter is like most adult children who want to see their parents with someone because they're afraid they'll have to take care of them in their old age. I told her that's why I work: so I can save enough money to live in an upscale assisted living facility with my own luxury suite, an indoor pool, and health spa."

"That sounds like a good plan. My plans include living in this house and dying when I'm a very old woman."

"How old, Hannah?"

"One hundred."

"That's all?"

"Okay. One hundred one."

"That's better. I hate to be a party pooper, but I have a date with a bed who has been calling my name. Those hurricanes are lethal."

"I know. That's why I didn't have a second round."

Tonya stood up. "Good night."

"Good night."

One down, two to go. She'd scaled one hurdle, the most important one. She'd hired a professional chef for the café and supper club. Hannah knew there were accountants and personnel specialists looking for positions, but her concern was trust. She wanted to hire people she could trust to work in the same place where she lived.

Her instincts were right when she'd invited Jasmine, Nydia, and Tonya to her Manhattan apartment. The camaraderie between them was still evident when they laughed and joked like a group of schoolgirls. She didn't want to believe she had to wait four decades to connect with women she now thought of as friends.

Everything in her life was falling into place. There were only a few missing pieces, but she was confident those, too, would soon fall into place.

Hannah sat in the parlor with her friends,

watching and critiquing talk shows. She rarely watched television, and when she did it was usually documentaries, classic movies, or an all-news channel. Her recommendation they spend the day at home was a good one when temperatures were predicted to top one hundred degrees. Meteorologists were urging those who didn't have to venture outdoors to stay inside.

Everyone, including herself, had slept late. When she finally walked into the kitchen at nine-thirty, she quickly brewed a pot of coffee and selected the items she needed to prepare brunch. She was drinking her second cup when Tonya joined her, complaining of spending a restless night because of hot flashes.

Hannah recounted her experience with hot flashes, mood swings, and vaginal dryness. She told the chef she only wore cotton nightgowns, took an over-the-counter homeopathic hormonal medication for the hot flashes, and used a lubricant to offset the dryness.

Tonya confided to her about her failed marriage, her decision to become a chef, and her reluctance to remarry, while Hannah shocked Tonya when she gave her an intimate view of her ancestors, beginning with Etienne and Margit and ending with her parents. They'd become two women who needed to unload about things they'd never revealed to anyone. Hannah knew her relationship with Tonya wouldn't be as employees, friends, but co-owners.

The doorbell chimed throughout the house and everyone looked at Hannah. "Are you expecting company?" Nydia asked.

She glanced at the time on the cable box, gasping. She'd forgotten she had a dance lesson with St. John. Unfolding her legs, she scrambled off the loveseat. "I'll be right back."

Hannah opened the door to find St. John smiling at her. "Please come in. I forgot about the lesson. Please give me a few minutes to change."

St. John caught her arm. "Don't bother, sweetheart. I told you to call me if you needed to cancel."

"I woke up late and the morning just got away from me." Her excuse sounded trite even to her ears.

Lowering his head, he kissed her forehead. "I'll leave you to your friends, and I hope to meet them Saturday."

Hannah took his hand. "You don't have to wait for Saturday. Come with me and I'll introduce you to them."

■ ■ ■ ■

St. John didn't want to impose on Hannah and her houseguests, but knew from her expression that she wasn't going to be denied. He didn't realize how much he'd miss her until it was time for him to go to bed. He marveled at how quickly he'd gotten so used to her sleeping beside him.

"Okay."

He entered the parlor, and the attention of the four women was transferred from the television screen to him. "Good afternoon, ladies."

Hannah took charge of the introductions. "St. John, these are my friends from New York and Atlanta. The lady with the dimples is chef extraordinaire Tonya Martin. The young woman sitting next to her is her daughter, Samara, who is currently a student at Spelman College." She pointed to a young woman with a mass of curly hair framing her face. "Nydia Santiago is a brilliant accountant and CPA, so if you want someone to balance your books, then she's the one." St. John laughed along with the others. "Finally, but definitely not least, is Jasmine Washington, who was our HR specialist before all of us were unceremoniously dismissed from our positions. Ladies, this is my very good friend, St. John Mc-Nair."

Tonya angled her head. "It's nice meeting you, Mr. McNair."

"Please call me St. John."

"How do you spell your name?" Nydia questioned.

"It's spelled like the prophet St. John, but pronounced SIN-jun. My mother named me after a character in *Jane Eyre.* Therefore it's the British pronunciation."

"Was your mother a teacher?" It was Samara's turn to question him.

"No. My mother is a retired nurse."

The interrogation continued with Jasmine asking, "What do you do?"

He gave Hannah a quick glance. It was apparent she hadn't mentioned him to her friends. "I'm a teacher."

Samara sat straight. "Where do you teach?"

"I teach at Barden College."

"What do you teach?" Samara asked another question.

"History."

Hannah patted his chest. "I think you'd better sit during this inquisition. I'm going into the kitchen to bring everyone something cold to drink."

Tonya popped up. "I'll help you."

CHAPTER 20

Tonya literally pulled Hannah into the kitchen. "Where did you find *him*?"

She halted opening the refrigerator. "What are you talking about?"

"Don't play obtuse with me, Hannah Lowell. I'm talking about the man in your parlor who, besides being gorgeous, is as smooth as Skippy peanut butter."

"I didn't find him anywhere. We went to high school together and reconnected at our fortieth reunion. He takes ballroom dance lessons during the summer, and he asked me to partner with him."

Tonya watched Hannah as she took out a pitcher of lemonade from the fridge, then took down iced tea glasses from an overhead cabinet and placed them on a tray. "Is that all that's going on between you two?"

"We're friends, Tonya. What else do you want me to say?"

"That perhaps you're sleeping together?

And if you are, then good for you. That gives me hope that someday I'll meet a man with as much class as your St. John."

Hannah stirred the lemonade with a long-handled spoon, then handed off the tray to Tonya. "I thought you have someone."

"I like Darius, even though I'll never be in love with him. That's why it's so easy for me to talk about moving here."

"How do you think he's going to react when you tell him?"

"I don't know. Darius isn't an easy man to read, because he holds so much inside. Back to St. John. How serious are the two of you?"

"Not serious at all. I'm widowed and he's divorced, which means we don't need to be married to have a relationship."

"Does he have kids?"

"No. He and his ex-wife never had children."

"Remember when I told you that day in your apartment that once you go black you don't go back, and you said you didn't know anything about that. I'm going to ask you one last question, and I'd appreciate an honest answer."

Hannah felt heat in her face because she knew what Tonya was going to ask. "What is it?"

"Is he as good as your husband was in bed?"

"Better," she said without guile. And he was. When St. John made love to her, Hannah experienced emotions of unbridled desire and ecstasy followed by a contented peace that made her want to lie in his arms forever.

"Good for you," Tonya whispered. "Enjoy it for however long it lasts, and I hope for you it will last forever."

Hannah nodded because she was too emotion-filled to speak. Talking about St. John made her aware that she was in so deep that she couldn't differentiate between liking and loving. She found in St. John everything she'd sought in a man but hadn't been aware she'd wanted until reuniting with him.

She returned to the parlor and filled glasses with the cool citrus drink, then settled down to listen to Samara tell St. John about the research she'd collected for her thesis. The man with whom she'd fallen in love went up several more points when he told Samara to email him what she'd written and he would look it over and give her his feedback.

Hannah placed her hand over his. "Tonya is smoking brisket and a pork shoulder in the outdoor kitchen and I'd like to invite you to eat with us. Tonight we're going to have an international dinner because Nydia has volunteered to make Puerto Rican–style rice and beans. Jasmine is going to make a dessert of caramel flan, while I've been assigned the task of making a Greek salad."

Attractive lines fanned out around St. John's eyes when he smiled. "I'm never one to turn down good food, so count me in."

The kitchen was filled with activity and laughter as Hannah, Jasmine, Nydia, and Tonya prepared their dishes while Samara stayed in the parlor with St. John.

"It's a good thing this kitchen is so big; otherwise the four of us would never be able to work together," Jasmine remarked.

Nydia nodded. "I still can't get over the fact that there's an outside kitchen."

Hannah crumbled feta cheese in a ramekin, then set it aside and covered it with plastic wrap. It was the last ingredient she'd put into the salad. "Years ago, before there was air-conditioning, many houses in the south were built with outdoor kitchens in order not to heat up the main house."

"And of course it was slaves who did the cooking," Jasmine spat out.

Hannah gave her a withering glare. "There

weren't any slaves at DuPont House."

"How did that happen?" Jasmine asked.

Inhaling a deep breath, Hannah held it, and then finally let it out, knowing she should have waited until everyone was together to recount her family's history. She captured Jasmine and Nydia's rapt attention when she repeated what she'd told Tonya about the DuPonts, watching their expressions change to disbelief when she told of the number of mixed race relatives she'd never met.

Jasmine wiped her hands on a dish towel. "Are you saying that everyone named Du-Pont, whether white, brown, or black, is your relative?"

"I'm not saying that, Jasmine, because other than Etienne and his brother Jean-Paul, I don't know how many other Du-Ponts from France settled here. St. John will probably be able to authenticate this because he's involved in writing a comprehensive history of free people of color in Louisiana."

Nydia smiled. "That's what I call a trifecta, Hannah. The man has looks, brains, and he's sexy as hell. Now if I could meet a younger version of your St. John, I'd . . ." Her words trailed off as she shook her head.

"Don't you even try and play yourself,

mija," Jasmine crooned. "You weren't even coming down here with us because you didn't want to leave the love of your life back in New York."

Nydia pushed out her lips. "The love of my life has been *fucking* up lately. I told him if we're going to move in together, then he has to save his money, because I'm not going to subsidize his portion of the rent. The last time I asked how much he'd saved, he gave me some lame-ass excuse that he had to loan one of his homies some money because the idiot took some woman home with him and when he woke up his wallet was missing. I lost it, calling him every name I could think of in English and Spanish, and in the end he walked out."

"What did I tell you about a man not being able to match what you bring to the table?" Tonya reminded Nydia. "I usually don't get into other folks' business when it comes to their love life, so I'm going to say this once. Get rid of the bum, block his number in your phone, and move on with your life. You have too much going for you to let an anchor weigh you down. He's never going to progress any further than he is right now, and he's always going to look for a woman to take care of him."

"Preach, sister!" Jasmine shouted.

"Amen," Hannah intoned.

Tonya dropped an arm over Nydia's shoulders. "Now repeat after me. I'm going to get rid of the bum."

"I'm going to get rid of the bum," Nydia repeated, eyes downcast.

Tonya gripped the back of her neck. "Say it like you mean it."

Nydia's hazel eyes were filled with determination. "I'm going to get rid of the fucking bum!" Everyone applauded and then dissolved into uncontrollable laughter.

"Y'all know you're crazy as hell," Hannah said as she struggled to catch her breath.

Jasmine pointed at her. "You better include yourself in that equation. If you hadn't invited us down and plied us with an evil drink that had me dreaming of all sorts of naughty things, I probably would still be in my condo watching endless mindless reality shows and commercials for drugs to cure every ailment known to man."

"Tonight we're going to skip the alcohol and have sweet tea. I don't want you to leave here blaming me for turning you into drunks."

Nydia raised the lid on a pot of pigeon peas and rice and then quickly replaced it. "Is it true people can drink in the street down here?"

Hannah nodded. "Only if it's in a plastic cup. If you order a drink in a bar and you don't finish it, then you can ask for a go-cup."

Jasmine smiled. "This place is party city twenty-four-seven."

"Are you changing your mind about relocating?" Tonya asked Jasmine.

"Not yet," she replied. "I have to see more of the city before I make that decision. What I did like when we drove through the French Quarter was the architecture." She waved a hand. "And this house is incredible. If I were appraise the contents, I'm certain they would sell for high seven figures. I noticed some of the plantations we passed on the way down were either abandoned or burned-out shells. Hannah, why did this place remain intact?"

"New Orleans was under the control of the Union Army for the duration of the Civil War. And because the DuPonts didn't own slaves, it wasn't burned or looted. Stephen DuPont allowed a Union colonel to use the house as his headquarters with the proviso his men not steal or ruin anything. He was able to save the house, but his business suffered. He couldn't ship sugarcane out of the city because of the Union blockade. He would've gone completely bankrupt if he hadn't employed blockade runners who were operated by British citizens making use of neutral ports like Havana, Nassau, and Bermuda."

Nydia whistled softly. "There's so much to history I never learned."

"If there's anything you want to know about history, then just ask St. John. He's the chair of the history department at the college."

"And I know my daughter is talking his head off about everything that pertains to government and politics," Tonya said.

Hannah opened the wooden chest filled with silver. "I'm going to set the table in the dining room so we can have more room."

"I'll help you," Nydia volunteered.

Ninety minutes after St. John walked into DuPont House, he sat down at the opposite end of the dining room table from Hannah. The aromas wafting from the various dishes reminded him that he'd only had a cup of coffee and a glass of juice earlier that morning. Conversation had become a lively banter as he watched Hannah laugh and joke with her former coworkers.

The only time he'd witnessed her that uninhibited was when they were in bed together. He smiled at her as he raised a glass of sweet tea to his mouth. At that moment he felt a pang of regret that he'd stayed in a loveless, one-sided marriage for more than half his life. The day Lorna asked for a divorce she was finally able to reveal the trauma that had left her scarred for life. The week before, she'd driven to Kenner to visit the aunt and uncle who'd raised her. When she returned, St. John knew without asking that she'd changed completely. That's when she revealed that her uncle, who had lost his leg because of diabetes, had begun touching her inappropriately when she turned eight; it escalated until she was thirteen. The touching progressed to penile penetration, and by the time she was fifteen he came to her room several nights a week to have intercourse with her. The one time he didn't use a condom he got her pregnant. Her aunt took her to a woman who gave her a concoction that put her in a semi-conscious state while she underwent an abortion. Lorna never told her aunt that it was her uncle who'd gotten her pregnant, because he'd threatened to kill her if she ever told anyone about their secret liaisons.

The abuse only stopped after Lorna and St. John were married, and by that time guilt made it impossible for her to allow another man to touch her.

Instead of comforting his wife, St. John flew into a rage, shouting that she didn't love or trust him enough to tell him the truth, and her silence had turned him into an adulterer.

The divorce was quick, uncontested, citing irreconcilable differences. What St. John found strange was that Lorna sold the house where they'd lived as husband and wife to move back into her abuser's home to care for him and his wife, who'd been diagnosed with dementia.

His reverie ended when Hannah asked him to pass the rice and peas. "I must congratulate the cooks sitting at this table, because everything is delicious."

"Where is your family reunion?" Tonya asked him.

"It's going to be at my house."

"How many are you expecting?" Nydia questioned.

He lifted his shoulders. "It varies. Sometime we have as many as seventy-five, and in other years it's been like twenty-five to thirty. My cousins are doing the cooking so I urge everyone to bring their appetites. And come early, because we always have breakfast to tide us over before we sit down to eat dinner."

"I don't mind helping out with the cooking," Tonya volunteered. "I need to keep my skills sharp now that I'm not working."

St. John gave her a long, penetrating stare. "I'm sure Eustace and Gage wouldn't mind extra help, especially from someone who's a trained chef." He paused. "Hannah, why don't you and your friends spend the night at my place?"

"Is there enough room for all of us?" Jasmine asked.

"If there isn't enough room, then we can always double up," Samara said quickly.

St. John smiled. "There's more than enough space for everyone to have their own bedroom."

Tonya cleared her throat. "How about it, Hannah? Are we checking out of this venerable establishment to check into another hotel for one night?"

She narrowed her eyes at St. John. "I suppose we can see what the owner of the other establishment has to offer his guests."

"Oh, I forgot to ask," St. John continued. "Is anyone here allergic to cats?"

Samara's expression brightened. "You have a cat?"

"No, he doesn't have a cat," Hannah said. "He has *my* cat. Don't look so smug, St. John. You know you hijacked my kitten."

"I thought he was your cousins' kitten."

"Damn," Jasmine drawled. "They're not even married and they're arguing about who gets the cat."

Everyone laughed except Hannah, and St. John realized she was still upset that Smokey hadn't come back to DuPont House with her. Dinner continued with everyone but Jasmine recalling stories about the pets they'd had. She said her mother was allergic to pet dander so she didn't grow up with a dog or cat.

St. John couldn't remember when he'd had a more enjoyable evening. It did boost his ego somewhat, because he was the only male in the company of attractive professional women. Dinner concluded with slices of a custard dessert that literally melted on the tongue, and cups of the chicory-laced coffee favored by most New Orleanians.

Hannah ushered him out the door when he offered to help clean up. "Now I know I can't get rid of you," she said as they stood on the porch together.

"Why would you want to get rid of me?"

"I don't. But if I attempted to do so, those ladies in the house would probably tear my throat out. You have to know you charmed the panties off them."

St. John splayed a hand over her bottom.

"I'm not interested in anyone's panties but yours."

She rested her head on his chest. "One of these days I'm going to come to your house butt-naked under my skirt and you won't have to take off my panties."

He was reminded of the time they made love in the garden when he hadn't worn a pair of briefs under his shorts. "Maybe I should go commando more often," he whispered in her ear.

"Stop it, St. John, because talking about it will give me erotic dreams."

He nuzzled her ear. "I woke up this morning with an erection so painful that I masturbated into a sock."

"Go home, St. John, before I pull you into the garden and screw your brains out."

He pressed his groin against her so she could feel his hard-on. "I better leave now before your friends witness something they don't need to see." Lowering his head, he kissed Hannah with all of the passion coursing through his body. He wanted her more than he'd ever wanted any woman. Not only in his bed, but also in his life.

"Good night, darling," Hannah breathed out when he raised his head.

St. John smiled. "Good night, sweetheart."

■ ■ ■ ■

Hannah returned to the house, closing and locking the door behind her. Everyone was still in the kitchen, sitting at the table. "Well, did you give him some?" Jasmine asked, her eyes shimmering with merriment.

Hannah couldn't stop the blush rising from her chest to her face. "We don't do quickies."

Jasmine pointed at Nydia. "I told you they were sleeping together."

Samara pushed back her chair. "I think this conversation is a little too much for my delicate ears." She ducked, laughing when balls of rolled-up paper napkins were launched at her. "I have to go through my tablet to send Dr. McNair my research info."

Hannah sat down in the chair Samara had vacated. "I thank you guys for coming. It's been a long time since this house has been filled with fun and laughter."

Tonya shook her head. "Why do you always have to get maudlin, Hannah? You have a priceless historical home, a new venue that's guaranteed to be a success, and a fine-ass man any one of us would be willing to jump his bones."

She wanted to tell her friends that she'd grown up feeling alienated from girls and women her age, but she didn't want them to see her as someone who couldn't fit in. "If any of you think you're going to hit on my man, I'll cut you."

"Woohoo!" Jasmine screamed, then gave Tonya and Nydia fist bumps. "That's what I like. A woman who's willing for fight for her man — but only if he's worth fighting for."

They sat in the kitchen talking about the men they'd slept with when they shouldn't have given them a second glance. Hannah didn't have much to contribute to the conversation because she'd only slept with one man before St. John. But knowing they'd accepted her made their friendship even more special. Wakefield Hamilton did her a favor when they fired her. They'd given her the time she needed to plan for her future and, more important, they'd given her group of women who were friends *and* the sisters she always wanted.

Hannah was shown to a table at Broussard's. When she made the reservation for five she decided to eat inside because of the intense heat, which did not abate at sunset.

431

Everyone wore clothes baring a great deal of skin.

"This place is very French," Samara remarked.

"It's been a while since I've prepared a French dish," Tonya said.

Nydia glanced up from her menu. "How do you remember what to put in each dish?"

Tonya smiled. "It comes from years of practice." Her smile was replaced by a slight frown. She leaned to her right, her bare shoulder touching Hannah's. "Isn't that St. John sitting at the next table against the wall?"

Hannah's eyes shifted until she made out his face among the six people at the table. He was seated next to a very attractive woman with a flawless dark complexion and neatly braided hair, clinging possessively to his right arm. Hannah wasn't looking at her beautiful face, but the stunning engagement ring on her left hand. She tried telling herself he was single, they were not in a committed relationship, and therefore he could see whoever he wanted, but she found it hard to draw a normal breath.

Tonya rested a hand on her back. "It's not what you think," she whispered softly.

Hannah expelled an audible breath. "I'm in love with him," she said *sotto voce.*

"And you think he doesn't love you?" Tonya asked, pressing her head to Hannah's. "Don't jump to conclusions, because I've seen the way he looks at you, and it's not with indifference. So suck it up and don't you dare let him see you staring at him like a lovesick puppy. If you claim to be a grown-ass woman, then act like one."

Hannah squared her shoulders. "You're right. I am woman. Hear me roar."

Tonya smiled. "That's what I'm talking about."

"What are you talking about?" Nydia asked Tonya.

"Fifty-year-old shit that you don't need to hear."

Nydia had brushed her hair off her face, holding it in place with a narrow headband. She'd forgone makeup; she appeared no older than someone in their late teens. "I guess I have to wait eighteen years before I'm privy to fifty-year-old shit."

Jasmine patted Nydia's hand. "Don't let Tonya get to you, *mija*. She's probably talking about hot flashes and all the stuff women go through when they're in meno-pause."

"You're right," Tonya lied smoothly.

The waiter came to take their drink orders. When Hannah decided on a virgin mojito she saw the stunned stares from the others at the table. "Y'all go and order hurricanes. I'm willing to bet I'll become the designated driver tonight."

Jasmine made circular motions with her fingers. "They claim New Orleans is food, music, and drink, and I intend to sample all three tonight. I'll have a hurricane," she told the waiter.

Once they were given their drinks and entrées, Hannah managed to ignore the man sitting less than thirty feet away. The encounter turned into a laugh fest when Nydia talked about visiting her relatives in Puerto Rico and how she'd been chased by one of her uncle's pigs that would hump anyone standing close to him. She also revealed that she didn't grow up speaking Spanish, but once she entered adolescence her parents sent her to the island for the summers to keep her away from a boy she'd been sneaking around with. During the school year her older brother would follow her around to make certain she didn't see him.

"The one time I was able to evade my brother to meet Alvaro he found us. We hadn't done anything but Luis was livid. He told Alvaro that he would stomp a mud hole in his ass, then finish him off with an alley

434

biscuit."

Hannah angled her head. "What's an alley biscuit?"

"A brick!" the three women chorus in unison.

"Whatever," she drawled. "I suppose that's a New York expression. Did you brother ever stomp a mud hole in Alvaro's ass?"

"No, because at the time my brother was in the Golden Gloves, and if he hit him he was certain to break his jaw, and Alvaro was much too vain to have someone tag his face. Then I heard he'd gotten some girl pregnant. I knew if I'd come home pregnant, my father would've put me in a convent like they used to do back in the day. Then there was an epidemic of teenage girls having babies, and I wanted none of that, so I decided books were better than boys."

Hannah stole a glance at Samara, wondering if she had a boyfriend, but knowing what she'd gleaned about Tonya's personality, she was sure that if Samara dropped out of college because she was pregnant, the chef would cut her off cold turkey. She'd already mentioned she had one more year of paying tuition to the exclusive private female-only college before she closed her checkbook for good.

She detected the familiar scent of St. John's cologne, and when she glanced up he was standing next to her table. "Fancy meeting you here," she said, her words sounding false and slightly condescending. Hunkering down, St. John leaned in a brush a kiss on her parted lips. She could detect the taste of coffee on his breath.

"Hi, gorgeous. I noticed you when you came in, but I didn't want appear rude to my colleagues."

Her eyebrows lifted. "Those people are your colleagues?"

He nodded. "They wanted to get together before going down to their timeshare in the Bahamas." He rose to his feet. "Ladies. As usual, it's always a pleasure to see you." St. John pointed to Jasmine's drink. "Be careful or you'll find yourself lit up." He tugged playfully at Hannah's ponytail. "I'll see you Friday night." He was there, and then he was gone.

Jasmine stared at the liquid in her glass. "I was getting ready to order a second one, but I suppose I better stop now."

"That's up to you," Hannah said. "I thought we'd walk around to take in the sights before heading back to the house, but a second hurricane is not the answer if you want to remain upright."

Jasmine pushed the glass away. "To tell you the truth, I am feeling a little buzzed."

Hannah removed a credit card from her handbag. "Does anyone want anything else before I settle the bill? I truly will cut you, Tonya, if you're reaching in your bag for money."

Nydia smothered a laugh. "What's with our Magnolia Princess cutting folks?"

Tonya removed her hand from her handbag. "I dunno, but I'm not willing to risk it."

Hannah paid the bill, adding a generous tip. *"Ainsi, mesdames, sont vous prêt à voir la Nouvelle-Orléans?"*

"Oui," Tonya replied.

Nydia stared at Tonya. "You speak French?" The older woman nodded. "What did she say?"

"She asked us if we're ready to see New Orleans, and I said yes. I spent a year in France learning to prepare their dishes, and by the time I left I was fluent."

Hannah smiled. If and when Tonya moved to New Orleans, she had someone else with whom to practice the language. Pushing back her chair, she stood, the others following suit. It actually was still too humid to be outside, but touring the city at night was preferable to the oppressive daytime heat.

CHAPTER 21

It was close to midnight when they arrived at St. John's house. Hannah had called to let him know they were going to Jazzes and would come directly to his house from there. He'd assigned the four women the bedrooms in the rear of the house. Each of the bedrooms opened into a bathroom that was connected by a door to another bedroom.

"Where's my bedroom?" she asked as he led her down the hallway.

He dropped a kiss on her hair. "Where do you think? Where you always sleep."

Hannah handed him her overnight bag. "I have to shower and wash my hair. I feel clammy all over."

"Take your time. Smokey and I will be waiting for you."

She walked into the bathroom and slipped out of her dress and underwear, leaving them in the hamper with St. John's. Standing under the showerhead, Hannah turned her face up to the lukewarm water. She shampooed her hair and soaped her body, and then stood under the spray again to rinse her hair and body. Something startled her, and when she turned she found St. John standing outside the stall watching her. He was completely naked and semi-erect.

Tonya had asked if he was better in bed than Robert, and she hadn't hesitated because there was no comparison. Robert had never taken the time to arouse her, as if he was in a hurry to do the deed and get it over with. Most times, when it was over, he left her wanting more. His "more" was rolling over and going to sleep, leaving her sexually frustrated. The one time she mentioned this to him, he accused her of being oversexed. She hadn't been as oversexed as she'd been neglected. And she refused to compare the size of their penises, because again St. John came out the winner.

Smiling, she opened the door. "Are you coming in or staying out?"

He returned her smile. "I was waiting for an invite."

"Come onto my parlor, said the spider to the fly."

St. John stepped in and closed the door. "You are a spider who has me caught up in her web where there is no escape." He moved closer, nuzzling her neck and pushing his groin against her mound.

Hannah opened her mouth to his rapacious tongue as he simulated making love to her. Anchoring her arms under his shoulders, she writhed against him as the familiar sensations rippling through her belly settled between her legs, bringing with them a rush of moisture. The lubricant and her ability to relax made it possible for him to penetrate her easily.

Like the spider he'd likened her to, she kissed him, her lips trailing from his mouth to his chin, breastbone, and down his flat belly. The tip of her tongue tasted the moisture clinging to the tight curls in the inverted triangle of coarse hair between his thighs. She pressed light kisses along his inner thigh before reversing direction.

St. John reached over and turned off the water. He swept her up in his arms. "Open the door."

She complied, and taking long strides, he carried her out of the bathroom into the bedroom, placing her wet body on the bed, his following hers down. "May I love you, baby?" he whispered in her ear.

Nodding, Hannah closed her eyes, opening her arms and legs and moaning softly when his erection filled her. Her hands caressed the length of his spine, the firm flesh over his buttocks, her body arching to meet his powerful thrusts. It was flesh against flesh, man against woman. Ecstasy swept over them with the power of waves crashing against the rocks in a storm, sharing a pleasure so pure and explosive that for several seconds they had actually become one.

She welcomed his still-pulsing hardness and weight crushing her down against the mattress. This lovemaking was different from what they had previously shared. There was a wild desperation in their coming together, as if it would be the last time. Tears filled her eyes and leaked from under her lids, and she swiped at them before they fell.

There was nothing for her to cry about except that she had fallen in love with a man and wanted him to share her life and their future. She pushed against his shoulder. "St. John, you're crushing me."

He rolled off her, lay on his back, threw an arm over his face. *"Ês-tu certain que tu n'es pas une sorcière?"*

She went completely still. "Of course I'm not a witch. Why would you think that?"

St. John lowered his arm. "Because you

have bewitched me. I can't concentrate on my research because you're never far from my thoughts. I asked you and your friends to spend the night to act as a distraction so I don't have to spend the night sleeping on the veranda."

"Why are you sleeping out there? Don't you know the bugs will eat you up?"

"They don't bite because I light a couple of citronella candles. Even Smokey sleeps out here with me."

"Are you saying you don't sleep in the bed because I'm not here?"

"Oui."

"That's crazy."

"That's because I'm crazy about you, Hannah. You've gotten under my skin like an itch I can't scratch."

She kissed his shoulder. "I'm here tonight, and as soon as my houseguests leave, I'll be back."

St. John pulled her against his length, reached over and turned off the lamp, plunging the room into complete darkness. Sometime during the night Smokey jumped up on the bed and settled down at the foot to sleep.

The people from the party rental company arrived at seven to erect several tents in the garden. They'd just finished when another truck arrived with long tables, folding chairs, and tablecloths. Eustace was busy setting up portable stoves and gas grills, as his sons-in-law set out coolers stocked with steaks, fish, vegetables, produce, and dairy. Hannah introduced Tonya to Eustace, and he welcomed her with a bearlike hug.

She, Nydia, and Samara busied themselves covering the many tables with tablecloths while Jasmine stacked paper plates, plastic cups, and plastic place settings on a table. Minutes later, eight chafing dishes were heating as Eustace and Tonya grilled bacon, sausage links, and slices of ham. Dozens of eggs were scrambled, with and without cheese, while pots of grits simmered on the stove in the outdoor kitchen. By the time the first family members arrived, Tonya had baked several pans of fluffy biscuits.

Breakfast seemed to taste better in the open air as Hannah filled her plate with grits, scrambled eggs, sweet maple-glazed bacon, and a buttered biscuit. Jasmine had complained about gaining weight; she knew if she didn't curb her own eating, she wouldn't be able to fit into her clothes. She loathed having to buy a larger size when all she had to do was close her mouth.

The younger Toussaints and Baptistes arrived, and the noise escalated when one of them assumed the role of DJ and played music spanning several generations. Hannah lost track of time and names as St. John introduced her to his family. Most of them were comfortable speaking French; they were impressed when she was able to reply in the same language. After a while they referred to her as *la dame de St. John* or St. John's lady.

By early afternoon the ubiquitous New Orleans dishes had replaced the breakfast menu. The mouthwatering aroma of barbecued ribs, chicken, andouille sausage, pork chops, shrimp, crab, and oysters lingered in the humid air. St. John told her his parents and his sister and her family could not attend because of prior commitments.

One of his teenage cousins pulled her out to dance. Her initial self-consciousness fled once she was able to follow him as they danced to the classic hip-hop dance hit "Watch Me Whip/Nae Nae." She pulled away from him, shaking her head when the DJ played "Back That Thing Up." Flushed-faced and breathing heavily, she fell into St. John's embrace when he held out his arms.

"Now all the boys are going to want to dance with you."

"I don't think so," she gasped. "I'm done

for today, and I'm definitely not going to back my thing up for some young kid to rub up on me." She reached for a napkin off the table to blot her face and neck.

St. John rested a hand at her waist over the sleeveless white cotton dress that ended mid-calf. "My family really likes you."

Hannah closed her eyes. "I like them. I believe they're impressed because I try to communicate with my feeble French."

He kissed her shoulder. "Your French is far from feeble."

She opened her eyes, meeting his steady gaze. "You think that because you're biased."

"Damn right I am when it comes to you."

Hannah fed off St. John's strength as she leaned into him. She bit down on her lip to stop herself from telling him what lay in her heart. "Where's Gage?"

"I don't know. If he didn't show up, then he has to have a valid reason, because he never misses getting together with the family. Eustace's wife is also MIA. She sprained her ankle and the doctor put her in a soft cast and told her to stay off her foot. Many of the older folks decided to stay home because they're not able to withstand this heat. Maybe next year we'll hold the reunion at a hotel. Then we won't have to deal with the heat or rain."

The heat was beginning to take its toll on the revelers; they decided to leave to avoid dehydration or heatstroke. And in deference to the dangerous heat, St. John refused to offer anything alcoholic. Water had become the beverage of choice.

"Instead of a hotel you can use the inn. It has central air, the ballroom is large enough to accommodate at least sixty, and Eustace can use any of the kitchens to prepare food."

"What about your guests?"

"I just won't book any guests for that day."

St. John nodded. "I'll think about it."

"What's to think about? You won't have to pay for tents or tables and chairs because you'll be able to use the ones from the café and supper club."

St. John pressed his mouth to her ear. "I can't believe you came up with an alternative solution that quickly."

"If I'm going to become an innkeeper, then I have to think like an innkeeper."

Since Cameron's call, Hannah had come to regard herself as New Orleans's latest innkeeper. She told Tonya she would draw up a contract outlining the terms of their partnership so she could have her attorney look it over before accepting or rejecting what they'd discussed.

"I love you for offering your place for next year's reunion."

Hannah froze, unable to believe St. John had uttered the words branded on her brain like a permanent tattoo. Was he in love with her, or had he said he loved her in the same vein as someone saying they love an inanimate object? How many times had she said she loved the law, or she loved watching classic movies?

"Love you, too." She kissed his cheek. "I'm going to get some water." When he didn't respond to her declaration of affection, Hannah knew St. John wasn't in love with her.

Those assigned to the cleanup committee began clearing off and breaking down tables and stacking chairs. It took less than an hour to load vans and trucks with portable stoves and chafing dishes. The sun was beginning to set when Hannah said her good-byes to those who'd opted to linger as she and her friends climbed into Jasmine's SUV for the drive back to the Garden District.

Hannah sat on the back porch with Jasmine, Tonya, and Nydia. Samara, who admitted she'd eaten and danced too much, had retired to bed.

Jasmine patted her chest with a cold cloth. "Is it always this hot down here?"

Hannah ran her fingertips over a glass of ice water. "It is hotter than usual."

"Even with the heat I had a good time," Tonya said.

"Of course you did," Nydia said teasingly. "You spent the entire morning and afternoon with the chef who couldn't take his eyes off you."

Tonya made a sucking sound with her tongue and teeth. "Get your mind out of the gutter, Nydia. The man has a wife, children, and grandchildren, so the only thing we have in common is preparing food."

Nydia grimaced. "My bad. I thought he was hitting on you."

"One man in my life is enough," the chef countered. "Speaking of men, Hannah, I think you hit the jackpot with St. John. What's not to like about the man?"

Jasmine raised her hand. "I agree. I have to admit some of his male cousins were very nice. I couldn't understand a word they were saying when they spoke French, but it sounded sexy."

Jasmine talking about men reminded Hannah of the hint she'd made to Cameron. "Jasmine, are you serious about possibly dating again?"

"No. I still have to give myself more time to get over my ex's duplicity. I'm still carrying too much resentment to deal with a man, even if he's nothing like my ex-husband. It wouldn't be fair to him if I come at him like a crazy woman because of something he did or said to remind me of that snake I married."

Hannah agreed with Jasmine. It had taken her years to shake off Robert's infidelity and to learn to trust a man again. "How long do you guys plan to stay?"

"We'll probably stay until Monday or Tuesday," Tonya said. "I know we talked about staying two weeks, but if I'm going to relocate, then I have a lot of things to tie up. Nydia and Jasmine can stay if they want. I'll rent a car and Samara and I will drive back to New York."

Jasmine shook her head. "You don't have to do that, Tonya. If we came down together, then we'll go back together. I'm still not sure whether I want to relocate, but it's something I can definitely think about. Tonya, you and Nydia live in rentals, while I have to try and sell my condo."

Hannah pressed her palms together. "I'm sorry if you feel I'm putting pressure on you to give up everything that is familiar to you to move down here. I made the offer for you to come in with me because I feel I can trust y'all. How often to you hear of four women starting up a business together?"

"Not often enough," Jasmine replied.

"The doors to DuPont House are always open to you if or when you feel the need for a change of scene. I have to go back to New York before the end of September to pack up my apartment. Maybe we can get together again for omelets, mimosas, and Bellinis."

Nydia nodded. "Isn't that how this unlikely quartet got together in the first place?"

Hannah laughed. "We certainly are a motley crew. Now that you'll be leaving in three days and with this crazy heat we'll stay close to home."

It was early August when St. John got a telephone call from someone he'd believed he would never see or speak to again. Hannah had left his house to return home to meet with the engineer to ascertain whether they could install an elevator in the house.

He loved being with her, loved making love with her, and he was in love with her. And it was time she knew just how important she'd become and why he wanted her in his life. But that would have to wait until he returned to New Orleans.

It was Lorna who'd called to ask if he would come to Kenner to see her. Every imaginable scenario raced through his mind during the drive. When he maneuvered up to the house where she'd grown up, a chill raced over his body as he recalled what she'd told him about what had gone on behind the closed door.

Lorna was waiting for him when he got out of his car. She'd gained weight. It was enough to fill out the body that had always been much too thin for an adult woman. The chemically straightened coiffed hair bore few traces of gray, and there were no visible lines in her nut brown face. The beautiful young girl with whom he'd fallen in love on sight was now a beautiful mature woman.

He took her hands and kissed her cheek. "You look well, Lorna."

She smiled. "And so do you. But you always did. I can't invite you inside because I no longer live here."

"Why?"

"My aunt died last year and my uncle passed away four months ago. That's when I decided I could no longer live here and sold it."

St. John knew with the death of her abuser

Lorna could finally move on. "Where are you staying?"

"I have a position as a live-in nurse with a single father who has a child with special needs."

"Where does he live?"

"He's here in Kenner. I didn't ask to see you to tell you that, but to say I'm sorry. I'm sorry that I didn't trust you enough to tell you what my uncle did to me. I'm sorry I didn't go into therapy as you begged me to do. And I am truly sorry I denied you the family you always wanted."

St. John felt as if he'd been punched in the gut when he saw the tears streaming down her face. He reached into the pocket of his slacks and took out a handkerchief to dab her cheeks. "It's all right, Lorna. What's done is done."

She sniffled. "You forgive me?"

"I forgave you a long time ago. I know I lost my temper when you first told me about what your uncle had done to you, because all I thought about was what we'd lost. We spent more than thirty years together, and in all that time I felt as if you didn't or couldn't love me enough to open up about the abuse."

Lorna closed her eyes. "I was afraid."

"Afraid of what? Whom?

"I was afraid of what you'd do to him, St. John."

St. John stared at her, complete shock freezing his features. "Did you actually believe I would risk going to jail for that piece of shit!" He shook his head. "What hurts, Lorna, is you lived with me all those years and you never really took the time to know me. I would've confronted him, and if he ever touched you again, I'd make certain he'd spend the rest of his life in prison."

"He's gone. And when they put dirt on the coffin, it was if I'd buried all my demons with him. I'm in therapy with a therapist who deals solely with sexually abused patients. I have individual and group sessions and hopefully one day I'll be able to have a normal physical relationship with a man before I'm too old. If you check your bank balance, you'll find a check for what I got when I sold our house."

"I gave you the house in the divorce."

"I didn't need the house because I knew I was coming back here to take care of my aunt and uncle. The money I got for this house is more than enough for me to live on for a long time if I don't squander it. I have my own quarters at my client's home, so I'm able to bank most of my salary."

St. John smiled for the first time. "You

sound as if you're getting your life together."

"I'm trying. What about you, St. John? Have you met someone?"

"Yes, I have."

"Do you love her?"

"I love her very much."

Lorna smiled. "Then marry her, so you can have with her what you didn't have with me."

He winked at her. "That's my intent." Taking a step, St. John kissed Lorna's cheek again. "Call me if you ever need anything or someone to talk to."

She shook her head. "I can't do that. I don't want to go back when I need to look ahead. Seeing you, talking to you will remind me of what we could've and should've had, and I don't want to relive that again."

"Then I guess this is good-bye."

Taking his hand, Lorna gave it a gentle squeeze. "Good-bye."

St. John thought he'd been dreaming, and when he awoke he would be in his bed and not in his car driving back from Kenner. He probably would never see Lorna again, but knowing she was taking the steps to heal from the abuse she'd endured for years was comforting.

He wanted her happy and she wanted him

happy, and he knew his ultimate happiness would come from Hannah becoming his wife. He headed to the Garden District, knowing he and Hannah had reached the point at which their relationship had to be resolved. They weren't teenagers or twenty-somethings who could have a lengthy engagement.

Hannah answered the door, slightly taken aback when she saw St. John standing there. She'd left his house earlier that morning, promising she would return in time for them to share dinner together. "Come in. I didn't expect to see you until tonight."

Taking her hand, St. John led her into the parlor. "What I need to ask you can't wait for tonight."

"Why do you sound so mysterious?"

Sitting, he eased her down beside him on the loveseat. "Hannah, we've known each other a long time and I've probably been in denial for more years than I can remember. I'm saying all of this to say that I love you. I'm *in love* with you. Will you do me the honor of becoming my wife?"

Hannah stared, tongue-tied, as she attempted to process what she'd just heard. She loved St. John, had been in love with him for a very long time, yet she never could have conceived of being his wife. "You love me?" she asked in disbelief, recovering her voice.

St. John cradled her face in his hands. "Of course I love you. I wouldn't ask you to share my life if I didn't love you." He paused. "Do you love me?"

She rested her forehead against his. "You silly, silly man. Don't you remember me telling you about going to my mother to say I was in love with you and we were planning to marry? When I said that, I knew then I was in love with you."

"Does this mean you will marry me?"

She closed her eyes. "Yes, but on one condition." Hannah felt him stiffen.

"What's that?"

"You have to promise not to cheat on me."

"Why ask me that?"

"Because my husband cheated on me throughout our marriage. I finally found out when he had his first heart attack. He believed he was dying and he needed to unburden himself. I was forty-eight and I'd been married for twenty-seven years, and in all that time I never knew my husband was sleeping with other women. I need to know one thing before I give you my answer. Did you ever cheat on Lorna?" Hannah eased back when St. John hesitated. "You did, didn't you?"

He exhaled an audible sigh. "Yes. I didn't want to, but she didn't give me a choice."

Hannah jumped up, her heart pumping wildly. "You didn't have a choice?"

St. John stood. "Please, Hannah. Let me explain."

She shook her head. "I don't want to hear anything you have to say." She combed her fingers through her hair. "I can't believe it's happening to me again. How stupid can I be to fall in love not once but twice with a cheater." Hannah averted her head so he wouldn't see her tears. There's no way she was going to let him see her cry over him. "Please go. Now!" She turned back just in time to see him walk out of the parlor.

Her knees were shaking uncontrollably, forcing her to sit before she fell. Burying her face against the cushion, she cried until she had dry heaves. Just when she thought her life had righted itself, she had to duck a vicious curve.

Better you find out now rather than later. The silent voice gave her little solace. And despite his revelation that he'd been an adulterer, she still loved him.

CHAPTER 22

Hannah sat on the floor of her nearly empty apartment with Nydia, Jasmine, and Tonya drinking mimosas.

She'd returned to New York to donate all the furniture to her favorite charity. Boxes stacked against the wall contained her clothes and personal items that would be picked up by a moving company and shipped to New Orleans.

She hoisted her plastic cup. "Well, motley crew, this is it." They all touched cups.

Tonya shook her head. "We are a motley bunch. Drinking champagne from plastic cups."

"How's St. John?" Jasmine asked.

Hannah took a long swallow from her cup. "I don't know."

"What!"

"You don't know?"

Nydia and Tonya had spoken in unison.

"What the hell is that supposed to mean?"

Tonya asked.

Hannah was forthcoming when she told them about St. John proposing marriage and then his revelation that he'd cheated on his wife. "I lived with a cheating sonofabitch for twenty-nine years, and I swore that I'd never live with another cheater." She told them about Robert and how he'd admitted to sleeping with so many women he'd forgotten their names. "When he had his first heart attack, he was living with a woman in D.C., while he worked at the Pentagon. By that time his heart was too weak for him to fuck around. I wanted to leave him, but I couldn't because I'd married him for in sickness and in health. Believe me, if I'd found out he was cheating before he had that attack, I would've divorced his cheating ass."

Jasmine dropped the hand she'd put over her mouth during Hannah's passionate monologue. "Did St. John tell you why he cheated on his wife?"

Hannah shook her head. "He wanted to explain, but I didn't want to listen to his lies."

Tonya slapped Hannah on the back of her head. "For a supposedly bright woman you're stupid as hell! The man could've lied and said no and you wouldn't have been the wiser. The fact that he was willing to explain says everything about who he is. Now if you don't get your skinny ass back to New Orleans and listen to what that man has to say, I'm going to go to the Big Easy and fuck your man!"

Hannah's mouth dropped. "No, you didn't say that."

"Hell yeah, I did."

Jasmine rolled her head on her neck. "And when she's done, I'm going to have a go at him. I'm willing to bet he's never had some Filipino pussy."

It was Hannah's turn to cover her mouth. "I don't believe you women," she said through her fingers.

Nydia snapped her fingers. "And please don't forget that when I put this Boricua pussy on him, I'll have him speaking Spanish and French at the same time."

Hannah didn't know if they were joking or if they were serious. And she knew that, as a single man, St. John could sleep with whomever he wanted. "You would really sleep with my man?"

Tonya nodded. "Why not? He's no longer your man."

"But he is because I love him and do want to marry him . . ."

"Estúpida!" Nydia interrupted. "If that's

the case, why aren't you in New Orleans listening to what he has to say? Damn," she whispered, "I hope I'm smarter than you when I get to your age."

Hannah threw up both hands. "Stop it! You've insulted and disrespected me, and enough is enough! One more word about fucking St. John and I'm going to lose it."

Tonya clapped. "That's the fire I want to see." She hugged Hannah. "Go back home and fight for your man, and once you set a date, the motley crew will be there to witness your wedding to the finest man in Nawlins."

Hannah blinked back tears. "That's only going to happen if he still wants to marry me."

"It'll happen," Jasmine said confidently. "If he proposed once, he'll propose again." She raised her cup. "I raise my cup to the future Mrs. St. John McNair."

"Mrs. McNair," they all chorused.

Hannah returned to New Orleans. She waited two days before gathering the nerve to call St. John. She knew he'd returned to his position at the college, so she waited until nightfall to contact him. He answered his phone on the second ring, and she told him she needed to talk to him about something. His voice was laced in neutral tones when he told her he was available.

The first thing she noticed when he opened the door was his face. It was thinner, and she wondered if he'd been eating. "Thank you for seeing me."

"Please come in. We'll talk in the sunroom."

Everything about him came back like the rushing waters of fast-moving rapids. His smell, his softly modulated voice, and the way he looked at her. Could she hope beyond hope that he still loved her as much as she loved him?

She sat on the lounger she'd claimed when staying with him, while he elected to stand. She hadn't rehearsed what she wanted to say because she didn't want it to sound practiced. "I want to apologize."

His eyebrows lifted slightly. "For what?"

"For not listening to you. I judged you unfairly, and that's something I'll regret for the rest of my life."

"Why?"

Hannah wanted to scream at him to show some emotion. That he cared about her and what she was struggling to say. "Because I love you, St. John. I've loved you forever, even when I told myself I was in love with another man, and even when you were in love with another woman. I don't care why you cheated on Lorna, because the past is the past. Ask me again."

St. John crossed his arms over his chest. "Ask you what?"

"Please ask me again to marry you."

"I asked you once, and I'm not going to beg, if that's what you want, Hannah. I told you before, I'm too old to play games, and if that's what you're into, then I'm not the man for you."

Hannah didn't want to believe he was rejecting her. She had laid aside her pride and come to him, and his rejection had stripped her bare. "I'm not playing a game." Her hands tightened into fists. "I came here because I want to know why you cheated on Lorna."

St. John wanted to hate Hannah, but he couldn't. Not when she was everything he'd always wanted in a woman. He knew what it had taken for her to contact him again, and she was right. He did owe it to her to let her know why he'd cheated on Lorna.

"Lorna wouldn't let me make love to her because she'd been sexually abused as child by the uncle who raised her." He told Hannah everything Lorna had disclosed to him about her horrendous childhood, his heart turning over when he saw Hannah cry, knowing she was crying for an innocent child who hadn't had anyone to protect her from a monster.

St. John felt her pain as surely as it was his own when she buried her face against the cushion and sobbed. Closing the space between them, he took her in his arms and comforted her as he would a small child.

"It's okay, baby," he said over and over, rocking her gently. "She's better now. She's getting the help she needs."

"Oh, St. John. What she had to endure from that monster is unimaginable."

He kissed her hair. "I didn't want to sleep with other women —"

Hannah stopped his words when she placed her fingers over his mouth. "You don't have to explain. You did what most men would have done if they were denied their wife's body. I understand why you didn't leave her."

"I wanted to, Hannah, but there was something in her eyes that wouldn't let me, so I stayed in a cold, loveless marriage until she had enough. If I marry you, I'll never cheat on you even if you deny me your body. I love making love with you, but sex isn't at the top of my list for wanting to marry you."

She blinked slowly. "What is?"

"You, Hannah. It's your inner strength, your passion for life, in and out of bed. I watched the way you interacted with your friends and my family, and everything about you is so real that there're times when I don't believe how lucky I am to have you in my life."

"That goes double for me."

"I think it's time I make you an honest woman. I'm not going to sleep with you again until you're Mrs. St. John Baptiste McNair."

She stared up at him through her lashes. "Are you proposing to me?"

He nodded. "Yes, I am. And this is the last time I'm going to ask you. Will you marry me?"

Hannah threw her arms around his neck. "Yes! Yes, I will marry you."

St. John kissed her with all of the passion he could summon within himself. "When and where?"

She pulled her lower lip between her teeth. "Next month and in the garden at DuPont House."

"Okay. That should give us enough time to send out invitations and tell our families that the Baptistes and Toussaints can add the DuPonts to their family tree." He stood, pulling her up with him. "Come into the office so we can decide on a date, then I'll call my parents and sister to let them know the news."

"I have to call my son."

"Don't forget we have to shop for rings."

Hannah clung to his arm. "I want something simple."

"That's not happening, because nothing about you is simple."

St. John never would have suspected that when he walked up behind Hannah at the reunion, months later she would agree to become his wife. Both had been given second chances, and this time they were going to get it right.

Hannah held her arms out at her sides. "How do I look?"

She had selected a simple platinum gown with a squared neckline that barely skimmed her body. It was her second wedding, and tiny orange blossoms were pinned into the elegant chignon on the nape of her long neck. Her son had flown in with his wife and children several days earlier, and he'd offered to give her away. She'd opened DuPont House for out-of-town guests who'd been invited to witness the nuptials of Hannah Claire DuPont-Lowell to St. John McNair.

She'd chosen Tonya, Nydia, and Jasmine as her attendants, while St. John had asked his father to be his best man, and his cousin Eustace and brother-in-law, Kenny, to be his groomsmen.

"Beautiful," Nydia crooned. "St. John is a lucky man."

Hannah rested her right hand over her throat, and the exquisite cushion-cut emerald set in platinum and surrounded by brilliant diamonds caught the overhead light. When they'd gone shopping for rings, she'd told St. John she didn't want the traditional diamond. In the end they'd decided on an emerald because he said it reminded him of her green eyes.

During the rehearsal dinner she informed him that her cousins would have to live with them at his house while the mansion underwent the renovations to turn DuPont House in DuPont Inn. He said he didn't mind because DuPonts were going to become a part of their extended family, and although he never envisioned himself becoming the spouse of an innkeeper, he wouldn't have it any other way.

Wyatt walked into the room, resplendent in his tuxedo. Her son had inherited his father's dark hair and eye color, features, and complexion, which tanned easily. She'd noticed women staring at him because of his movie star appearance.

Wyatt offered her his arm. "Are you ready, Mom?"

She wanted to tell her son that she had been ready more than forty years ago, but didn't want to shock him. "Yes."

He escorted her down the staircase. Tonya, Lydia, and Jasmine followed in their flowing burnt-orange slip dresses. Several tents had been erected in the garden, and chairs covered in white organza and tied with orange ribbons were set up theater-style for their guests.

Suddenly everything became a blur as a string quartet played what she recognized as one of St. John's favorite songs: Anita Baker's "Just Because." Recalling the words filled her eyes with tears, and she blinked wildly before they fell and ruined her makeup.

She and St. John had planned every phase of their wedding from music to the menu. They'd taken private tango lessons with Mrs. Duarte because their first dance as husband and wife would be a tango, and knowing this, she'd selected a gown with a flowing skirt. They would marry in the garden, then retreat to the rarely used ballroom in the house for the reception.

The minister stood under a pergola of climbing white roses waiting to begin the ceremony. The song ended and Wyatt led her down the rose-strewn flagstone path to where St. John stood with his best man, his father Daniel McNair, Eustace, and Kenny. The mustache and goatee were back. He looked delicious in his tuxedo with a satin vest, matching bowtie, and boutonniere. She smiled when he mouthed *beautiful.* Even if she wasn't beautiful, she *felt* beautiful.

Time passed at warp speed when the minister asked who gives this woman, and Wyatt's deep voice echoed clearly when he gave his consent. There was an exchange of vows, and the haze cleared when St. John slipped a diamond eternity band on her left hand. She repeated the action when Daniel gave her a plain platinum band which she slipped on St. John's beautifully formed hand.

"You may kiss your wife."

Hannah felt St. John's heart beating against her breasts when he pulled her against his body and kissed her. His arms tightened around her waist, and he continued to kiss her as he lifted her off her feet to thunderous applause.

Her face was nearly the color of the orange blossoms when they traversed the path amid a shower of flower petals. It was a long time coming, but she'd finally found love with her best friend.

Her arms went around his waist inside his jacket as she leaned into him, her eyes shimmering with a joy that made her slightly light-headed. "I love you so much, Dr. Mc-Nair."

"Not as much as I love you, Mrs. Mc-Nair."

They stared into each other's eyes. The photographer caught the tender moment on film. The photo would be on display for future generations whenever they walked into their private suite at the DuPont Inn.